CW00460606

Harry Treasure, among other things is a rough artist, a sculptor of barbed wire and a writer of short stories. This is his first full length novel. He works a mixed farm in Cowra, a town in the Central West of NSW to pay the bills.

To my wife Heather for her tireless patience and daughters Kim and Cathy for their help and guidance.

Harry Treasure

KING'S SPUR

AUSTIN MACAULEY PUBLISHERS™

LONDON • CAMBRIDGE • NEW YORK • SHARJAH

A CIP catalogue record for this title is available from the British Library.

ISBN 9781398485419 (Paperback)
ISBN 9781398485426 (Hardback)
ISBN 9781398487451 (ePub e-book)
ISBN 9781398485433 (Audiobook)

www.austinmacauley.com

First Published 2023
Austin Macauley Publishers Ltd®
1 Canada Square
Canary Wharf
London
E14 5AA

Chapter 1

Atlas died just before daybreak.

It happened in a little clearing in the Victorian Alps between two great boulders that stood like sentinels among the mountain ash. Men from the Royal Dargo mine had set up camp for the night, sleeping in wet blankets around a small fire. The pack-horses moved restlessly from foot to foot, still fully loaded, while Atlas, a giant pie-bald gelding stood shivering, legs bowed, foam drooling from his mouth, a ton of cast iron strapped to his back.

Charley Nash held the night shift, tossing a stick of wood on the fire from time to time as he soothed the animals. He loved the horses and knew the big piebald was in trouble long before the end came. Probably Atlas knew it too, having carried a large section of a rock-crushing mill on his back for the past sixteen hours.

When Charley felt the final shudder, he had his hand on the neck of the great beast. He tried instinctively to hold the animal upright, but this was like trying to hold back the tide. The whole mess fell, showering dust and sparks into the air as parts of the mill broke free and skidded into the fire.

The clearing was alive in an instant. Wild figures in oilskin coats with wet blankets tangled about their legs. Emanuel Trask, the foreman, let out a roar that could wake the dead. His head had been no more than five feet from where the mill had landed. Saddle horses reared and snorted among the trees.

Atlas's near side hoof gave one final thrash and then lay still. Emanuel circled the body in disbelief, then stumbled to an outcrop of rock, dropped to his haunches and held his head in his hands.

"God Almighty, the poor bugger!" His face was haggard in the half light. Hooked nose, wild eyed and full beard. "It was too damn long with that much weight. We should have brought block and tackle to unload the damn thing!"

His mind wandered back to the small village of Dargo from where the horses had been forced to carry their loads up the treacherous grades into the mountains towards the mine. No wagon could handle the terrain. When forced to stop for the night, there was no way to unload the animals as they would not be able to reload them in the morning, so the horses were forced to stand all night, waiting for first light to begin the journey again.

Emanuel cursed himself under his breath, "I thought we'd make it in a bloody day!" He still found it hard to justify the mistake. "Bloody Major Terry, I told him we should have cut through a road to bring a wagon up!"

The fire, flared up by the flying mill lit up the scene in a flickering yellow glow, picking up the shocked faces as the men, looking down at the fallen animal, prodding it in the stomach with their boots to test that it was fully dead. The stomach shuddered with late nerves, but that was as close to coming alive as Atlas would ever get. Pink foam bubbled from the nose and the eyes were wide open.

On the rock, Emanuel hunched the blanket around his shoulders and stared into the darkness. But there was no way to cover his own guilt. The first light was just stirring the tree tops that dropped away to the South. Mist was still hiding in the valleys. They had travelled two dangerous miles in darkness as it was, before being forced to stop to wait until daylight.

"How's the rest of the horses," Emanuel mumbled, never turning from beneath the blanket.

"The mare's about done, boss, but the bay's still alright. Course they didn't have near the weight to carry that Atlas did!" Charley had no teeth down one side of his mouth and the lower part of his jaw didn't seem to fit right. The result of a wild colt and a rail fence when he was a lad. His legs were bowed and his back didn't seem to fit right when he moved. Only on horseback everything came together.

Emanuel snapped a dry twig between his fingers, his jaws still working beneath the rough beard. "We broke the machine down as far as it would go. There was no other way we could have loaded it." He stared off into the distance though he could see nothing but the vision of the dead horse in his mind. He heard the soft sound of a boot in flesh.

"Keep your damned boots to yourself!"

The accent was broad Yorkshire, always more evident when he was upset. "And get the rest of the mess to the mine as soon as you can see. Get straight back and bring another pack horse, the strongest one you can find, you might have to go into Grant to get one. And bring a block and bloody tackle!"

Emanuel wrapped the blanket tightly and watched the sky lighten up in the East. "God Almighty, what a mess!"

It was almost eleven o'clock when Charley and two others arrived back with a bay Clydesdale, block and tackle and a half empty rum bottle.

By that time, Emanuel had freed the harness from the dead animal and cleared a path some thirty yards to the butt of a giant mountain ash with a good sturdy limb that he thought might support the stamp mill. The work had been hard, as there were many large logs to clear away. Emanuel's hands were blistered from the axe and his beard glistened with sweat. He was not used to manual work since he had become foreman of the Royal Dargo.

He sat on a fallen log like a beaten dog, running a line of spit into the dirt between his feet. A racking cough tore at his lungs and this left him half spent.

Three years ago when he quit the coal mines in Lithgow, a doctor had told him to get out of the mines. Get work in some dry place, somewhere like Bourke, or perhaps move into the mountains where the air was clear.

Emanuel's reply was quick, as he had spent quite some time in Bourke. "I expect I'll be going to Hell soon enough, so I'll take the mountains!"

At least, the lungs were not as bad as they once were. There was no blood nowadays.

They dragged Atlas into a gully off the edge of the clearing then fixed chains to the Mill and with the Clydesdale, dragged it to the base of the mountain ash. The most agile of the men, a strong young lad named Groves, climbed to the limb and brought the pulley up. By noon, they had the cast iron machine strapped securely into place. The great horse's legs buckled under the strain, but he remained upright.

"Jeez boss, I hope we don't lose this one," Charley would have prayed to some God had he known a God, "I hate doing this to no animal!"

"You think I bloody-well like it? The faster we get going the better."

There were only a little over three miles to the mine, but they were hard miles. The path was boggy and rough as it climbed steeply across the spur, weaving between timber and outcrops of rock. At places, the track was too narrow to take the wide load and the timber had to be cleared away to let them through, at others they ploughed through mud where water cut the track, through soft bracken filled with leaches that clung to boots and fetlocks alike.

But despite the isolation, many travelled this track to the diggings at Crooked Creek and Grant. Emanuel had been trying to persuade the mine to cut a new road through for many months. A road that could carry a wagon, but so far had met with little success.

The Royal Dargo was owned by a syndicate of three men—Terry, Watts and Maloney—all based in Melbourne. It was a sluice mine and there were many who didn't like the method of sluicing. Emanuel was one of them. Watts and Maloney spent little time at the mine, their only interest the ledgers and the gold the ledgers told them had been taken out.

Major Terry though, was around more often. More often than Emanuel cared for. Riding a half Arab mare, carrying a riding crop, a sharp temper and a biting tongue, his main contribution to running a profitable mine was cutting costs. He liked things neat and run with military precision and order. But there was little of that around a gold mine.

The men could hear the sounds of the Royal Dargo long before they arrived. The first thing they saw was the spray. A mist rising above the timber washed with a rainbow of colours.

The water was channelled from a stream, half a mile higher up the mountain. It travelled along timber chutes, before being channelled into a large canvas pipe that narrowed in size until the water burst through a nozzle with such force that two strong men could barely hold it.

The jet of water directed at the mountain side, gouged out timber, mud and rock, and, hopefully, a little gold. The buildings of the Royal Dargo clung to every spot on the hillside where a footing could be found, tin and bark shacks, tents, clinging like vermin among the timber and rocks. The administration building however took pride of place, sprawling low and flat, built of rusty corrugated iron on the only narrow clearing. The sign 'Royal Dargo' scrawled across the front, and below in smaller letters, 'Props. Watts, Malloy and Terry'.

The sign was black and looked as if it had been painted with a tar brush.

Jock Hoolahan met them in front of the building, a monster of a man, with a tawny mass of ginger hair that had not seen a pair of scissors for many years and craggy eyebrows that ran across the front of his forehead like unravelled rope. Jock and Emanuel went back a long way. He had been the one who had brought Emanuel to this high country mine in the first place. "Hey boss, you son of a bitch, I never thought you'd get here! Major Terry's been giving me Hell!"

The sound of the water crashing against the cliff face almost drowned out the words.

"We're here now, so you better get that damn thing off that animal's back before Terry kills him too!"

"The gelding that you sent in earlier is almost done boss. Completely broke. He won't be no good any more. Terry's about to have a fit!"

Emanuel wheeled his mount around towards the cook house. "I'm going to get some grub in my belly, then head out to Harrietville to collect the wife and kids. I'm a long time behind already. Tell Terry that I'll be back in a few days."

"Jeez boss, you'd better not go yet!" Jock was dumfounded. "Tell him yourself if you mean too. He's already pissed off!"

Emanuel spat in the dust. "Tell Major Terry to get fucked!"

Chapter 2

She always had trouble with corsets.

The hooks on the back instead of the front. A man must have invented them. Of course arthritis in her fingers didn't help. Her mother had died riddled with it. She glanced at her reflection in the mirror, lit up in the yellow glow of a kerosene lamp. The lamp was low on spirits and the wick was starting to blacken. Emanuel was careful with little things like that. He didn't like to waste kerosene on a light they would soon be leaving behind.

She wound her hair up into a tight bun, set a hat in place, then secured it with the needle she carried in her mouth for the purpose, then knotted the hat firmly beneath her chin. Her face had well-formed features, considered handsome by some when she was young.

Especially when she smiled. But Emily felt little cause to smile nowadays. Her body was thin, hard and strong, strapped firmly back into place after three hard births.

Wearing a heavy knitted jumper beneath a long, grey coat and a woollen skirt above buckled up boots, there were no trousers for Emily. Even if they were more practical astride a horse. If the Good Lord meant you to wear trousers, he would have made you a man. She found that she and the Good Lord shared the same views on many things.

Emily scooped up the porcelain pot with rambling roses scrolled over the side, half full of a yellowish liquid. The day was just breaking light when she emptied the contents out the back door.

She would have gone further, but rain had fallen during the night, and rivulets of water ran through the mud. She rinsed the pot under the broken gutter above the doorway. She'd miss that pot, once the property of her mother, but then they couldn't take everything. Out across the yard she could see the shaggy white rooster searching, a little bewildered around what was left of the fowl yard. But the hens were gone, loaded into a wire cage strapped to the side of a pack horse.

This was done while he was away, visiting the neighbours. The rooster would have to stay as she had no time to bother with it now.

Her breasts, full of milk, were beginning to pain, and she could hear the whimper of the baby, just about to wake in the basket at the foot of the bed. When fully awake, Harry had to be fed at once. He had felt this an undeniable right from the instant he left the womb. At nine months, he didn't have the patience to wait, and this trait was to stay with him until his death. Emily wrapped a heavy shawl around her shoulders, scooped the child up and made a nest for him in it, pulled up the jumper and opened her blouse, adjusted everything to fit, all as she moved about the room. Time wasted was the work of the Devil.

The basket would have to stay, a baby crib was already strapped to one of the horses. She lifted the top plate of the stove where the fire was banked and almost out. The family had already eaten and were ready to go. A quick look around for any forgotten items found the hat box full of old papers to deal with on the kitchen table.

She sorted through the box as the baby feasted on her breast. There were letters from her sisters. One married a railway fettler living somewhere in Queensland while the other, Harriet, was still single and lived with her mother in Newcastle.

Into the coals went the letters. She would like to keep them, but there was no room for sentiment in the place where she was going. Next came a crumpled photograph that Jim had tried to eat when it fell from the mantel-piece when he was still an infant. It showed her mother standing wide and stern, dressed as always in black, her father Albert, tall and thin with the back-turned collar of a Methodist minister riding below a prominent Adam's apple.

The only record she had of her parents. Into the fire went the photo. The flames had caught and the sides of the envelopes were turning up. A few old cards, and then the envelope wrapped in a piece of ribbon with a few strands of dark hair inside. Emily froze as she ran the strands through her fingers. Jacob. She already had the name picked, so sure it was a boy. Jacob came still-borne, three weeks early, perfectly formed with a strange head of dark hair. Emily was alone when it happened, one early morning when the pain struck her down and the mess flowed between her legs. She made it into the bathtub and that was where Mrs O'Brien found her some hours later. The only birth that ever came easy. Jim, standing in his cot screaming to be fed had brought Mrs O'Brien from next door.

Emily tried to find a place to carry the envelope, then remembered the few vicious words she had picked up in the corner of her hearing all those years ago, *Strapped in corsets too long…*

She tossed it with her other memories into the fire, stirred the ashes so everything would burn then closed the lid.

So this was it then.

Emanuel was moving about like a large animal in the lean-to, a skillion roof that clung to the side of the house. She could hear the snort of the animals, the slap of harness, the high-pitched, excited voice of Nell.

Emily killed the light and carrying the burden sucking wolfishly on her breast, went out to join her family.

There were six horses in all. A large roan gelding belonged to Emanuel, the rest on loan from the cattleman, William King, including the little bay filly that Emily was to ride. The bay, Jenny, belonged to King's wife. Old William King had a soft spot for Emily. In fact, from what Emily heard, had a soft spot for most women.

The horses were loaded high with household goods. One with armchairs strapped to each side, with the legs removed so that they could pass easily between the dense timber.

Emanuel had removed the legs with a wrench and Emily could see the track-marks in the timber. Huddled inside the chairs were two children. George, her younger son in one chair and her daughter Nell in the other, while the eldest son Jim, sat wedged between bags of chaff on the next horse, his face pinched, cold and serious. Jim's face was always that way and his mother worried about him. She thought he was a little weak in the chest.

George sat sulking, only half awake, holding the hand-carved gun he always carried on a journey. Nell bubbled with excitement, at last close to her father which, she felt, was like being close to heaven. Emanuel had difficulty keeping her inside the chair and eventually had to tie her there, then strapped her brother in for good measure.

He patted Nell on the knee. "Quiet down lass, we're in for a long journey and I'd hate to have to tie that tongue of yours down, less we'd all be deaf before we reached the spur."

He squeezed her knee again before moving on, checking the pack horses. An uneven load could spell disaster on this journey. The horses were loaded with chicken cages, chickens still intact, bedding, baby crib, food, tools and clothing.

Even a sewing machine. The whole thing looked like the picture of a camel train Emily had once seen in biblical magazine.

Emanuel helped her into the saddle and she drew her skirt up to fit. No side saddle for Emily. But her corsets were killing her. Maybe she should have done away with them for the journey, but she gritted her teeth and adjusted Harry to the other side. He burped and spat milk all over her. Emily always milked well. The smallest heifers always gave the best milk, Emanuel often said. She always felt like hitting him when he said that. Of course old King had told her he'd rather carry a fifty pound bag of flour on a horse than carry a baby. But that was a man for you.

"All set lass?" Emanuel, in unusually high spirits, winked at his son sitting between the chaff bags, "The big journey begins then." He patted the roan on the rump and led the pack out onto the street.

There were a few lights in the windows of Harrietville as the sky began to soften in the east. They passed the Blacksmith shop, a bark-roofed skillion open to the street, where fat Carl worked at the forge, stripped to his singlet, stomach hanging over his belt. A buggy stood off to the side with a missing wheel. They could hear the ring of hammer on anvil as Carl worked a strap of white hot iron. They heard the sizzle of steam as he lowered it into a bucket.

"Tell King I'll be back with his horses in a few days." Emanuel bellowed as they passed.

Fat Carl's only reply was a grunt and a scratch of his stomach.

Water trickled down the wheel-ruts of the street and a line of fog hung a few inches above the ground. The horses' hooves were lost in a soft cloud.

Chapter 3

The road led up the mountain towards Hotham Heights before winding down the south side towards Omeo. But five miles up the road Emanuel led the party off to the right onto a track that wound between heavy scrub and snow gums.

Emanuel rode in front on his roan gelding, leading two of the pack-horses, the first with the two children aboard. Jim followed next, entrusted to lead the last of the pack while Emily brought up the rear. Further into the journey, they would turn the pack-horses loose to follow along behind as they had been trained.

The track was narrow and heavily timbered and Emily soon saw the wisdom of removing the legs from the chairs. Progress was slow and torturous as they followed the tops of the ridges, deeper into the mountain. They picked their way carefully around the moss-covered logs, through gullies, between outcrops of rock and it wasn't long before Emily was completely lost. By lunchtime, the small party had only reached the hollow on the south side of Mt St Bernard. Here Emanuel decided to call a halt as Emily was exhausted and the baby crying.

"We'll take a break here and boil the billy."

He had learned a little as foreman at the mine and knew not to push a man beyond his limits. He seemed a little softer than usual as he helped Emily from the saddle. It was only her iron will, or perhaps her stubbornness that stopped her collapsing on the grass.

The baby was wringing wet and had dirtied both himself and his mother thoroughly. Emily laid him out on the snow grass and went to work on the mess while Emanuel untied the two children and helped them to the ground. They had fought all the way from Harrietville and no sooner had her feet hit the ground than Nell kicked her brother in the shins. He chased her off into the scrub and Emanuel winched when he heard the sounds that came from the bushes.

Jim was the eldest, and therefore found himself with most of the work, and most of the abuse. "Tie the horses up lad and look lively about it!"

Emanuel tried to make small talk as he started a small fire, realising that Emily was completely exhausted. "By nightfall, we'll be well out on the Dargo High Plains. There's only four families own the leases to this part of the high country."

His eyes played out across waving snow grass, covered with wildflowers.

"Thousands of acres of it. It's fine grazing land in the warm months but murder during the cold. Some of the homesteaders winter their stock on runs down on the low country during the cold months. Those cattlemen think they are kings up here."

The billy was bubbling. He threw in a handful of leaves and swung it around his head by the handle. It was a trick he liked to show off. One he'd learned from the Colonials.

"When we break over the divide, off to the east is the Bogong High Plains, they run clear down to the Cobunga River, down towards Omeo."

His eyes drifted off across the waving grass and the twisted Snow gums. "You'll like the hut me and old Jock built on the spur."

"Anything you did with Jock Hoolahan would have to be a worry," Emily said.

"You're pretty hard on old Jock. He's a pretty handy man at times. Never seen a man better with an adze or broad axe. You got him terrified, you know? Could hold you out in one hand like a rag doll but he's still scared of you!"

Emanuel was too, in his own way. "Only thing Jock Hoolahan's terrified of is a good wash."

Nell and George burst out of the scrub and Nell hit him behind the ear with a clod. The howl was deafening—but not as loud as Emanuel's voice. And for a while the whole mountain went quiet.

Emanuel changed the subject, "We put up the hut at the bottom end of King's Spur, not far from the mine."

He kicked the ashes in with his boot. "You know why they're called spurs?"

He held his hand out, palm down with the fingers spread. "Imagine the top of my hand as the mountains and the fingers are the spurs running down to the valleys below. That's the best way I can describe it. You'll love the spot. You're so high if it wasn't for the trees you could see the ocean to the south on a clear day."

After they had eaten, Emanuel found it hard to get his crew moving again. Everybody had had enough and he well knew the journey had barely started. They would not reach the spur before the next nightfall, and this was a worry.

They climbed up one ridge, weaving between timber and rock, then down the other side, then up the next, always climbing higher into the mountain. They reached Mt Freezout at about three in the afternoon, then on to Blue Rag. The range began to drop off to the east as Emanuel drove them on, horses floundering over moss covered logs and through heavy timber and bracken. Emily pleaded to stop. By this stage, she carried little if she lived or died, but Emanuel knew that it would be impossible to set up camp in this terrain. They continued on until at last the country began to level out a little and it was here in late afternoon that Emanuel called a stop on a small rise near a grove of trees, a spring breaking out beneath some rocks some twenty yards away.

By now, George was asleep in the chair and even Nell had lost her fight. "Unpack those horses Jim, hobble 'em and turn 'em loose while I set up camp! Look lively, lad!"

Emily did collapse this time. She just folded up on the snow grass holding the infant beside her.

Emanuel knelt down and softly felt her cheek. With his left hand, he checked the baby. "I'm sorry, lass, I expect I drove you hard. But I'll soon get a fire going and rig a tent."

He stretched a canvas between two saplings and spread a tarpaulin over a bed of snow grass. It wasn't long before he had the fire burning. Jim still struggled with the pack horses, an ever growing pile of gear spread out on the ground beneath the scrub. The sewing machine was too heavy for him and it crashed to the ground.

George and Nell now fully awake were playing in the mud beside the spring, slapping at the mosquitoes. Emanuel carried an armful of blankets to make up the beds. "Come here Nell, George, you can help with this. You're not completely useless you know!"

Emily had almost recovered by now and lay propped up against a saddle feeding the baby. "I never knew old King had ever carried a baby, let alone a bag of flour!"

Emanuel laughed. He'd never seen Emily so beaten before. "Then he don't know what he missed!"

The pan was over the coals and he had managed to find some bacon and a few eggs that were unbroken. He sent George to the spring for water and found a place for the blackened billy among the flames.

"There's been aborigines camped here. See those stones down by the pool, lass?" He said, drawing Nell onto his knee. "Don't see many this far up the mountain as a rule. Too cold."

Emily was a little concerned. "Where are they now?"

"Don't know. They only take little girls anyway!" he said, jiggling Nell on his knee. Then more seriously, "Probably weeks since they were here. But we won't have any trouble with 'em anyhow.

Sometimes down on the plains the cattlemen loose an occasional steer. But they won't trouble us up here."

The mosquitoes came in droves with the coming dusk. Emanuel threw green leaves onto the fire to make it smoke. Smoke in their eyes were better than the mosquitoes. But still their hands slapped steadily into the night.

Awake at dawn, it was a full hour before the horses were loaded. Breakfast was stale damper, corned meat and tea. The sun was well up before they started, mist covering the mountain peaks to the South.

The country was changing as they moved lower onto the plains. The wild white clover and softer grasses grew right up to the roots of the timber. Wild flowers were everywhere, along with Heather and all manner of mountain shrubs. These were not really plains as such, just country a little less wooded with rolling green hills cut by deep chasms. When they passed close to an escarpment in one place where the timber opened out, they could see the mist below them like thick cloud covering the ranges that spread as far as the eye could see to the South, sharp peaks cutting through in places, one tall granite spire looking like a tomb-stone in the cloud.

Emanuel did not call an evening stop. There was only six miles to go, but tough miles. The moon was late rising and was often darkened by drifting cloud. During the dark times they picked their way blindly, feeling their way through the scrub. Emily could hardly recall what happened at this time, but she knew they were travelling downhill, the horses sliding and slipping between boulders and timber. She remembered asking how far it was to the hut.

"Not far," Emanuel lied. It was pitch black when they reached the place the locals called Angel's Leap. No one knew where the name came from, but Emanuel was afraid to attack it in the dark. He dismounted and walked back along the line. The pack horses were uncoupled now and had followed along in procession at their own speed, making their own way between the timber. "Let your pony have his head and try not to look down, I'll go along on foot. We'll be fine, let the pony take his own footing. The young 'uns are asleep so that's the better." He patted Emily on the knee. "Look sharp, son," He said to Jim, "and let the horse have his head!"

They waited until cloud cleared the face of the moon, then Emanuel began the descent. The track was only a few feet wide, loose gravel sliding underfoot, skipping over the edge, they could hear the stone rattling down the hillside. When the sky darkened they halted, then when it lightened again continued on, at times glints of the river some three thousand feet below could be seen between the timber.

It took almost an hour to gain the bottom of the leap. The country became heavily timbered, with snow gums giving way to Mountain ash and Woolly butt with the odd Red Gum. They were on King's Spur.

They travelled on further through the thickening undergrowth through light and darkness, then the clouds cleared for a moment as they broke through onto a small clearing with a huge red Gum in the centre, and a small cabin on the far side. It was like sighting the Holy Grail.

The baby let out an almighty squall.

Harry Trask had arrived at King's Spur.

Chapter 4

The cabin was built from logs of Mountain Ash, stripped of bark, trimmed by adze and axe, mortised and fitted at the corners. The cracks between the logs were plastered with a mixture of red clay, horse hair and just the right amount of lime. It had a bark roof held in pace by narrow rails, with a veranda clinging to the South side. There had been no shortage of good bark during the months it had taken to throw the building together and Emanuel had become quite expert at peeling it off the logs, loosening it first with the back of an axe, then standing on top, driving in the bar to peel the bark off in long strips. That was how he almost lost three toes, when his foot slipped just as the crow-bar was driving down. A good set of boots saved the toes. As it was they were blue and broken for the many months it took to fix themselves. But they were never quite right again and he was to carry them that way for the rest of his life.

There was a kitchen and two rooms, divided with a roll of new hessian. A dirt floor, levelled and swept clean. A chimney at one end and a water tank at the other. The tank, a square steel one, salvaged from the mine, was to be filled from a small spring some three hundred yards down the spur, carried on a sled built from the fork of a handy-sized tree, the water then bucketed into the tank. At least that was Emanuel's plan.

The bark roof was no way to run drinking water into a tank.

A rough lavatory stood against a granite bolder, an easy walk from the back door. There was a horse yard made of stringy-bark rails close to the hut, where the horses stood hobbled. Emanuel had not quite completed the job as yet. There was also a barn that needed to be built.

Emily inspected her new home on aching legs, finding it difficult to even stand, while Emanuel followed behind like an eager puppy, waiting for a pat. A very large puppy with a full beard and a hooked nose. But praise was a hard thing to find with Emily.

"We'll get a new floor down before winter," he said. "In this room at least. I'll get timber from the mine." Emanuel, although an honest man, found anything going to waste at the mine as fair game.

"Terry's got a mind-set on replacing the floor in the Assay room. He's got a thing about people dropping small bits of gold between the floorboards. I think the man's mad."

Emanuel's excitement grew when they came to the chimney. He considered this a masterpiece stoned up to the height of a man with the shape to make it draw well. Jock Hoolahan had designed the whole thing and Emanuel had hauled the stone on a sled drawn by his roan saddle-horse. His hands were still blistered from the job. The fireplace was huge, large enough to carry the butt of a small tree. He had left it loaded with firewood before travelling to Harrietville and Emily had almost cried with joy after Emanuel fired it up when they arrived, almost frozen last night. It never ceased to amaze her how her husband, usually as considerate as a house brick, could sometimes do something as thoughtful as that.

There was an iron bar set into the stonework just at the right height to hang the cast iron cook pot that they had carried all the way from Harrietville. *That would do for a time*, she thought. But she would still miss her stove. The hob was huge and would easily carry the old blackened water fountain.

Except for the two armchairs they had bought with them, the furniture was all handmade. A wooden frame for a bed was built of rails with hessian stretched between and a table had been built from slabs of milled timber from the mine, while a couple of boxes that had once held dynamite, stood as cupboards against one wall.

From outside, they heard the sound of Jim's voice followed by a loud slap.

"Didn't hurt y' rotten maggot!" Then the thud of a boot and a high, piercing scream.

Emanuel winced.

Emily knew she would miss the small house in Harrietville. Would miss the few friends she had made and particularly miss the schooling for the kids. They'd have to do something about that, even up here, else they'd likely grow up like a pack of wild animals.

Jim had been coming along well at the school in Harrietville. Could read better than his father already. Emily tried to rub the pain away from her buttocks. They'd best start setting things up. The goods that they had carried with them were still dumped under the shelter of the veranda. She could hear King's horses stamping around in the rail yard at the back of the hut. So much to do and her legs were killing her-and the baby would be awake soon.

She had dreaded the thought of coming into the mountains, but what had to be done, had to be done. If it were God's will to lead her family into the wilderness, then so be it.

There was to be one life change, however. She had flung her corsets off, and off they could stay. That was letting her values slip, but little by little she felt things had been slipping lately. Now they were in this wilderness she may have to develop a new set of rules to handle life.

"You better help me get these things inside," she said. "Then you best take those horses back to King."

As they moved their worldly possessions inside, Emily marvelled at the work Emanuel had done during the past summer. She had barely seen him for months on end, and though he explained that he and Jock Hoolahan were working on the hut every spare minute, Emily felt a little dubious. She had never trusted the pair together. Emanuel was not a drinking man, but he often smelled of alcohol after he had been working with Jock Hoolahan. And Jock didn't get those red veins in his nose from drinking tea.

She paused holding her back, then lay her hand gently on Emanuel's arm. "You did well here," she said. "You and old Jock Hoolahan."

Emanuel sat astride the big roan gelding to deliver a list of instructions for the rest of the day. A stern sermon in his best Yorkshire accent. His accent seemed to change with his moods.

William King's horses were strung out behind him on a rope.

"Now Jim, you're the man of the house while I'm away, so act like it and don't fight with your brother, or I'll tan your hide when I get back."

The horses stamped and moved their feet about.

"You see them stringy bark logs by the horse yard? Get the bark off them while I'm away. You seen me do it, lad. Use the back of the axe and mind you don't cut a foot off. The rest of you kids, help your mother and take notice of what Jim tells you!"

Emanuel wheeled the pack around.

"I expect to be back in about a week. I'll have to go to the mine after I drop the horses off."

He was talking to Emily now. She was standing in the doorway, hands working in her apron.

"I expect to pick up a milker in Grant before I get back. There's a widow there willing to sell a little Jersey. Lovely cow." He turned again to his oldest son, "So get those rails barked then we can throw up some milking bales when I get back."

He wheeled the roan towards the track that led up the hillside towards Harrietville, jamming his heels into the horse's flank. He turned to wave once, before he was lost between the timber.

At the doorway, Emily wiped her hands on her apron. Life always seemed easier for men, with everything laid out before them. She knew she would be lonely up here, even with the kids. Even now she missed the big oaf with the heavy beard and the hooked nose. She felt a rare rush of affection.

And this was about as close to love as Emily would ever get.

Chapter 5

The Royal Dargo Mine was strangely quiet when Emanuel rode into the clearing. A few men lay about, smoking in the shade of a tree, but these were the only people Emanuel could see. Over by the cliff face he could see the canvas pipe, weaving like a long snake leading to the giant brass nozzle that stood idle and silent. It was like a small cannon, mounted on a trolley, the whole thing imported from California at an expense that made Terry shudder every time he thought about it. It worked on a swivel base, manoeuvred by a wooden beam. When spewing water there needed two men to control it, by rights, but Terry said one man worth his salt should be able to handle the thing. Terry liked to save money. The water gouged rubble from the hillside, washing it into a pit further down the valley, from where a team of tip-drays carried it to the mill-race to be drained onto a series of sluice trays. As many as a dozen men worked these trays at a normal time, but now the whole thing stood idle. It seemed like a ghost mine. The stamping mill he had brought up from Dargo stood assembled on a small plateau, the formwork for a slab of concrete laid out beside it. This was the only change Emanuel could see as he rode towards the administration building.

Jock Hoolahan, wild-eyed and half-crazy, met him at the door.

"What the hell's goin' on Jock? You lot taking a bloody holiday?"

"Holiday my arse! Them bloody Crayes wrecked the water race!"

Jock's eyes were wild and not quite focused. "We seen that young bastard Henry Craye mustering steers yesterday, and now there's a section of the damn race down, trampled to hell and back by cattle. Them Crayes don't like the mines about. Think they own the whole damn world!"

"Where's Terry?"

"Gone back to Melbourne, thank God. You know it really shook him up losing those horses!"

"Bully for Terry. It didn't do me much good either. How's the gelding?"

"Dead."

Emanuel swore. "Then we better go look at the mess. Maybe we can save something of the damn mine!" He hitched the roan to a sapling, then turned to the men laying beneath the tree.

"Get off your bums, you lot and start shifting rubble up to the chute. It won't kill you to be a few loads in front!" *And a lot easier to work with a dry arse*, he thought. Normally you'd be working under a cold spray most of the time.

Emanuel followed the empty water race back up the steep incline into the mountain, so steep he had to scramble on hands and knees in places. Jock Hoolahan found it difficult to keep pace and talk at the same time.

"Only good thing, the Major finally decided to cut that road in from Dargo. Losing them horses really got to him."

"About bloody time!"

"We got everyone up there working," Jock panted, his bad knees no match for Emanuel, weaving between the trees and rocks, following the track that hugged the wooden water race. "I got Jimmy O'Brien in charge!" It was a steep climb. They had gone almost half a mile straight up before they came to the spot. The race, joints sealed by tar had crossed a small ravine on a wooden trestle. The trestle was down, the timber scattered and trampled, water roaring like an avalanche from the broken trough. It had already gouged out a gully, carrying rocks and dry timber before it, piling up around brier bushes and bracken, washing aimlessly down the mountain side.

Twenty men worked at the site with crowbars and shovels. Axes, hammers, nails and tar to seal the joints in the new timber.

They heard Charley Nash coming up a track from the North—the long way around from the mine, leading a draft horse, dragging a bundle of sawn timber on a sled. There was very little room for the sled on the rough track and the horse stumbled and scrabbled, hooves tearing at the shifting stone.

Emanuel was squatting, examining the cattle tracks.

"You see the mess we get into when you're not around boss!" Charley bellowed. "Won't old Major Shit be pleased?"

"I'm not pleased either. We better have an armed man patrolling the run in future," Emanuel said. "If you see one of Craye's steers in the area, shoot it. Maybe that will tell 'em something."

"Hell I'd rather shoot a Craye than one of his steers!" Jock muttered. "The steers got more brains."

"Maybe. But it's not quite as legal. Old Rube would miss one of his steers more than one of his sons anyway, most likely!"

Emanuel doubted Jock would shoot anything anyway. Despite his size and despite his talk, Jock Hoolahan was a gentle giant. A man so shy he could barely speak to a woman. Although he had heard, though he'd never seen it, Jock was said to be a regular bull in a whorehouse. But in the company of a respectable woman, a real woman as Jock called them, he could barely manage a word.

If Jock had the gun and Henry Craye came back with his steers, the man would probably be quite safe.

Chapter 6

The weather changed rapidly in the high country, often with four seasons in the one day. But the summer of eighty six was an unusually dry one, and as the high country dried off, fires ravaged a great area of the western side, from the Dargo River to Mt Tabletop.

The Trask holding had grown over the summer. The milking herd that had begun with a single jersey heifer had swollen to an old Illawarra shorthorn, heavily pregnant with udder almost rubbing the ground and a sway-back mare of questionable age called Bess. These Emanuel had purchased from widow O'Brien from the tiny gold mining village of Grant.

Later, two Hereford cows joined the herd.

William King lost a great many cattle that year and often arrived at Emily's door with a spare poddy calf slung over the pommel of his saddle. Emily reared so many of these that winter that her small herd soon spread out over the hillside and Jim found his time cut out holding the cattle close.

The snow began in early June, first a little flurry, then the winds came and the cold fronts swept through, blanketing the high country in white. At times, the mine closed when the water froze in the chutes.

Herds of cattle were moving down from the high country, driven to the lowlands around Dargo and Omeo, where both King and Lee Paterson had their winter holdings.

When the mine was closed, Emanuel found himself with more time to make improvements to the homestead. He put down timber floors and even a veranda floor. Built a set of milking bails under a small bark-roofed barn and finished the horse and fowl yards. A pile of firewood grew against the back wall, almost as high as the wall itself. He divided off one section of the veranda with hessian and installed a tin bath tub standing on second hand bricks. Outside in the yard stood a second hand copper mounted on a rough, stone fireplace. Emanuel was well pleased with himself.

By this time, Harry had been weaned and another baby, Bess, was on the way. Emily bred better than King's cattle and her breed were certainly better fed.

It was late winter when Emanuel was away at the mine that a man called Gordon Jones called at the homestead. This was not an unusual practice, even in such an isolated spot as the road from Dargo to the mine was partially finished and passed not a mile below, while there was also a track from the north west that miners often used on their way to the diggings at Crocked Creek and Grant.

The wind rattled the front door on its leather hinges and snow swirled against the new glass windows when Gordon knocked at the door.

He was half frozen as he backed up against the fireplace, rubbing his hands behind his back to circulate blood in the fingertips. When Emily offered a cup of tea, the man accepted it readily. This chance meeting to change the Trasks' lives forever.

Jones was a small man with sparse, ginger hair and sun-damaged, pale skin. He warmed his hands around the mug as he sat at the table, now scrubbed almost white with soap and pumice stone.

"I'm finally giving up my lease on the high plains, you know," he said. "I've had enough. It's always something in this damn country. Sorry for the language missus. This drought was the finish. If it don't starve you out, it will freeze you. Thought I'd go live with my sister up in Newcastle." He blew a cool breath across the tea. "Be warmer up there. I've been leasing the run from Lee Patterson for nigh on ten years now, but I've finally had enough. Had enough."

Emily wiped her hands on the apron, "You've been in the mountains a long time, Mr Jones?"

"About twenty years now. But it's a young man's game. I'm going in to Omeo now to see Patterson. Give back his lease."

"How many acres are there in the lease, Mr Jones, if you don't mind me asking?"

"Near about four and a half thousand. You and old Emanuel ought to take it over." He laughed. "Emanuel's still young."

Emily thoughtfully wiped her hands on the apron. Yes, Emanuel was still young.

"If you don't mind me asking, just how much do you pay for the lease?"

"Thirty pounds a year. And not worth a penny of it in this weather."

Emily's gaze shifted to the fireplace. High up on the right side there was a loose stone with a biscuit tin hidden behind it. In the tin was about thirty pounds.

"Well, I better be on now. Thank you for the tea, ma'am. Dreadful day out there. It'll be a lot better up north I expect."

"Yes, I'm sure it will Mr Jones." She wiped her hands until the cloth was half worn away. "I'm sure it will."

Chapter 7

There is a fork in the road from Omeo where it turns up towards the mountains, joining the road from Swift's Creek in the south.

The weather cleared just as quickly as it had closed in and Emily urged the sway-backed mare along through the cold winter morning. A buggy coming towards her from Swift's Creek pulled to the side of the track and the man sitting high on the seat tipped his hat.

"Morning ma'am. The name's Mackenzie. Jim Mackenzie. You're out early and alone I see. What brings a lady out here on a day like this?"

"Oh I've seen worse days Mr Mackenzie. I'm just back from Omeo. Live at King's Spur, up above Dargo. You might know my husband, Emanuel Trask, foreman at the Royal Dargo gold mine."

"Can't say I know the man." Mackenzie was tall with handlebar moustache, stiff collarless shirt buttoned up to the neck. He had cold, grey eyes.

"You've travelled a long way madam. What brings you to Omeo at this time of day?"

Emily considered it no business of his but still replied, "I've just signed a lease with Lee Patterson on the Dargo high plains."

"The deuce you have?" Mackenzie was out of the buggy so quick he almost tripped on the lower step.

"Why the blazes would you do a fool thing like that?—Excuse me ma'am. But God damn that's the very reason I'm going to Omeo!"

"Sorry Mr Mackenzie, but you're a little late." She slapped the document in her pocket, mainly to check it was still there.

"But God Damn ma'am! Excuse me, but why would a women need a cattle lease?"

"Oh I expect my husband will find a use for it Mr Mackenzie."

"But so help me God I only learned of the lease yesterday and I was up at dawn to get to Omeo to see that blasted Patterson!"

"Well, I'm sorry but you were still late Mr Mackenzie."

Mackenzie was almost frothing at the mouth as he clutched Emily's saddle. Behind him the buggy horse was fidgeting. "What did you pay the mongrel, if you don't mind me asking ma'am?"

"Not that it's any of your business, I paid the man thirty pounds."

"Thirty pounds? Thirty pounds? I'll pay you forty on the spot. Forty pounds!"

"I'm sorry Mr Mackenzie, but the lease is not for sale. Good day to you."

As she rode away Emily heard him wrench the reins of the horse, heard the slap of his fist against its head. The horse reared and Mackenzie had difficulty getting him back under control again. He could have broken his hand.

"Four and a half thousand acres?" Emanuel's boots thundered through the house. "Four and a half thousand acres? What are we going to do with that—you must be mad, woman!"

Emily let the man rave. The children looked on in awe, having never seen their father quite like this before.

"And money? What did you use for money, woman?"

"Oh we had thirty pounds in the tin. I used that."

Emanuel found the biscuit tin. Sure enough there was only a little change left. He dropped to his chair and clutched his head in his hands. The biscuit tin upside down on the table.

"You must be mad, women." Emanuel reached for his pipe. He didn't smoke much now-days, not with his lungs.

"How far is it to Omeo?" He tamped tobacco into the pipe bowl with shaking fingers. "It must be nigh on thirty miles. That old mare was lucky to make it that far."

Emily could see that he was beginning to slow down.

"Four and a half thousand acres." Emanuel lumbered to his feet, threw open the door and walked out into the cold. He collapsed onto a stump near the front door.

"Cattle," he mumbled.

As he drew on the pipe it lit up his face. "How the Hell we going to stock that much land?"

He sat there looking out into the frosty night. "Cattle."

Chapter 8

Wangaratta was some eighty miles to the north west and Emanuel and Jim made the journey in two days, camping one night beside the roadside near Bright.

Jim, swollen with pride, sat high in his saddle all day, clutching a raw-hide whip he had platted himself. Jim was always good with his hands.

His father had seldom treated him like a man. Not a real man, and Jim was to discover a side of his father on this journey that he had never seen before. Or perhaps he had seen it, but always around other people.

Around the campfire that night, with pipe drooping from the side of his mouth, Emanuel recited poetry from the old country in a mongrel mix of Yorkshire and Australian accent. Jim was in heaven.

They would have made better time, but Emanuel slowed himself to the speed of the old bay mare, as this was a long journey for the tired, old sway-back.

They rode up the main street of Wangaratta in the late afternoon, stopping in front of the Royal Hotel.

"I'll find a room first, lad, then we'll take care of the horses later."

He booked a room at the office, then taking his son by the shoulder, led him into the bar.

"We best not tell 'em how old you are, son," he said with a wink.

"I'll have a pint of ale, my good man, and a small one for the young fella here!" The barman, walrus moustache, sad eyes and heavy stomach, cast an eye at Jim as he drew the drinks.

"Mind you say nothing to your mother, lad. She'd likely skin us both alive. But if you're man enough to drive cattle, I expect you're man enough to have a drink!"

Jim saw a lean, dirty cattleman at the far end of the bar, a cigarette hanging from the side of his mouth and wished he could look like that. But perhaps the cigarette was going a bit too far with Emanuel at his side. Still he tilted his head back and took a long swallow of the beer. It got up his nose and he nearly gagged. But he felt better than he'd ever felt before.

At the sale the next morning they bought forty head of heifers, a cross bred Hereford bull and an unbroken chestnut colt. Emanuel had seen the boy's eyes on the colt and when it came up for sale asked, "You reckon you could break it, son?"

Jim's throat tightened so he couldn't speak. The auctioneer paused for the second time of asking, hammer in the air. Jim almost choked. Emanuel threw in the final bid and the hammer fell. He slapped his son on the shoulder, "I don't suppose you can be a cattleman without a horse!"

But Emanuel's mood turned sour, as it often did, in the afternoon when they took delivery of the herd. They drove them out of town, Jim leading the unwilling, frisky colt, shying at every opportunity, at every barking dog, often wrenching the boy's shoulder half out of its socket.

The First National Bank was the thing that had upset Emanuel.

"That upstart manager!" He spat. "Young whelp. Hardly old enough to wash behind his ears."

He cracked the whip to keep the mob in line.

"Gives me a form to fill out and knew I couldn't read half the garbage written on it! Hell, I told him I was foreman at the Royal Dargo more summers than he'd had hot breakfasts!"

He cracked the whip across the bull's rump, and the bull resented the treatment. "Keep up boy! Let that pony know who's boss!" He gave the bull another lick with the whip, "I'll likely buy that rotten bank one day, just to put that young whelp out of a job!"

Eventually, in a red brick building down a side street, he had found a money lender by the name of Solomon Slone, who loaned him money for the cattle at seventeen percent interest.

Emanuel angrily took more skin off the flank of the half bred bull.

"Two hundred pounds at seventeen percent"—and the way he was travelling with Major Terry, he would soon most likely be out of a job.

It took them almost a week to reach the high country, the colt travelling easily by that time. Only the bull gave trouble, sometimes propping, refusing to move any further, then tossing his head, trying to find the soft underbelly of a horse or an unwary leg in a stirrup. Emanuel almost wore out its hide with the whip.

"That bull's got a head like old Jack Emery," he once remarked, thinking of the cranky old nozzle-man at the mine.

So that's how the bull got the name, Cranky Jack.

They left the herd grazing in a valley close by the old homestead block on the high plains, then rode down to the spur, down the track of an almost sheer cliff-face called Angels leap. At places, the horses almost slid on their rumps on the gravel until they reached the bottom.

Now comes the hard part, Emanuel thought. To explain to Emily about Solomon Sloan and the loan of money at seventeen percent.

Two hundred pounds.

Chapter 9

Early the next morning, Emanuel left for the mine, hoping that he still held a job, leaving Jim with the task of checking the new herd.

Jim was swollen with pride as he set off with his brother George sitting behind him on the flank of the old bay mare. To leave the new colt behind was a worry, but not to Nell. She was eleven years old now, almost twelve and could ride as well as either of her brothers. She loved the new horse and could hardly keep her hands off him.

The boys had to dismount when they reached Angel's Leap, to climb the cliff-face on foot, leading the old bay mare.

A cold front was spreading across the mountains that day, with light snow drifting down, whipped by small gusts of icy wind. When they finally broke through the snow gums to the homestead on the high plains, the snow was piled high around the rocks and backed up about the tree trunks.

There had once been a fence around the old homestead but that was long gone. A few bushes clung to rotten sections of rails and the gate was off its hinges.

The boys pushed through the overgrown shrubs down the front path, but found the door locked. There was new wood piled beside the front door and a wisp of smoke from a dying fire rising from the chimney. Mystified, they remounted the old bay mare and rode to the valley where the cattle had been left the day before.

But the cattle were gone.

They had no clue as to the boundaries of the high plain's run, so all they could do was search all day through the snow. By mid-afternoon had found only a dozen cattle grazing on a small plateau far to the west. They didn't know if this was part of their own run or not, but as the weather was closing in, they decided to turn for home. The wind blew stronger and snow swirled about them as George sat clinging to his brother almost frozen. When a total white-out enveloped them, they were dangerously close to a sheer cliff. They stopped, blind and lost, not knowing which direction was up, which direction was down. It was difficult even to keep balance without side vision. But eventually the cloud cleared a little and they were able to pick their way along the cliff face.

Then out of the mist, like out of a dream, a man's face appeared. Then his body, draped in heavy oilskin coat, bent forward in the saddle of a very tall horse. A hammerhead pie-ball that stood sixteen hands at the shoulder.

The man nudged the horse towards them, never taking his eyes from their faces, wisps of long blond hair coated with snow sprouting from beneath a shapeless hat.

"What are you two cubs doing up on this mountain?" His eyes were pale and cold. "You whelps belong to the Trask fella—the foreman at the Dargo mine?"

Jim tried to keep the old horse from slipping from the cliff top. The man sent shivers down his spine.

"I'm Jim Trask and this is me brother, George."

The man kneed his horse up beside them, bent before the wind like a half opened pocket knife. He was younger than they first thought. Eyebrows were pale like an albino's with a little snow clinging to a pale beard. They could taste his breath. He healed his horse close beside them and the old bay could barely keep her step beside the cliff face.

"Why don't you kids stay where you belong on a day like this. Your old man ain't no cattleman. You lot got no cause to come up here." He nudged the giant horse closer while his knee pushed against the old bay's side. They heard him laugh. A soft rattle in his throat.

"They say old Trask leased old Patterson's block. He ain't got no business here. He's just bloody mining shit. Why don't he let cattlemen run their own business. We been after this block for years. Bloody deserve it too!"

George's teeth were shivering against his brother's shoulder. "Get back where you belong boys, and tell your old man to keep his damn cattle off my old man's run!"

Then he wheeled away and they could hear his laughter as the snow swallowed him up.

Chapter 10

"That sounds like Henry Craye," Emanuel chewed the corners of his beard. "From what I've heard of him. I've never met the man, but I've seen his father, old Rube Craye. Him and his other son, a half-wit named Albert. I seen 'em one day at the mine. We might have trouble with that lot!"

Emanuel sat in front of the fire, his boots on the hob. He loaded his pipe thoughtfully, tamping the tobacco in the bowl as his temper slowly mounted. "If they've got my cattle they'll soon know about it!"

Emily stood behind him with a heavy iron pan in her hand, holding it like a weapon.

"Threaten my boys they'll know more about it!"

"You say he tried to ride you off the cliff?" Emanuel turned to his oldest son. Jim, his pride badly hurt, shuffled his feet.

"I reckon he did."

"He did alright!" George blurted. Now that the whole thing was over, George was full of fight. "Mighta killed us. Come any closer I would of hit him with something!"

"Better saddle up the horses, lad," Emanuel said to his oldest son. "We'll go straight up there and sort this damn thing out."

"And get those cattle back!" Emily slammed the pan down on the table, dislodging two mugs and a pepper pot.

The day had cleared with a covering of snow blanketing the high country when they arrived at the homestead block. Emanuel rattled the door once, then reared back and lashed out with his boot. It took three blows to splinter the latch, the door swinging open on one damaged hinge. There were dirty metal plates on the table, some covered with smatterings of food, along with dirty tin mugs and a piece of stale damper. There was new wood beside the fireplace and in it the coals were still warm. Emanuel swore and wheeled towards the door. He jerked the big roan's head savagely as he swung into the saddle and spurred the horse off into the timber. Jim followed as best he could on the old bay mare.

It was not hard to follow the tracks in the new snow. At last, they crossed the divide, pausing on the crest of a rise, looking down over the Bogong high plains. They could see three horsemen half a mile below them, driving a herd of cattle through a deep snow drift towards a gap between two cliffs. A place known as the Gap. It looked like a natural holding yard with rails and hessian partly across it. Further to the south two riders were driving a smaller herd of a dozen cattle towards the same spot.

Emanuel was quite calm now. He turned his horse and nudged him away from the crest.

"We best find our cattle, lad. If there's any short, then we'll check that herd and sort a few things out!" He kicked the roan savagely in the rump and turned towards the north east. "Left to their own will, the mob probably went before the wind!"

By sundown, they had recovered all except four of the heifers, scattered to all points of the run and by dark had them back to the homestead. The yards were in poor shape, but Gordon Jones had carried out some repairs during the summer. Within half an hour, they had it shored up enough to hold the cattle for the night.

"You better get back home lad. And go easy at the leap. Tell your mother I'll be staying here the night." He unsaddled his horse in a tumbledown yard out back. Someone had left a bag of chaff. "Very kind of them I must say. Now go along lad, and ride careful, mind!"

Emanuel propped the broken door closed with a chair and lit a fire with the wood provided, then helped himself to a can of beef he found in the cupboard. Then he filled a billy from a snow-drift outside and set it on the fire to boil. He found tea in the same dirty cupboard, then slumped on a chair, threw his boots on the hob and waited.

They came an hour later, the noise travelling well before them. There was an argument, when they found his horse in the yard.

The door rattled. First a pause then a shove and the door swung open. Ruben Craye stood wide legged in the doorway. "Who the Devil are you?" he roared.

Ruben was almost as wide as he was tall. A huge bear of a man in dirty woollen coat, with hat down over his eyes. He carried a leather raw hide thong looped around his left wrist.

"I'll ask the same question," Emanuel swung his boots to the floor. "I'm Emanuel Trask and I own this damn place!"

Ruben moved into the room on heavy legs, the leather thong beating against his leg. The rest of his crew moved in behind him. Five men in all.

"Might interest you to know Trask, if that's your damn name, but this hut ain't in the lease. The homestead block's been surveyed off. Nobody owns it."

"The Devil they don't. It's the homestead block. That's that. A homestead goes with the lease."

"Check the records you old fool," Ruben moved over to the fire and slumped into the chair Emanuel had vacated. "Me and the men been using the place while we muster. Ain't nobody owns the place. It's who's here first. Now you're trespassing, so get the hell out before I lose my patience!"

One of the men kicked the door shut. A stiff breeze had blown up and snow was falling again. The door blew open again so he had to jam it shut with the broken chair.

There was a lean and arrogant man that Emanuel took to be Henry and a much heavier man, probably Albert, his elder brother. There was a hard man with pockmarked face and another, quick moving with a head like a rat. Emanuel watched them move around the room with rage building up inside him. Henry found a jar of half-eaten peaches in the cupboard, speared a piece with the knife then swung a leg insolently across the table as he worked at the half empty jar.

"Why don't you scum get out. This is my lease of land and you have no right to be on it. Either running your cattle or using the hut for a camp. You are not welcome here!"

"We got more right to this land than you have you Pommy bastard. We was born here. Been here all our lives. You come here buggering up the country with your stinkin' mine and think you own the place. We been usin' this hut to camp for years!"

"Not anymore. You scattered my cattle and threatened my sons…"

The man with the pockmarked face moved up behind and kicked Emanuel's feet from beneath him. He crashed to the floor but regained his feet in an instant, swinging wildly.

There was not much science to the way Emanuel fought. Only piston fists driven by blind rage. Except for the rage he would have landed more blows. But a few found their mark and a tooth and a smattering of blood found the floor. Then Henry moved in with his boots and the rat man moved in too. Then Albert, slow at first, caught the blood lust and joined in. Chairs crashed and the lamp spun from the table, spilling burning kerosene across the dusty floorboards. They battled around the room until Emanuel went down, boots finding his sides as Henry held fast to his beard. Ruben heaved himself from the chair to stamp the burning kerosene out with his boot. The cuffs of his pants caught fire and he had to beat them out with his hands. The battle carried on by firelight.

Henry held a hand-full of Emanuel's beard high, a piece of skin as large as a florin clinging to it. Emanuel's screams were terrible to hear.

"His face comes off easy. Must be pommy blood!" Henry laughed. He hadn't enjoyed himself so much in years.

The boots kept going in while Henry dragged the fallen man around the floor. More beard came away with skin attached. It came out more easily when someone planted a foot on his stomach as Henry pulled.

Finally they ran out of breath. Emanuel lay on the floor, covered in blood. Some of his parts seemed to go in the wrong direction.

Ruben towed the fallen man with his boot. "Throw him out!" he bellowed. "Can't say we didn't warn the man!" They took the limp body by the arms, dragged it across the floor, kicked the chair away from the door and flung him out into the snow. "And shut that damned door again!"

Later they drank tea and ate the last of the beef. Henry had eaten the last of the peaches.

"It was trespass," Ruben muttered. "A man ought to sue. Charley, go into the back room and see if you can find another light."

A few minutes later, the rat man arrived with the lantern. "There ain't no kerosene left boss. This thing ain't worth a damn!"

Ruben flogged the side of his leg with the leather throng.

"The rotten old fool. A man should sue him for trespass!"

Chapter 11

Emily tightened the heavy woollen coat about her and tied the hat down hard around her chin. She bent to lace up her boots.

"Now look after your father, Lass," she spoke out of the corner of her mouth, bending to lace the boots. The baby was growing.

"I'm leaving you in charge now Nell. Keep your brothers in line and send Jim up tomorrow morning with the things I told you. And change the dressing on your father. Often mind! If he gets worse send Jim for the doctor in Dargo."

The words tumbled out as she worked. She was in a hurry to get away. Nell saw her fumbling a handful of shotgun shells into her coat pocket. She couldn't see why she was in such a hurry as it would be near impossible to make the climb to the high country at night.

Nell glanced towards the room where her father lay. She had always worshipped the man, spent every moment she could on the pommel of his saddle, spent every moment she could with him, but now she hated to go in the room where he lay. She had seen the figure, not quite human, face half torn away, swathed bandaged like a Mummy she had seen in a picture book, arm tied in a splint her mother had made from old chair legs.

She remembered the sound the arm made as it came back into place. And there was the sound of his breath, short bursts, pausing for long periods then short bursts again. She could smell the pain in his breath. She didn't know how he got down the mountain last night. Could still hear him dragging across the veranda floor like a damaged animal.

"Now you're in charge Nell. You're a big girl now so I'm trusting you. Women are the only ones strong enough to take charge at times like this."

She was outside now, where Jim held the mare by the bridle. She swung herself into the saddle, drawing the twelve gauge shotgun up in front of her. "They'll not throw a women out of her own home. Mark my words!"

She turned the horse into the night with the shotgun resting across her pregnant stomach, following the line a dragging body had left in the snow. Occasionally there was a smear of blood, but probably most of it had bled out of him by then. Then the clouds closed in and she lost it all, letting the horse pick its way up the mountain in the dark.

She made the bottom of the leap when in a burst of half-light she found the spot where Emanuel's body had hit the ground. There was a mess in the snow and blood all over the side of a stump, then the marks where he had crawled away towards his hut. Instinct must have driven him on, crawling the rest of the way home. His big roan horse probably making it before him. Then the darkness closed in again and she pressed on, a little breeze and a sifting of snow on her face.

Nobody knows how she made the ride that night. It is a subject still talked about today. Waiting for small glimpses of moonlight while the clouds cleared momentarily, the mare picked its way up the steep grade, sure-footed, feet scrabbling like ice on the gravel, weaving between the boulders and the snow-tortured timber. Emily let the animal have its head, listening to the loose stone rattling and skidding into some unknown void between the timber. Occasionally she could see the glint of the river, some thousands of feet below before the clouds closed in again and she was forced to stop, breathing heavily, the shotgun still clutched to her swollen stomach. She tried not to look down, giving her faith to the good Lord. But the good Lord had better keep out of her way until she had finished what she had to do that night! But then the light broke free and she dug the horse in the ribs and gave it rein.

Finally when the sun broke the next morning, Emily found the place where her husband had mounted the big roan. She had become an expert tracker by now. Could see where he had dragged along, clinging to the horse's neck, feet dragging through the snow. Could see the scuff marks on the log where he had slumped across the animal's back. The rage continued to build up inside her, even driving out the cold as she arrived in sight of the homestead.

She dismounted before breaking through into the clearing, tied her horse to a tree and settled down to watch the cabin. Surprised how exhausted she felt.

A little smoke was rising from the chimney and presently a man appeared at the front door. He stretched then wandered out a few feet and she could see the flow of water into the snow with steam rising from it. He scratched himself then went back inside. Emily waited for over an hour until they left. She counted five of them. They threw down the rails of the cattle yards then rode off into the snow.

The door hadn't been repaired so Emily went quietly inside, made space between the dirty dishes and lay the gun down on the table, propped a broken chair against the door, then threw wood on the fire and settled down to wait.

It was dusk when the men came back. She could hear them shouting about smoke from the chimney. There was swearing and the rattle of spurs. The door shook but did not give against the chair. Then a lean face with albino eyes peered through the window.

He saw Emily sitting by the table, the gun resting across her stomach.

"It's an old bitch with a gun!"

Then Ruben's face appeared at the window.

"Well, I'll be damned!"

"We could easy throw her out. Come in from the back door."

Ruben pulled at his lip and smacked the leather throng against his thigh. There was still some latent chivalry inside Ruben. Or perhaps it had something to do with the gun.

"No, we can't throw a woman out."

"We could easy cover the chimney. Smoke the bitch out," the rat man said.

"Why don't you pack of curs just go away?" Emily roared. "I've got a husband near to death as a man's ever been—and you curs did it to him. But I swear you'll not throw a women out of her own home!"

There was silence for a while, then old Ruben said, "We'll wait her out. It's the only way."

He turned back down the overgrown path to collect his horse.

"We'll camp out tonight. But not for long. We'll wait her out."

But they didn't wait her out. Emily was still there the next night. Still there the night after and then the night after that. She was still there in the spring with the new baby almost formed in her stomach. Emily Trask had claimed for good, her part of the high country.

Chapter 12

The girl was christened Ellen but always known as Nell.

She was named after the heroine of a little green book with the back cover missing, called 'Nell of the Wilds', a book her father had once used to practise his reading. He never got far through it and it was one of the things left at Harrietville during the shift. Still, he called her Nell and the name stuck.

Nell was the firstborn girl and found from a very early age that, in the eyes of her father, she could do no wrong. So she grew headstrong like her father, a fountain of energy like her mother, and self-confident to a fault.

Jim was the firstborn of the family, so carried most of the weight, most of the expectations and caught most of the abuse. George came next but, as the second son, Emanuel found it much easier to concentrate on the first than try to train another. And then along came Harry, four years old and growing wild in the mountains. Another addition to the family was due sometime in the near future.

Jim had been handling his new colt for about two months, standing patiently for hours in the centre of the yard, driving him around on a long rein, flicking lightly with the whip to keep him moving, quietly gaining control while the mouth grew to accept the bit. Then he tied the horse with a short halter and slapped his tender parts with a hessian bag. He finally got to the stage where the horse stood, ears flattened, ignoring the hostile bag about his flanks.

Next came the saddle bag. The colt flattened his ears, bent back his head to grab the blanket in his teeth and threw the thing aside. He did the same thing again until Jim held it in place until he got the saddle on. The horse twitched his flanks and threw the saddle off. He did this about a dozen times before finally, grudgingly accepting it.

The time had come to ride him.

Emanuel was quietly pleased with the patience the lad had shown with the animal, but he could never let the boy know this. He walked slowly to the yard, arm still in a sling, the pipe gripped in the corner of his mouth. He used the pipe again nowadays. So much for his lungs.

George came along too, secretly hoping to see a little bloodshed if his brother was perhaps smashed against the horse yard rails. Nell sat balanced on top of the gate, imagining herself in the saddle. Harry crossed the yard with his kelpie pup, his pants hanging down about his knees and his nose running. Harry always seemed to have his nose running.

Charley Nash came along to watch the show and perhaps pick up the pieces. Since Emanuel had lost his job at the mine, Charley often helped out on the run.

He gave the girth a final hitch and held the ears of the colt as Jim swung into the saddle. He stayed up there for about five seconds, then hit the ground hard. He lay stunned for a while, then gingerly got to his feet, dusting himself off. His pride was well dusted too.

George yelled his encouragement as the colt bucked and thrashed about the yard.

"Get on again son and be ready this time!" Emanuel's only comment came around the stem of the pipe.

Jim got on again and was thrown off just as fast. He had to pick himself up five times before he finally gave up for the day.

Charley Nash had only one piece of advice for the boy.

"Get him out of the yard boy. Turn him up hill and kick him in the guts. A horse can't do a bloody thing pointing up hill!"

"And you can catch him again Charley." Emanuel said. "He'd be halfway back to Wangaratta in about ten minutes!"

Emanuel turned back to the house. "You better call it a day lad before you kill yourself. We'll have to get the animal cut, I expect."

Nell swung on the gate top. "No need to cut him. Jim's only got to learn himself to ride!"

Jim's pride was badly hurt. "Ride? You think I can't ride, you think you could do better?"

"Course I could. I could do anything with that colt, I bet."

"Oh yeah? Well, if you can ride the bugger, you can bloody well have him!"

And ride him she did. The next day when Jim was in the high country, with only George as witness, she rode the colt into the ground. Of course he threw her three times first. George screwed up his eyes hanging on the top rail of the fence and for the first time of his life felt a bit sorry for his sister. And he even found a little admiration for her. Perhaps more awe than admiration. But by the end of the day the pony was as quiet as a lamb.

From that day forward, there was always a dispute as to who really owned the horse. The colt they called Randy. Jim held that he was only joking, but Nell always claimed that the horse was really hers. Of course Emanuel backed her.

But they marked the colt a month later.

Emanuel's arm was out of the sling, not quite straight, but serviceable, as he sat on the steps of the veranda, drawing on his pipe and coughing a little.

They had brought the colt out of the yard to a clean spot in front of the house before throwing him to the ground. Jock Hoolahan took the head end, holding it across his knees, while Jim, down on his rump at the rear, planted one boot against the lower leg behind the knee, then pulled back the other leg. Charley honed his pocket-knife razor sharp, poured kerosene on the blade and set the bottle behind him in the dust, then kneeled down gently. His knees did not work so well anymore.

"Now hold fast to that leg boy, I don't want to lose no more teeth!"

He cut the purse and drew out the first testicle, talking all the while.

"You want to watch close boy, you'll have to do this next time, I expect."

He stripped it loose with the knife and threw it over his shoulder.

"The secret is to make a good-sized cut so it drains properly."

He started on the other side, the colt shivering and struggling, eyes white in their sockets. He stripped the next testicle out.

"Some people use their teeth for this, but I don't have many of them left."

He cast the used testicle over his shoulder and reached for the bottle of kerosene, flushing the purse clean. "Now turn him loose boys, he's a colt no longer!"

The pony gingerly regained his feet and stood there bewildered. Charley patted him on the shoulder.

"That will take the buck out of you boy, but you'll be as good as new in a few days."

Nell watched from a distance, seething with rage, hating Charley Nash like poison that day.

That night, a new baby was born in the log hut on King's Spur.

Jim was sent to Dargo in the pouring rain to bring the doctor but the baby arrived before he did. Emily, although small, had become practiced at delivering her own babies. All the doctor could do was clean her up and marvel at the resilience of the woman.

They named the girl Bess, after a distant cousin on Emily's side, or perhaps a favourite Jersey milk cow Emanuel owned. Nobody ever knew which. But the betting was, it was the milking cow.

Chapter 13

He came from the Omeo track to the south, a tall, sparse man with a hat like a moth-eaten saddle blanket, his legs spread wide over the pony that seemed too small to carry the weight.

Riding between the children, he stopped before Emily who stood in the doorway, wiping her hands on her apron. All the man's possessions were strapped in a pack behind his saddle. He swept the hat from his head.

"Good morning, Madam. Eric Hare, reporting for service to train this fine brood in the letters and maybe hammer a little religion into their head's as well!"

His head was bald and shaped like a bullet, with a large hooked nose and two deep furrows running down across his face. George stared at the man, at the fly crawling down his face. He thought that if it crawled into one of the crevices, it would surely be lost. But Hares hand was swift and effective. Hare did not tolerate obstructions.

"Welcome Mr Hare. All I want from you is to teach this lot to read and write and maybe add a few figures. We can manage the churching ourselves, I expect."

"Oh I'm sure you can my good lady. But I'll try my best to teach them the finer parts of the written word. And they'll be able to add better than your average bank manager in a few months, I'll wager. Not that I'm a betting man of course. Gambling is the downfall of many a good man!"

"I'm sure it is Mr Hare. There'll be three others from the mine here in the morning to help you earn your pay."

"Money is nothing, ma'am. Only the joy of bringing the enlightenment of the written word to the lives of these back-wood souls!"

"All very well Mr Hare. But I just want them to learn how to read and write. I expect they'll learn the rest of it in life. That's your lodgings up there beyond the horse yards. You can do your schooling there. So leave your gear and yard your horse. The boys will feed him later. Then come down to the house for a cup of tea and we'll talk. You can eat each day at the house." With that, Emily wheeled and strode back inside, well pleased with the new schoolmaster.

The hut that was to be the school house was built with rough Woollybutt logs, and like the homestead, had a bark roof. Emanuel and Jock Hoolahan had thrown it up in three weeks.

Hare slept in one end, divided off with a canvas curtain. He took his meals at the main homestead.

There was a blackboard, stolen from the mine. Emanuel could see no reason for a blackboard at a mine and two large logs were laid on the floor, one behind the other, to be used as seats. The logs were too big to get through the door, so were dragged into place and the building erected around them. They were squared with an adze in places to make seating easier. A large crate, pillaged from the mine took pride of place as the master's desk. So this was where schooling began for George, Nell and Harry. Jim, they considered, had had schooling enough. Besides, someone had to handle the run while Emanuel was at the mine. He didn't think he would be there much longer the way things were going. Besides the feel of running cattle on the high country was getting into his blood.

'Old rabbit' was the name George soon gave to the master of words. George was good with names.

Hare rode in every week on the little bay pony, administered his lessons with a fair smattering from the Good Book, then rode off to Omeo each Friday, to a long suffering wife with eleven children of her own. His wife, Lynda, dreaded him coming home. For too often, this led to another Hare on the way.

Chapter 14

Emanuel, Jim and Charley Nash were at the homestead block, stripping rails to rebuild the stockyards when William King and two of his men dropped by. It was a glorious day in the high country. Just a little chill wind blowing and the grass and wildflowers half way up to the stomach of a good-sized horse. Emanuel was stripped to woollen singlet with braces hanging about his waist. His whiskers had never grown back properly after the event with Ruben Craye, so now he wore a heavy moustache and mutton-chop beard that seemed to hide most of the trouble.

"Morning Mr King. What brings you here?" Emanuel still felt a little class distinction with King. The man was wealthy and seemed to own half the mountain as well as a property in the lowlands.

"Oh just passing through on the way into Omeo. Tell me, is there still that rotten cliff face to negotiate, or have you found a better way down?"

"I expect you better use the leap, less you choose to travel another half day. But a man of your horsemanship should have few problems. Especially with that horse you're riding." Emanuel could hardly keep his eyes from the magnificent black thoroughbred King sat astride.

"I expect I've been on more difficult paths than that in my days."

King wore a dark suit with shirt buttoned up to the collar. A full day's gear and provisions were strapped across the horse's rump.

"I see you're doing some running repairs. Old Gordon Jones was a good cattleman when he came to the plains some ten years ago, but of late he'd let things slide. No women you know. A man can't live in these parts for too long without a woman."

Emanuel wiped the sweat from his eyes and leaned against the rail fence. Charley dropped to his haunches to build a cigarette, while Jim counted the blisters on his hands. King's two men sat idly in their saddles swatting flies.

"It was the Pleuro that got him you know. Some years back now. Bought a mob of cattle down from Queensland. Old Jack Drew brought 'em in. Good man Jack. Damn animals brought the Pleuro with 'em. Lost the lot. The man never quite recovered from that. Burnt a lot of them in that hollow yonder. You could smell the stink clear to Mayford when the wind was right. Dreadful thing Pleuro. Especially when you got no women to lean on."

"I've never seen it but I expect it is."

"Good wife you got there Emanuel. God I admire the spunk of the woman. You're a lucky man."

Emanuel had never thought of himself that way before. "Yes, I expect I am."

"I heard of your troubles a while back. Bad bunch that. Old Rube's alright, in his own way but the idiot boy Alfred's probably the best of the bunch, but that young whelp Henry, can't stand the man!"

"We have a few things to settle, and I suppose one day we will."

"Just watch your back, and your cattle. He's a mean bastard that Henry."

Emanuel loaded his pipe and cleared his throat.

"I don't step aside for a brown snake and I don't step aside for Henry Craye!"

"Good man. Oh and a tip from an old cattleman. Salt. There's a lack of it up here on the high plains and the cattle love it. Can live perfectly alright without it, but they love the stuff. Run out a trail and they'll smell it for miles. Get 'em used to it and the wildest cattle alive will be eating out of your hand in no time."

"I'm a miner by trade, Mr King so I expect I've got a lot to learn from a true cattleman."

King tipped his hat and wheeled the thoroughbred down the mountain. "We must be moving less we'll never get to Omeo before nightfall. And good luck to you and give my regards to your good wife!"

Emanuel hitched the braces about his shoulders, spat on his hands and hefted his axe. He watched the backs of the three men ride off between the snow gums.

Chapter 15

There was a front log and a back log, with all the favourites sitting on the front one. Hare had arranged the seating so that Nell sat on the right side, close to his desk, where he could pat her on the knee sometimes as he walked past. Nell was almost fifteen now and maturing well beyond her years. Esma Elder sat on the left edge. He thought it better keep the girls apart so they wouldn't talk. Esma came from one of the mining families, a well grown girl, a little grubby but with grey eyes that hinted to boys of things in the world way beyond their years. George could not keep his eyes off her, and sat on the log just behind. There were two Coleman boys, Athol and Fred who also came from the mine, seated between the girls. George and Athol fought every day that summer in the gully behind the school and this forged a lifelong friendship.

Harry sat as far back on the rear log as he could get, while Jim escaped schooling altogether, because of his age. He could already read and write and he was needed to work the cattle.

Hare sat behind his desk. A cane lay across the desk in a menacing sort of way, an open jar sitting beside it containing castor oil and a table spoon. Hare believed a taste of castor oil was better than the stick on some occasions. He once taught a boy who showed no reaction to the cane, no matter how hard he flogged him. But reacted well to castor oil. Especially after a dead fly had floated in the jar for a few days. Hare considered himself a very humane and God fearing man.

Each of his pupils sat on their logs with a piece of broken slate and one piece of chalk in their hands. The chalk was very valuable. If you threw it at someone, you had to be able to find it again, less you were left without something to write with.

"Now the lesson today is," Hare began, "a man has three pounds and sixpence in his pocket, and he wishes to buy a bag of potatoes for eight shillings…"

"Why would he pay eight shillings for a bag of spuds?" Athol asked.

"I told you before, boy," Hare said patiently, "when you want to ask a question, put up your hand and say 'please sir'! Now, there is another man who owns potatoes and he has three piles of money in front of him." He drew the three piles of money on the blackboard with the stick figure in front.

"Now in the first pile are pennies. There are twelve pennies in a shilling. The second pile holds shillings. There are twenty shillings in a pound. Now the third pile has pounds. Now, the first man with three pounds and sixpence in his pocket says he wants to buy a bag of potatoes for eight shillings."

"Why would the man have his money in the dirt? That seems a stupid place to keep money…"

"Oh shut up you miserable boy! And didn't I tell you to put up your hand?" Hare turned his back and thought it over. "Now what matters is, the man with the potatoes…" He had lost his train, so he drew the stick figure working out the change.

Harry looked out the window at the high mountains. There was no glass in the window, only a hole in the wall. The pup was rolling in the dust beneath the red gum tree. George swatted flies. He rolled them down his face and flicked them into Hare's hat that hung from a peg on the wall. Mostly the flies found the target.

"Now as I have said there are twenty shillings in a pound and the first man wants to buy a bag of potatoes for eight…"

"He was robbed," said Athol. "He could have grown 'em in his own back yard."

"Be quiet you wretched boy! Now if we count the shillings…"

George noticed that everything had gone quiet. He looked up to the thunderous glare of Eric Hare.

"Come out here you miserable, revolting boy!"

George climbed over the front log while Hare found his cane. He considered the castor oil but decided on the cane, flexing it like a rapier. He delivered two mighty strokes across George's palms. George tried to draw his fingers away before the second blow, but was too slow and it caught him across the fingertips which was much worse. He hopped around holding his hands between his legs tears forming in his eyes, but afraid to cry because he was sixteen and Esma Elder was watching. He clamoured across the front log and regained his seat. Hands still firmly between his legs. Esma's eyes covered him with sympathy.

"Now that will teach you to respect other people's property." Hare emptied the dead flies from his hat. "Now, where were we…"

At lunch, they ate beneath the red gum outside the school hut. Emily had made it this way to be fair to the children from the mine. Hare took his lunch at the main house.

George sat on a log beside Esma Elder as she examined his hands. Then when nobody else was looking, she slipped them between her legs to warm them. At first, George went red behind the ears, then he began to plan how he could get the cuts again tomorrow, so he could get his hands between Esma Elder's legs again.

Chapter 16

Higher up on the Bogong high plains close to the headwaters of the Cobungra river, the Craye homestead spread out across a clearing between a stand of mountain ash. It was late May and the wind was up, coming in front of a cold change. The clouds moved across the snow-capped alps, forever changing shape as they rolled before the wind. Snow came in short flurries, promising more to come as the days shortened. Henry Craye heard a sheet of loose iron flapping on the roof as he stamped his feet into the boots at the foot of his bed. He rammed the grey woollen singlet into his pants, then found a shirt at the foot of the bed and still half awake, his knuckles brushed across the soft satin petticoat of his wife. The only piece of good clothing that she had. He could hear her in the kitchen, built a few feet away from the main hut, could hear the cry of the baby. Henry felt a strange sensation at the feel of the material. Then a kind of fury. A fury directed at himself. He threw the garment to the floor.

"Can't you shut that damn kid up!"

He splashed cold water on his face from a basin near the door to clear his eyes then shook his hands dry. "A man's got a hard day in front of him and can't get a moment's peace. Take the kid outside!" There were only two steps to the kitchen, where a fire burned fiercely in the stove. Ida stood pale and restless, trying to nurse the baby quiet. Henry threw bacon and eggs onto a tin plate then broke off a piece of damper. The wind rattled the loose iron as a pale sun broke from behind Hotham.

Crossing the yard towards the main homestead, Henry Cade hitched his braces into place and pulled on a heavy woollen coat. The Tasmanian Bluey. An oilskin coat swung over his arm.

Old Rube was just shuffling out onto the veranda to slump into the cane bottomed chair beside the doorway. The chair burst a couple of strands as his weight sank into it. Henry could not understand why the old fool would come outside in weather like this.

Ruben's hips were shot. Too many years in the saddle and too much weight. He carried a stick nowadays and seldom mounted his horse to ride among his cattle. He spent much of his time just sitting in the ancient chair looking out across the mountains.

Albert just breached the door, adjusting his belt.

"I think we'll go clean up those cattle on the Dargo side. Think there's about forty head there." Henry said, "This weather's closing in so we best get the cattle down to lower country on the east side." Henry was the youngest brother, but he had taken control, especially now old Rube was down.

"Just be careful you don't get no Trask cattle with 'em. We don't want no more trouble with that lot. The old girl would most likely take a man's head off with a gun." Ruben had gained a grudging respect for Emily.

"Bugger the old girl. But we'll leave her bloody cattle alone. Albert go down and roust those lazy buggers out of bed, the day's half over."

Albert took orders readily from his younger brother. He was born a little slow, but perhaps a kick in the head from a horse when he was only four years old didn't help. Already at the far end of the clearing there was activity at the workman's hut. There was the whinny of horses and the stamp of feet, the slap of leather at the horse yards.

Ida was out in front of her cabin, thin and cold rocking the baby on her hip, looking towards the men.

"You want to look after that woman of yours you know." Ruben had noticed the bruising beneath her left eye. "It's hard on women in this country. Damn hard without a woman."

Ruben had buried his wife two years ago. He paid her no respect when she was here but found life very hard without her now that she was gone. Especially with the bad hip.

Henry was in no mood for lectures. "Mind your own damn business old man!"

Henry wheeled about and strode towards the horse yards.

It was magnificent on the high country. There was snow already on the high peaks, laying about in drifts, the grass bent before the coming winter.

They had reached the bottom of Blue Rag when Henry called a halt. "Now you lot go ahead into the Dargo plains. You'll be on the Trask run, but there's a herd in a valley behind Mt Tabletop. Muster 'em and bring 'em back. Try not to get any Trask cattle, unless there's an odd cleanskin among 'em. I'm going to inspect the holding yard. I'll catch you up later I expect."

Henry watched the men ride away up the incline, then swung his leg over the pommel of the saddle and began to roll a cigarette. Henry loved to be alone on the high country. He loved to be alone anytime. Basically he hated people, especially those who didn't live in the mountains. Lice he called them. When the tobacco pack was empty he stopped himself flinging the empty pack onto the ground. Instead he shoved it into the pocket of his coat. To pollute the high country was much worse than smashing a man's face. Henry drew the smoke into his lungs and blew it out, then swung his leg back into the stirrups and rode down across the ravine. His three dogs followed in the snow behind.

Across the ravine, there was a natural opening between two steep cliff faces that led to the holding yard. A track some twenty yards wide wound between the cliffs, beneath a huge overhang of loose rock, fragments of which sometimes fell into the valley, then the track opened to a natural clearing covering more than an acre. The place, known as the Gap, led to a perilous track that wound down into Grant's valley. The area had been settled long ago, once owned by a man named Greasy Willis. An old cabin still stood in the valley where Willis lived with a rail-thin and silent wife, Edna, two strapping sons and one half crippled one. One night, during a storm it was said, because the kerosene ran low, the lantern glass began to blacken, Edna had lived under a great deal of pressure in the wilderness. The only luxury she ever asked for was kerosene for the lamp. So she took an axe and killed her husband and two sons as they sat at the kitchen table. The cripple managed to escape with only part of his ear missing. Then she ran out into the storm to drown herself in the pond some hundred yards away from the hut. After that, the place was said to be haunted. Henry had heard the story many times as a boy and the thought still raised the hairs on the back of his neck, and although Henry never believed in ghosts, he always treated an axe with great respect.

Miners were said to have used the track to cross into the valley in the old days, but that was before Henry's time and now wild horses and stray cattle were the only occupants of the valley. Henry rode carefully, checking that the rails they used to seal the entrance were still there, lying half covered in snow. Where the gap narrowed at the back, a log fence was still in place. He wheeled the horse up the hill towards the Dargo high plains as a rock dislodged by the snow came bounding down the incline. Albert had been hit by falling rubble some years back but when he suggested dynamiting the overhang to bring it down and make the place safe, Henry flew into a rage. "This mountain was here a damn-sight long while before half-wit people, you useless oaf!" He never forgot the look on his brother's face when he said it. Never forgot the surprise of his own reaction to the thought.

He met the rest of the crew in mid-afternoon, crossing a broad plain covered in snow. There were about sixty head of cattle. As Henry rode in from one side, he saw three riders were coming through the snow from the south. Henry adjusted his eyes against the driving snow that seemed much thicker on the open plain. He saw another herd of cattle further to the south.

It was the Trask girl who came in first, on a smart chestnut pony. "What are you doing on this run?" She called into the wind.

Henry tipped his hat, something he wouldn't do as a rule. He liked the way she sat a horse. He really liked the way she sat. "We're just rounding up a few of our strays, Miss Trask—or may I call you Nell?" He flashed her a broad smile. The girl took his breath right away.

Nell said nothing as the horse fidgeted between her thighs.

"Sorry we're on your land. Just gathering a few strays." He couldn't keep his eyes off her. She was a natural just like the country she rode in. She took Henry's breath right away. He thought with disgust of his scrawny wife. Ida couldn't throw her leg over a horse to save her life!

Charley Nash was already riding through the herd, checking the brands. Jim was close behind. "Don't seem to be much wrong here boss," he said to Jim.

"Course not!" Henry snapped. His tone changed talking to the old man "We don't want no trouble. Just collecting what's ours."

"Seems you were looking for trouble when you beat up my father," Nell said coolly the horse moving nervously below her.

Henry was taken aback by the boldness of the girl. The last time he had seen her she was only a child. "That was only a misunderstanding Ma'am. My old man Rube got out of line. I wanted nothing to do with it all. Least it's all in the past now, I expect."

"Maybe to you mister, but not to me. Or the rest of the family. That thing is not settled yet. Now get your cattle off our run!"

Henry tipped his hat with a faint smile. He'd never been spoken to this way before, especially by a slip of a girl. It was a strange experience that set him right back on his heels.

He sat with leg across the pommel of his saddle and watched the cattle ploughing through the snow drift in the valley below, driven by the ring of stockwhips along the track into the hidden ravine. Henry pulled a stub of pencil from his pocket and ripped the tobacco carton apart to expose a piece of manageable cardboard. He licked the pencil and began to write. He had learned to write from his wife Ida who had been a schoolteacher down in Dargo when he married her. He wet the pencil stub with his tongue and began to painfully write.

Poetry came to him sometimes alone on the high plains.

"She came like an angel out of the snow,

Riding a horse like the waters flow."

Chapter 17

The winter was closing in, so this was to be Hare's last day on the Spur. He was due to return the following spring.

His going was a great relief to everyone, especially Nell. She had no trouble learning the fundamentals of reading and writing, but still considered the past few months a general waste of time as it kept her away from her horse and away from the high plains. George was a little concerned because he would not see Esma during the winter months. And he would miss his fights with Athol, but this was heavily outweighed by the fact that he was rid of Hare for the next few months. This would give his hands a time to recover.

Sleet drove in through the open window of the classroom, as Hare held his last lessons. There was no glass to stop the rain so he had to move his desk to stay dry. He wiped the cane carefully so that it would not rot. A good cane was hard to come by and this one had lasted him well. He emptied the jar of castor oil out the window and rinsed it in rain water. He had only used it once on Athol and that didn't seem to have much effect on the boy. Some kids were just strange.

He took out the well-worn little brown book. "Now in the sentence 'The cat sat on the mat'." He drew a cat with his piece of chalk on the blackboard. Hare drew cats very well.

"What's a mat?" asked Athol. That was enough. The kid was only trying to get at him. He seemed to actually like the cane!

"Everyone knows what a mat is, you stupid boy. A mat is a sort of a rug thing people put on the floor in front of the fireplace!"

"Why would anyone have a rug thing in front of a fireplace. Wouldn't the hot coals burn the rug thing?" Hare prayed silently to his God. He didn't want to kill the boy—he wasn't a violent man.

"Look boy, I couldn't care less if it burned or not. That's not what this lesson is about. The cat is a noun, and a noun is a person, place or thing. The mat is also a noun. When the cat sat—'sat' is a doing word, a verb."

"Why would anyone let a rotten cat in the house. We had a cat in the hut once and it stole meat right off the table. Mum said she should'a killed it."

"Will you be quiet boy and pay attention to the lesson?" He paused in desperation. Athol was getting to him. Still, this was his last day, only a few hours more—he gave Nell a friendly pat on the knee. He would miss Nell. 'My little Queen of Sheba' he often called her. He had pet names for both the girls.

One rotten apple makes it hard on the rest, he thought. Still there was more than one rotten apple. He reassured himself again with a pat. "It's pleasing to know some pupils are keen to better themselves." He tried to remember where he was at.

"Oh yes, now where was I? The verb is a doing word. A doing word, right? Now can anyone tell the class another verb? Any verb?"

Athol's hand shot up in a flash. "Killed." He felt washed in his own brilliance. "If ma killed the cat…"

With school at last over for the winter, the pupils watched with relief as Hare rode away on his little bay pony, his slate and chalk and canes strapped in a pack across the horse's rump.

Nell felt nothing but disgust for the vile old man with his dirty hands as he rode away between the Mountain Ash.

Harry sauntered back to the homestead, the cattle dog pulling at his pants, while the Coleman boys mounted their old half draught mare, bareback, one behind the other and turned for the mine, trying to beat the rain. Athol had decided not to fight today, as he was so relieved to be through with school for the winter.

George followed Esma into the stable to help saddle her horse.

It was warm in the stable, among the loose hay, quite easy to brush his hand against her as he helped with the saddle. She pushed lightly back against him.

"Don't suppose we'll see one another again till spring?" George felt a little rise in his pants.

"Na I don't suppose we will." She tightened the girth and George pressed up close behind her. Despite the cold, he was beginning to sweat. He thought he felt her bottom wiggle.

The rain was falling now, the wind lifting bark on the roof.

"You go'na get real wet out there. Maybe you should stay longer till the rain blows over."

"Maybe I could stay awhile. Ma won't be expecting me till late in this rain."

"It would be awful warm down in the straw." George suggested hopefully. Suddenly she had her arms around him with one leg hooked around his. She pulled him down with her into the straw, searching for his mouth. Her teeth were like an animal all about his face. George searched clumsily for her lips as he rolled on top of her. His fingers were all thumbs as he fumbled for her clothes. He felt the buttons go on his fly and something burst from his pants like an angry animal, gouging between her legs. There was a desperate rising feeling, then quite suddenly, the worst thing happened. Wetness spilled out over them. George shuddered like a whipped mare.

Esma, bewildered, raked her fingernails into his flesh. George stumbled to his feet, not knowing what to do or say. "Jees, I don't know what happened."

Esma looked coldly at him. It was a hard look. "I guess you're still only a boy," she said. And then she laughed. George wished she hadn't laughed. "Well, that was the greatest fizzer I ever knew. Think I'll take my luck in the rain. It's better to be wet by rain than an awkward boy!"

George was totally devastated by the laugh. "That's never happened before, honest!"

Esma laughed a wicked laugh. "Na,' bet it never happened before. Bet nothin' ever happened to you before!"

"Bugger you!" George threw at her back as she rode away in the rain.

Chapter 18

They had agreed to meet at the outcrop of rock and twisted snow gums that rose out of the flats of Hobbles plains. They had been in the saddle for two days, Emanuel, Nell and Charley Nash, mustering the run to the west, sweeping down as far as the headwaters of Crooked River. They arrived back at the knoll with over two hundred cattle, waiting there in a protected spot to boil the billy and have a bite of lunch, waiting for the return of Jim, George and a new man named Anderson to come in from the north. It was only early in the month of May but the bite of winter was in the air and they were desperate to beat the cold front closing like a frozen fist from the west. They planned to move the cattle back to more protected country, lower down the mountain.

By mid-afternoon, the rest of the crew arrived, driving a mob of sixty cattle through the snow. When the two mobs were boxed, Emanuel rode between them, the oilskin coat wrapped firmly against the wind.

"We're still about forty head short." He made two more passes before he was completely satisfied. "I don't see the Wangaratta bull among them either. You sure you got 'em all?"

Jim wrapped his frozen hands around a mug of hot tea and stuffed a piece of dry damper into his mouth. He hadn't eaten for nine hours.

"I'm pretty sure we got them all. We swept up clear to Tabletop, right across to the Bogong plains. Maybe you lot missed 'em."

"We don't miss anything, boy." Jim hated the 'boy', "You check that spot where the headwaters of the Dargo forks? We found a pocket of cattle in there once. There's a little protected valley this side of Tabletop."

"Well, we swept through most of that country. There's a lot of snow there and there was no sign of cattle anywhere."

"Well, we best check it again." Emanuel weaved his horse through the mob again. "Nell, you, Charley and Anderson start moving the mob down. We're about out of tucker so we better try to get back by tomorrow. You Jim, better finish feeding your face and George, you better come along too."

They reached the headwaters of the Dargo by late afternoon, crossing it where the stream was not much deeper than the horse's fetlocks. Jim was surly as he felt sure he had missed nothing. The old man always doubted him.

But they found the cattle an hour later, stuck in a bed of Sphagnum moss, some floundering belly deep, trying to reach the harder ground at the edge. About a dozen had been there for a long while and were making little progress, churning the moss into mire. The remainder of the mob stood about, testing the surface, calling for those in the bog to join them on higher ground. The Wangaratta bull was in the moss, exhausted and almost spent. They plunged their horses into the bog as far as it was safe to go, wielding their whips. But with little success, only moving the mob a few feet towards the edge. Eventually, almost exhausted, they were successful driving three mud soaked heifers to harder ground.

Emanuel steadied the big roan in the mud, "George, you take 'em towards higher ground. Don' let 'em turn mind! Box the others and hold 'em on the high ground."

The heifers were frustrated by the whip and the ordeal in the mud. One turned to charge the boy. George swung the whip and drove them up the snow embankment.

Emanuel and Jim turned back into the mire, managing to get a rope around the neck of the nearest beast. Jim, withering in shame, shed his oilskin coat, kicked free of the horse and waist deep in the moss, threw his shoulder behind a floundering rump, twisting the tail for purchase. One by one they managed to get the cattle to the edge, where George took over and herded them to safety.

Only Cranky Jack remained, sullen and desperate. Emanuel got a rope around his horns, while Jim after two throws got his rope there too, and both horses managed to drag the animal clear. They shook the ropes free.

"George, mind the bastard don't turn back in. He's just contrary enough to try anything!"

The bull stood shaken but not beaten. His eyes were mad and saliva spilled from his mouth. When George tried to move him, the bull charged. A muddy, stumbling charge. But the old bay mare, stuck to the knees in mud and snow, was not fast enough. One horn took the boy in the lower leg, opening him up to the knee.

The mare floundered off into the snow drift, the boy reeling in the saddle, blood spilled like water.

It happened so fast that Emanuel barely saw it.

"Jim, get these animals up on the high ground. Christ, what a mess!" He had George down in the snow. "Get 'em back to the main mob. Don't camp for the night till you get 'em clear of this bloody place. And next time damn you, do your job right!"

He tore off his coats and then his shirt, ripped it to strips then bound the leg tight. Blood filled the bandage and spilled into the snow. Emanuel couldn't understand how a body could have so much blood inside it. He struggled back into his clothes, unaware of the cold, swung the lad like a bag of chaff across the neck of the big roan, found the saddle and spurred up the incline.

"Now don't lose those cattle mind." He yelled at Jim. "You've done enough damage for one day!"

Emanuel had to take his frustration out on someone.

He caught the main mob camped at the edge of Hobble's plain. George had passed out long before that time and the big roan gelding was almost beaten.

"Charley, best lend me your horse!" He lowered the boy down to Charley's arms. "And you Nell, ride for home. Be careful in the dark mind, but get your mother and bring her up to the homestead block. Tell her to bring all her medicine stuff. Go along girl, and for God's sake be careful. We have enough troubles for one night!"

"Charley," He said quietly, "You best ride back and find Jim. The boy might need help. He'll need food and some dry clothes. You'll have to help get a good fire going somehow on the plain to camp for the night. He's been in the mud and must be near frozen." Emanuel tightened the girth on the fresh horse. "I fear I may have been a bit hard on the boy!"

He's not a boy, Charley thought grimly, but kept his views to himself. He's been a man for over two years now.

With the help of Charley, they loaded the boy into the saddle of the fresh horse with Emanuel up behind him. He spurred off into the snow, not quite sure if the boy was alive or dead.

Just before daylight Emanuel lay the boy on a bunk in the old homestead. He had lost so much blood that the skin around his lips was white. Muscle and proud flesh hung from the gaping wound in his leg.

Emanuel lit a strong fire, filled a basin from a drift of snow by the door and set it above the fire to boil. He cut away the bloody bandages and what remained of the trouser leg, then spent the best part of an hour cleaning the wound. All the while the boy slipped in and out of consciousness.

Emily arrived when the sun was up, carrying a chaff bag full of supplies. Emanuel was nearly as white as the boy and completely spent.

"God, am I glad to see you girl! The lads almost done, I fear."

"No need to blaspheme. Get a hold of yourself man till we see what we've got. Good gracious-men! How on earth did you manage to do that?"

"It was easy." Emanuel, more squeamish at the sight of other people's blood than he was of his own, felt ready to collapse. "It was that damn Wangaratta bull." He was even past the fear of swearing in front of Emily.

"Now hold fast to the boy while I get a good look at this mess," she said. "Good Lord, there isn't much leg left!"

With the boiling water, she diluted Condys Crystals, and when she doused the wound, George almost left the bed. Then she sprinkled sulphur powder into the wound. She only had a little of it and had to be careful. Next she drew a large needle, threaded it with black cotton and sterilised the lot in the boiling water.

"Now hold fast to the boy's leg. This is bound to hurt." The boy was shaking with fever. "In the bag, you'll find that half bottle of rum you had hidden! Give the lad a shot of that. I expect it'll do him more good than it would have done you."

Emanuel never ceased to be amazed at how the woman ferreted out everything that he had hidden.

George almost gagged as the liquor tore his throat. Emanuel had a little drink himself.

The boy lifted from the bunk as the needle went in. Emily had three stitches in before he passed out again. This made things much easier. Emily stuffed the muscle and the proud flesh back inside the wound, snipping pieces of unnecessary flesh away with a pair of dressmaking scissors. There were more than twenty stitches when she finished the job. Emanuel was as pale as George by that time. Emily cleaned up the wound, coating it with a liberal amount of Rawley's Universal Salve. It was the magic salve that fixed all things on horses and men. She was exhausted by the time she bandaged the wound. She slumped in a chair near the fireplace.

"See if you can make yourself useful enough to make a cup of tea. Lord I don't know how you men get yourselves into so much trouble!"

Chapter 19

George enjoyed his recovery, some weeks later after most of the pain had gone. The leg healed with a long and ugly scar that left him with a small limp. A limp he played up, as he thought it made him look more distinguished.

Bess spoiled her brother rotten. In the second week when the leg became infected, she bathed it in hot water until it almost dissolved, then applied liberal quantities of methylated spirits, ignoring George's agonising shrieks, then blowing cool air on it to soothe the pain. He swore she was the cruellest sister ever born, but quickly forgave her when she smothered him with homemade buttered scones.

By the third week, he was walking with the slight limp, thinking himself a hero. Nobody else but him had a rip like that and lived!

Jim thought George was only malingering, and told his father as much. Emanuel agreed and said the boy had best come back to work the next day.

With his time of ease coming to an end and the others away in the high country, George decided to test the leg with a ride to the mine to see if he could shake up Esma Elder. There was still unfinished business. And now he was a hero.

The water still thundered against the hillside, gouging out mud, rock and gold, while the mist filled the air like rain. The sound was deafening, with people scurrying around like ants.

George rode on through the mist and some quarter mile past the mine site, found the slaughter yard owned by Eli Elder partly hidden in a small clearing in the scrub. Through the open door of the bark-roofed shed he could see a recently butchered beast hanging from a rafter. Below it, the earth was a mud pile from where the carcase had been washed down. There was a set of rough yards behind with a few steers penned inside. He rode past the fowl yards where moulting hens scratched around in the dust, and an overgrown vegetable garden, also filled with moulting red hens.

There was a gate hanging open and a path chipped through the weeds leading up to the door of the hut, a wisp of smoke climbed from the chimney.

"Hello, Mrs Elder," he said to the thin, hard and haggard woman who opened the door.

"What do you want?" was her only reply. He could see a man slumped in the chair further back in the room. His singlet was stained from the blood of the slaughtered steer and his braces hung about his waist.

"I'm looking for Esma, Mrs Elder. I was just ridin' past and wondered if she was around."

"Well, she's not. Went out a while ago and I dunno where she went. Dunno where that girl goes much of the time!"

Back in the room the man looked up through bloodshot eyes. There was a tin mug in his hand that seemed to be half full of black coffee. He splashed a liberal amount of rum into it from the bottle before him and quickly lost interest in the boy.

"Well, I'm sorry to waste your time, Mrs Elder, so I better be going along."

George felt the day had been wasted but, just as he turned away from the door, who should be walking up the path than Esma herself. She had filled out from her school days but seemed a little more scruffy in a torn cotton dress.

Perhaps she cleaned herself up a bit for school. "Georgie—Georgie Trask!" There seemed to be that same snigger about her lips that had pained George so much at the time in the stable. He still smarted at the memory of the incident. But he felt he was much older now. Particularly with the leg. And he was sure he was more experienced.

"Just ridin' past, testing the leg. Got gored by a bull you know" He showed her the scar. "Damn near died," they said. "Nobody thought I'd live."

Esma seemed only mildly interested as she walked him back to his horse. Mrs Elder had a face like thunder.

"Don't you be too long' young girl. You got things to do back here mind!"

Esma gave a hostile toss of the head. "How's the leg now?" she asked George, to change the conversation.

"Oh it's healin' alright." He exaggerated the limp. "Mum had to shove half the muscle back inside and sew it up with a blunt darning needle."

Esma wrinkled her nose. "God, that must have hurt!"

"Ah it was nothin' much. Just one of those things that happen when you're working cattle. It was a hell of a wild bull!"

By this time he had unfastened the horse and they were walking back by the fowl house.

"I'll show you the scar closer if you like." He hitched the horse to a post and lifted his trouser leg. Esma was more impressed by the angry scar this time, running from ankle to knee. She ran her fingers over the scar. George pretended it didn't hurt.

"You must have been very brave. I think I'd die if I had somethin' like that!"

"Oh I suppose I could have easy died. But you just got to go on. Wouldn't mind sitting down for a while though, out of the sun. This is the first time I been out since I did it."

He thought he sensed an opening. "Thought I'd just test the leg and look you up. Gotta go back to work tomorrow. Don't matter to the old man in this job if you're half dead, you still gotta go to work!"

He sat resting on a half empty bag of grain in the fowl shed. Esma asked to look at the scar again.

"You musta had a thousand stitches!"

"Yeah Ma gave 'em to me with only a slug of rum to stop the pain. Most people would have died, but it was nothing with the rum." He looked around at the dirt floor, covered with fowl feathers. There were several empty bags in the room. Enough to make a useable blanket.

"You just gotta put up with some things in life when you're a cattleman."

George rolled back his trouser leg, feeling a lot more confident than he had at school as he went about his business.

He'd give Esma bloody Elder something to laugh about!

Chapter 20

The muster on the high plains began in early April and continued well into the month.

Close to four hundred cattle, steers, heifers, bulls and calves trampled the yards to dust. Many of the cattle were wild because they hadn't been handled since the last muster while a few hidden far back in the hills had missed the last muster entirely.

The yards sprawled beneath the scattered timber. The largest, of dog leg design built with Woollybutt logs, held the main mob. Here Emanuel and Nell, cut through the mob, moving cows and calves into the marking yard. Nell rode the chestnut gelding, Randy, that she now claimed as her own. He was as nimble on his feet as a dancer, easily outperforming the ageing, big roan that Emanuel rode.

The marking yard was a much smaller one, with a high rail fence, where Jim and George roped the calves, threw and dragged them to the branding fire. Sometimes an irate mother cow charged, causing a wild scramble for the rail fence. They welcomed the high fence at a time like this.

Harry had become handy with the branding iron. The first day he had carried it gingerly from the fire to let Charley finish the job, but by the second day he had become quite proficient himself, burning the 'Circle Lazy T' into the rump until the flesh singed. He quickly got the timing right. The calves kicked and their mothers bellowed. Charley, on his knees, was quick with his knife on the bull calves, before cutting a clover leaf with a pair of pliers in the point of the left ear before turning the calves loose.

He had just straightened himself at the rails, stretching the feeling back into his legs, when he caught sight of riders on the horizon. Charley's eyes were better than most men. Only his knees were suspect.

"Hey boss," he called, "Somebody's coming. Seems like three men with a bunch of wild horses."

Emanuel rode over to the rails, squinting into the sun. "How the Hell can you see that from this distance?"

But Charley was seldom wrong. When they finally arrived at the yards there were three men, the first leading a large chestnut stallion that reared and fought at the rope. The two other riders were driving nine horses and six foals. They had been driven hard for two days, but were still difficult to control.

The first rider was young and smartly dressed, with fancy leggings and a leather waistcoat. He looked a little flash for Emanuel's taste. He wore a short, well-trimmed beard and had wild blue eyes. Nell rode over to the fence, weaving between the cattle, looking at the newcomer with interest. He didn't look too flash to Nell. He looked about just right. She didn't like the look of the other two though.

"I go by the name of Rang. The name is Bell. Harvey Bell. But most people just call me Rang." The flash young man waved in the general direction of the other two. "This here's Haselburger and Nates. We been trapping wild horses in the Grant valley. Hope you don't mind us passing through your run. We're heading in to Omeo to unload 'em."

Emanuel would have agreed with Nell. He didn't like the looks of the other two. Especially the one, Haselburger, with a wild beard and dark, heavy eyebrows that met in the middle. The third man had a shifty look, reminding him of someone he had once fired from the mine.

"The name's Trask. I own this run."

The horse skipped around as the stallion reared back. Rang fought for control.

"Of course they're all for sale if you should want to take 'em off our hands. Save a lot of driving."

Emanuel was interested in more horses so he glanced casually over the mob. They were still hard to control, probably only captured in the past few days, but clearly driven hard since that time. Some of the mares had manes half way to their knees, six foals and two horses that appeared to be station bred. They clearly hadn't run with wild horses for long.

"You won't get far with those station bred horses in Omeo," he said casually loading his pipe.

"They was running with wild horses," Haselburger growled, "Probably have been for years-so they're fair game!" he spoke in a guttural accent. His German heritage was not far away.

"Maybe. Maybe not." Emanuel ran his eyes over the animals. He was becoming more practiced in his assessment of stock since he had left the mine.

"Look, three mares are probably a bit far gone. You'd never break 'em. The foals look alright and the stallion looks as though he might have a bit left in him- if you could ever handle 'em. Dunno if I could take the risk of the station breads though."

Charley was only interested in the stallion. It reared back from his hand when he tried to touch it.

"The mark of the prophet," he said, noting the small indentation in the animal's neck, just up from the shoulder. An indentation about the size of a thumbprint.

"Supposed to be the sign of good Arab blood. Though don't know if I believe that or not."

Emanuel chewed the stem of his pipe. "Look, I could probably give you ten quid for the foals. Maybe fifteen for the stallion and thirty each for the rest, providing you break 'em first!"

"And how the Hell you expect us to break 'em?" Haselburger growled.

"Well, I'm short a man." Emanuel said, glancing at Rang. "I could maybe give you a job young fella and you could do it in your own time. That way I could take 'em off your hands."

"I ain't looking for no job mister," said Haselburger.

"I'm only looking for one man." Emanuel said coldly. He couldn't bear the thought of the other two men on the place. He turned towards Rang. "You look like you might be handy, lad. Look like you could ride a bit." Nell thought he certainly could.

"Ride? I can ride anything that moves. Reckon I could ride a bolt of lightning!"

"Don't think there'll be much call for lightning." Emanuel ran his eyes over the lad again. He was certainly flash. "You're not bringing trouble? Not running from anything?"

"Not from anything in these parts. I come from dirt farmers in the Malley. Me and the old man parted company two years ago on not real good terms. Been droving to Queensland since. Done a lot of things, but no troubles you have to worry about."

"Hold on Bell," Haselburger growled, "if you stay me and Jack ain't. What about our share of the horses?"

Emanuel let his eyes drift over the horses again. "I expect we could work something out. How about we come to an agreement on your share and I'll write a note to Jack Haynes and Son. They're agents in Dargo. Got an office there. Present 'em the note and they'll make good the money."

The horses were restless and hard to keep under control. The stallion reared and pulled. Emanuel didn't like the way the third man kept his eyes wandering over the stock. And over Nell. He wished they were off the place.

"A note? What good would a note be when we got down the mountain and this Jack Haynes of yours told us to go to buggery!"

"If you knew me in these parts you'd know that my word and my notes were good enough."

"Still a hell of a lot of trouble." But it would save them putting the horses through the saleyards. And he was a little worried about the station breads.

"Well, that's my offer. If you want to accept it, you best pen the horses in the yard yonder, if not I'll bid you farewell."

Haselburger chewed his beard, leaned over the pommel of his saddle and ran a line of spit into the dust. "You drive a hard bargain, old man."

"Then if you accept it, you best come over to the house, and you Jim, come too. You can write better than me."

A price was eventually reached, and Jim, deep in concentration at the kitchen table, wrote out the note to Jack Haynes.

Emanuel watched with relief as the two horsemen rode away. The flash young man, calling himself Rang, stayed.

"If we don't get our money, expect to see us back." Haselburger threw over his shoulder.

"You'll get your money!"

"Can't say I'm sorry to be free of that lot myself." Rang mumbled to himself as he followed Emanuel back to the cattle yards. "I only run with 'em for the past month and they were startin' to get to me."

"It's your own doing who you run with son. But just do the right thing here or I promise you won't last long!"

It took almost a week to prepare for the drive to Maffra. Horses had to be shod, while provisions such as flour, baking powder, salted meat, tea, sugar and treacle were carefully loaded onto the packhorses. The loading had to be precise in this country, travelling over wild terrain on a drive that would last at least ten days.

Harry was desperate to go on the drive, but everyone said he too young. He sulked and kicked his favourite cattle dog in the stomach. A thing he deeply regretted. He loved that dog.

They set off before dawn, towards the south east, planning to reach a place called Matheison's Flats on the Dargo River. Following the unwritten law of a cattle drive to set up camp well before nightfall. They had seventy head in all, counting steers, a few cull heifers and cows. This was to be Emanuel's biggest drive to the markets to date.

He thought back to the year when they first took over the run, luckily mustering forty head of strays, left there by Jones after his last, rough muster. The cattle had been in poor condition after spending a hard winter on the high country, but their sale had helped keep the wolf from the door that first year. The herd had steadily increased since then, but Emanuel felt there was still a long way to go.

He rode along it front, a bag of salt slung over the pommel of his saddle, calling, "Salt. S-a-l-l-t. S-a-a-l-l-l-t-t." Some of the animals were already partly used to his voice, and these followed along easily. Nell and George rode at the wings while Jim and the new man Rang took up the rear.

The terrain was steep and rugged with the herd difficult to control in the dense scrub. Still they reached camp before nightfall and set up in the rough holding yard. A yard that had never been quite completed. They spread a sheet of canvas between two trees as light rain was beginning to fall. Jim, George and Rang were appointed to take turns to control the outside perimeter during the night.

The second day was tougher, following the Dargo down to Phelan's Plains. The track turned away from the river in places to climb into the range, often on a path not five feet wide with a sheer drop of 1000 feet to the river below. Man or beast would only go over once. At the bad places, the mob was split into small groups, the drovers keeping them as tight as possible, keeping the animals moving at all times. Often an aggressive beast would try to turn and horn the animal pressing close behind. The rogue beast had to be identified at once and held close. They finally reached the next small river flat, rested the mob for a while before climbing the next range.

At last, they wound down the track, crossed over the bridge into the small village of Dargo. The cattle were an interesting sight to the locals, but a familiar one. A string of cattle, led by a salt carrying drover like some type of pied piper, winding down the crooked street between the buildings. The cattle tried to break into the side streets, some climbed onto the raised footpaths, their hooves rattling the floorboards, sometimes their shit splattering out behind them. Dogs and children gathered in the side streets and followed the mob along in the dust.

Then on to Waterford. Here Emanuel rode ahead, returning well before nightfall to stop the drive in a clearing some two miles from the old Bulgoback Hotel.

"We best set up camp here lads. The holding yards south of Bulgoback are full. Old Lee Paterson got three hundred head penned up there. We'll make camp there by the creek."

Rang was growing tired of a steady job. "How about we give the mob a break for a day or two, boss. Maybe have a few beers at the pub?"

"You were hired to drive cattle lad, not drink beer." was Emanuel's only reply.

The next section was the long stretch of nineteen hard miles called Anderson's track, across broken and stony hills. Then late on the sixth day they broke out of the hills where the small township of Maffra stretched out below them.

Rang rode along in the dust beside Nell. He found himself riding close to Nell more often of late.

"Your old man's a tough boss. Recon he'll let us have a few days off in Maffra?" Nell laughed, shaking her full mane of red hair.

"I wouldn't count on it, Rangy boy! Just consider yourself lucky you caught him at a very good day."

"Jees, you call this a good day?" He threw Nell an easy smile. "I wonder what he'd do if I got fresh with his daughter?"

"Why don't you try it. But he'd probably kill you, I bet!" Nell said with a toss of her head.

Chapter 21

Emanuel stopped over in Maffra to attend to some business after the sale, so Nell stayed with him to wander through the shops. George had met an interesting girl at a local cafe and decided to take the day off as well.

On their way back to the spur, Rang and Charley stopped for a drink at the Dargo hotel. Jim was riding with them but he was not interested in drink, so he decided to ride on to the homestead.

Rang and Charley leaned against the bar, nursing their glasses and talking about Emanuel, now that there were no members of the family about.

"I don't know how young Jim takes all the shit the old man heaps on him," Rang mused. "I left home for a damn side less than that."

"Yeah but you ain't Jim. It takes a lot of guts you know-sometimes it's harder to stay than go. Old Emanuel's alright though. He's square. I've known the old bugger a long time."

It was not until the second drink that they noticed the two men sitting at a table at the dark end of the room. Nates and Haselburger, the men Rang had travelled with, trapping wild horses in the Grant valley.

He nodded in their direction and couldn't help notice their eyes never left him while he talked to Charley.

"Steer clear of that lot," muttered the old man. "I never liked the look of either of 'em, the moment I seen 'em."

"They're harmless enough. The German thinks he's a rough bastard, but he's harmless enough. Saw him cry like a baby one day when his horse kicked him on the knee. The other one, Nates, done a little time in jail I hear. But he still lets the German push him around. But I don't care. I'm going a different way nowadays."

Charley rode on in the late afternoon, taking two bottles of cheap whisky in his saddlebag. He always bought two bottles because it would be a long while before he saw civilisation again. And he knew when that lot ran out, he'd wished he'd bought more.

Rang stayed on. It had already been a long time between drinks.

Charley had barely left when Haselburger sidled up beside him.

"How's it going young fella, workin' steady with dat Pommy toff?"

"Alright. He's a hard old bugger, but fair."

"Not as fair as that daughter of his, I bet!" sniggered Nates. Rang could have punched the man in the face.

"You know dat wild valley, Grants I think they call it, where we trapped them horses?" Haselburger's voice still carried a heavy accent, despite the fact he had been born and bred in this country. "Bloody waste of time dat. Didn't even make tucker."

His family had come out from the old country early in the century and settled in the marginal wheat country of South Australia. Haselburger, part of a large family, was the only son not interested in farming. He left home at an early age, with a broken-down horse and ten pounds he had stolen from a tin can that his father had hidden that contained the family fortune.

"Dat's wild country back in dere. Too wild for most people I say."

Rang began to feel uneasy. He didn't quite know where this conversation was leading.

"What's it to me. I know the country, I was there, remember?"

"Just thought you might be interested in a little proposition. There's a lot of cattle in the high plains. Too many by all accounts. Dem toffs up there wouldn't miss a few. Great place to hold up. Old hut to camp, too. And yards. Thought it might be great opportunity for a smart young chap like you."

Rang slammed down his empty glass. "Count me out, Haselburger."

"Mine Got! Got upperty, haven't we? You weren't so almighty proud when we found you hiding in the scrub from dat copper out around Bourke!"

"That was different. It was a mistake" Rang didn't want to think any more about hiding in the scrub from the copper outside Burke. Enough scrub to hide in around Burke was hard to find.

"Yeah a mistake," Nates sniggered. "A copper's daughter is always a mistake when you're caught in bed with your bloody pants down!"

Why did he always feel like smashing the man in the face?

"And dare seemed to be a little something about horse theft, too, I remember," threw in Haselburger.

"I give the horse back. Turned him loose just outside town. It was only the publican's horse anyhow." Rang vividly remembered the policeman at the door and the wild clamour out the open window. "And the horse was just there!"

But that was a long time ago and now Rang was determined to stay in one spot for a while.

"I got a good job now, so I'm sticking to it."

Like Haselburger, he had been born to dirt farming parents, this time in the Mallee country. Rang's father was lean, small and poor, with a fetish for horses. He had built a little track on the farm to train his own horses, and this kept him poorer than the wheat he tried to grow. He often rode his own horses at the country meetings and found himself better at this than farming, and not much good at either. He often told his long-suffering wife that he never drank or smoked, so a little gambling would not hurt him. He bet on everything that moved.

That was what caused all the trouble. When Rang found himself with five pounds in his pocket, he took a bet on Tarcoola in the Cup at forty to one. This seemed a fortune to Rang. His father wanted the boy to put the money into the place as this would answer a lot of their problems. But Rang spent the lot on fine clothes, a good horse and a new rifle. He didn't stay long on the farm after that and soon lost the horse and had to sell his rifle. But he kept the clothes.

"You're stayin' wouldn't have nothing to do with that piece of Trask skirt?"

"Will you shut your bloody mouth Nates, or will I shut it for you?"

"Settle down, Nates. Can't you see de man's too good for us now."

He slopped his beer. Haselburger was a little drunk. "But I tell you something though, fancy boy, if anyone comes lookin' for us, we'll know where da word come from. And we'll sure as hell come looking for ya!"

"Don't try to threaten me, Haselburger. I don't give a damn what you do, or your sleazy friend, just leave me out of it. Just don't come onto the Trask run!"

When at last Rang had enough to drink, it was too late to make the ride up the mountain, so he slept on two chairs in the dark at the back of the room. By that time, he didn't feel good enough for the trip anyway.

Chapter 22

Dargo celebrated Federation with a ball held in the Catholic Church Hall. The hall was on the outskirts of town, standing proudly, clad in new corrugated iron. It was the only hall in town.

Emanuel, Emily and Nell drove down from the spur in the new sulky they had purchased in Omeo, drawn by a fine bay mare called Queenie. The horse and sulky were a birthday present for Emily to celebrate her last child, bought at a time when Emanuel was in a rare good mood. They had recently cut a better track through from the spur to the road from Dargo and could make the trip now in less than two hours. Emanuel was well pleased with the rig and the feeling of prosperity it bought with it.

George and Rang followed to town on horseback, while Jim stayed at home with the children. He had little interest in town people and much preferred to stay in the mountains. Charley would have nothing to do with the hype of Federation, and chose to celebrate it in his bunk with a bottle of cheap whisky.

A large group of the cattlemen from the mountain came down to celebrate the big event, along with a few dusty miners in serge suits they had found somewhere in their swags. Most of the local town people came along with some from the surrounding lowland farmers there as well. The small hall was almost bursting, decorated with balloons and bunting, with a huge picture of Edmund Barton on the wall. Barton was the man to lead the first federal parliament. Save the colony in fact, some said, although others thought, save it from what?

Billy O'Riley, the local butcher was a strong advocate for federation and the self-appointed mayor of Dargo. Having arranged the Ball, so fully expecting to lead the proceedings, he mounted the small stage at the front of the hall. A short wide man who had to stand tall for anyone to see him, hooked his thumbs under the braces of his new suit, cleared his throat and began a well prepared speech.

"As we gather here tonight on this auspicious occasion, the foundation of our new Federal Government…"

Emily bustled into the small kitchen to help the local ladies prepare food while Emanuel stood in the crowded hall to listen to what O'Riley had to say.

The stylish Una Lund struggled onto the stage with her piano accordion. Struggled with the help of several willing men. Una was a handsome woman. Blackie Davis tuned his fiddle while his wife settled her ample bottom at the piano to test the keyboards. The butcher, annoyed by the interruptions, continued with his well prepared speech.

"While I know there has been a lot of fierce debate, and misguided fear, I might say…"

Rang soon tired of the speech and wandered outside to build a smoke. He wore a fancy waistcoat and stiff collared shirt. He had even found a tie. Back in the crowd someone yelled, "Sit down Billy!"

George soon found his old sparring partner Athol, and as their attention span was not very long, they wandered outside as well.

A netting fence ran along beside the building, enclosing a small yard where buggies and sulky's were held. A few saddle horses were tied to a rail. There was a pie-ball mare hitched to a sulky by the fence. Everyone knew the horse and rig as the butcher drove it everywhere. George unhitched the horse while Athol drove the shafts of the sulky through the netting fence. They led the animal through the back gate, backed it into the shafts where they stuck through the netting and reharnessed it. The whole operation took only a few minutes.

Rang sat on the front steps rolling the tobacco between his palms, laughing around the cigarette paper held between his lips. From inside the hall, the speech rolled on:

"Federation, my friends, will give our State the prosperity that we all deserve. That lot up North have been taking all the cream from our hard earned sweat for far too long…"

Someone called again, "Sit down Billy!"

The band found a tune, stuttered for a while, then gaining strength, drowned out the butcher.

'Sweet Rosy O'Grady', the popular song sweeping the country at the time, announced the first barn dance. Everyone seemed to know the tune. Cattlemen, free of their spurs, miners and a few townspeople selected partners and formed the circle. Light and dust spilled out through the open doorway.

The family of Henry Craye passed by the two boys in the dark before they even noticed. He kicked Rang's feet as he stepped over them, leading his wife into the hall. Ida walked a few steps behind her husband, carrying a small child on her hip, a heavily pregnant stomach leading her through the doorway. Ida knew the hall well. She had taught school there before the lack of numbers caused the school to close. She still had her looks then, before life with the wild and strange cattleman took them away. Marrying Henry Craye had seemed a good way to move up in the world at the time. But life in the mountains had not lived up to expectations. She had only left home twice since she had been there. Once to have her baby. The second time to have a broken leg set by the local doctor. Henry had been in an unusually good mood all day, but it had still taken a great deal of persuasion to get him to the ball. Henry didn't give a damn about federation.

Emanuel saw them at once and couldn't think of anyone else he least expected to see at a ball. He was talking to William King at the time, pausing in mid-sentence. He couldn't take his eyes off Henry Craye.

King noticed at once. "Let it drop, man," he said. "Tonight's not the night."

Across the hall, a group of eager young men had gathered like flies around Nell. She didn't dance as well as she sat a horse. She hadn't had that much practice. In fact, she had no practice at all, her legs moving straight, stiff and formal. Still this didn't seem to worry the locals, who danced little better than she.

Henry Craye was different. She was taken completely by surprise when he asked her, formally, with a faint bow from the hip, to take the floor. Confused, but curiously flattered, Nell let the man take her arm. The band was gathering confidence when it broke into the strains of 'Roamin' in the Glomin'.' Henry swept her around the hall on feet that seemed to glide across the floor. It was one of the strange gifts that Henry was born with. It was as if things that were designed for other people accidently landed on Henry's shoulders. Gifts he never really cared for or particularly wanted.

"What about your wife?" asked Nell breathlessly. She found it difficult to cope with his speed across the floor. "Shouldn't you be dancing with her?"

"I'll dance with whoever I please. And you please me at the present, my girl!"

Emanuel elbowed his way through the crowd, grabbing Nell by the arm, almost throwing her to the floor. Henry followed them, still holding one arm.

"I'd ask you not to lay your dirty hands on any daughter of mine!" Emanuel roared. Much of the dancing stopped, and so did the fiddle. Una, deep in her work kept playing the accordion. Then the piano petered out.

"Settle down you old fool. I'll dance with who I please," said Henry Craye.

"Like Hell you will. You got a wife-go dance with her, if she's fool enough to have you. Just get your hands off my daughter!"

The accordion finally stopped. The last feet shuffled to silence on the floor. Nell felt the eyes of everyone upon her.

"I'll do what I please you old goat. I only asked the girl for a dance. I see nothing wrong with that!"

"There's a lot wrong you, you young cur. I remember you well, Henry Craye. We have some unfinished business!"

"That was only a misunderstanding. Happened a long time ago, so get over it!" The room had gone completely quiet, "The whole thing was my old man's doin', anyway."

"I know who was there Henry Craye. Don't any of your lot go near my daughter. And keep your filthy cattle off my land!" In rage the old Yorkshire accent took over completely.

"You Trasks is all the same. You been in the mountains a few years and think you're Almighty God. Well, we Craye's been here for generations, so don't go looking down your noses at us. We been running cattle in these parts for more years than you've had hot breakfasts, you pommy bastard!" Emanuel drew back his arm but King grasped it in time.

"That will be enough you two. Settle this later!" He dragged Emanuel kicking and fighting towards the door. "Come outside man and settle down." Then he whispered as he led him away, "I got a little something under the buggy seat that will do you good."

Nell moved nervously back to her seat, cheeks flushed with shame. Henry rocked on the balls of his feet, glaring at the two cattlemen leaving the hall. Then strode to his wife, grasped her by the arm and drew her to her feet. His young daughter clung to her mother's side.

"Let 'em have their bloody ball!" he spat.

Outside King led Emanuel, still shaking with rage towards his buggy, standing beneath a pepper tree by the fence. He drew a full bottle of whisky from beneath the seat.

"This will make the night flow better!" He took a long pull of the bottle and handed the rest to Emanuel. "You nearly caused some excitement in there. So much for peace and Federation!"

"That filthy rat-faced little turd." Emanuel mumbled, drawing on the bottle. "I should have smashed his face."

"I probably did you a favour." King said with a laugh. "I hear he can go a bit. And he's thirty years younger than you."

The band struck up 'Danny Boy', faulting at the beginning, but finally getting into the swing.

George had watched the argument from the doorway, feeling disappointed that events had ended so quietly. He felt that it mattered little how young Henry Craye was at the time. His father's rage, could have murdered anyone on the night.

"This Federation is not all bad, you know," King was saying around the bottle of whisky. "People think that a federal government will channel too much money away from us. But the tariffs will go and that will do nothing but good in the long chalk. And this Barton fellow, I think he's a good man…"

George had found the Chalker twins sitting quietly with their mother on a bench by the far wall. His father had made him somewhat of a celebrity that night. He managed to pry one of them from under her care-the prettiest one, Bella. He knew nothing about dancing, but shuffled about the floor with the girl, generally getting in the way of everyone else. Rang had found Nell and coaxed her to her feet. The crowd had thinned out around her since the episode with Henry Craye. Rang didn't dance as well as Henry, but Nell found there was much less fuss about it.

Out by the buggy the two cattlemen were getting drunk. "You know it's funny how money changes a man. When I first came to the mountains, I was just a bloody drover. Brought a herd in for Lee Patterson's father. I was only Billy King then. Now I'm William." His words were slurring and the bottle was half empty. Emily appeared briefly in the doorway, looking for her husband. The sound of the accordion drifted through the board walls. He didn't know why his thoughts turned to Una Lund. "A strange woman that Lund woman. Some said she was once some kind of a dancer. All sorts of stories going around at the time. You'd think she was too much for old Whitey Lund to handle!"

"Can't say that I know the man." Emanuel slurred his words.

"He owns a nice parcel of land out on the road to Bairnsdale. But she's a strange lady, can't say I don't find her attractive."

"A fine stamp of a women!" Emanuel said, his Yorkshire accent completely back.

In the early hours of the morning when the ball was finally over, the butcher's curses coloured the night air.

"Who did this to my bloody horse?" Some ladies stood in shock in the yard. Some were mounting their buggies, some carried empty dishes to their sulkies. Billy's horse backed up in fear against the netting, lashing out with its rear hooves, rearing forwards until the sulky fouled the fence. Billy at last got his horse under control. "Bloody kids I'll be bound. Look at the paint ripped off the bloody shafts?" The horse backed up and his feet kicked the netting fence again. "I'll kill the rotten brats when I catches 'em!"

William King nudged Emanuel in the ribs. "I wager that kid of yours, young George, knows something about the butcher's horse." He laughed a slurred laugh. "God we was all young once!"

"A man should tan his hide." Emanuel said, not quite convincingly and now fully drunk.

Mrs Chalker had some trouble finding one of her daughters, but at last found Bella, a little flustered, trying to think of some kind of alibi.

George was nowhere to be found, so Emanuel and Emily left him to find his own way home.

Emanuel slumped drunkenly in the seat while Emily, sitting straight and rigid, drove the sulky home. He sang quite a lot along the way, while Emily steered the sulky wheels into as many ruts as she could find.

Chapter 23

Mustering the west side of the run near McGovern's hut, Nell and Rang blundered onto the stray steers. Wild and rangy, they had clearly missed the last autumn muster and probably the muster before that. At the sight of the two riders, they turned into the heavy timber and were soon out of sight, crashing through the undergrowth down the spur.

"I bet it's a long time since that lot has seen people!" called Nell.

"Probably never has seen people-and probably will be a long time before they see 'em again!" Rang pulled his mount back on its heels. "We'll never head 'em in that country. Probably halfway to the Wonnangatta River by now!"

Nell dug her spurs into her horse's flank. "Not in my books. You say you can ride, Rang boy-now's the time to prove it!"

The chestnut horse burst down the incline and Rang soon lost sight of her in the timber. It was madness the way she rode, sitting the horse as if joined to it. The pony's hooves clipped the moss covered fallen logs and small stones flew like shrapnel as she weaved between the mountain ash. Rang could not come close to her, but could hear the sounds of animals crashing through the scrub. He weaved between the timber, jumping rocks and fallen logs, doubting the bloody strays were worth the effort. A few wild bullocks were hardly worth your life. The ground turned boggy as he plunged into a ravine, the mud flying from his pony's hooves. There were running springs in the gully bottom and as they climbed the further bank, the hillside seemed to be bleeding water everywhere. They were almost to the bottom of the next spur before he sighted Nell again, this time riding towards him, slow, crest-fallen, mud stained from head to foot.

There was no sign of the strays, and no sound, until he heard them crashing through the scrub, well down the mountain, maybe half a mile away.

When Rang brought his horse up, its rear legs slid on the soft earth. "I thought you said you could ride?" he laughed, secretly relieved that the girl was still alive. "Do you realise you near broke your fool neck over a few worthless strays!"

"I did not nearly break my neck, Rang Bell!" She peeled a glob of loose mud from her shoulder and flicked it away. She looked more shaken than Rang had ever seen her.

"Well, it appears you made a pretty good attempt at it."

"I did not fall. I never do!" The mud was all over her saddle and down the shoulder of the horse. She knew her story was lame and blushed at the shame of it.

"You could have fooled me. Did that mud fall from the sky?" Nell spurred past him, the shoulder of her horse striking him on the knee.

"I told you I did not fall off, Harvey Bell!" She only used his given name, Harvey as a weapon. He wished he had never told her of it. Nobody used the name nowadays.

"And what about the cattle? Did you have a talk to 'em. Make 'em promise to come back by themselves?"

"Shut up Harvey. I decided they just weren't worth the trouble!" he watched her back, straight and haughty, covered in mud as she rode up the mountain side. "Besides, it's going to rain. Look at the clouds."

Indeed when he looked up between a break in the trees, the sky was starting to blacken. The weather never ceased to amaze him on the mountains. Rang, although having lived in the high country for more than a year now, had been born and raised in the flat Malley country, and was still not used to the mountains.

As they rode on towards McGovern's hut he couldn't help smirking at the hurt pride showing in the set of her haughty back. The mud clung to her red hair, covering her checked shirt, and he wanted to rub it off.

The hut came into view, resting among the bushes in a small clearing, tumbled down cattle yards running into the timber behind it. The clouds were thickening and thunder rumbled a long way to the west. *It was almost midday, time for a bite to eat*, Rang thought, in the shelter of the hut.

These mountain huts were built at strategic spots over the high plains and were great cover in times of emergency. Stock yards were often built near the huts, handy when handling cattle miles from the homestead.

Jack McGovern's hut was not built for the purpose, it was just used because it was available. Built a long time ago, with only an iron roof added in later years to replace the bark that had first covered it. There was a chimney built of flattened kerosene tins attached to the one log room, an old bathtub at one end to catch some of the water that ran off the roof. Old Jack was known to have had a dubious reputation as a cattle duffer. This was in the early days when Gordon Jones owned the lease. Jones was losing cattle and it was rumoured that one day, liquored up on rum, some of his men found the hide of one of his cattle nailed drying to the wall and dragged old Jack from his hut and hung him in the gully behind the house. But this was all hearsay, and no one knew if the story was true.

Rang quickly got a fire going in the fireplace to boil the billy, while Nell scraped some of the mud from her body. The sky was quite dark now, thunder rumbled like an upset stomach and a flicker of lightning travelled across the sky.

"I'm going out to clean myself up." Nell had calmed down and was beginning to see the humour of it all.

Rang found a few rashes of bacon in his saddlebag. He loved his bacon. There was also damper and the ever popular treacle. An old saucepan was hanging on the wall, so he carried it outside to wiped it clean with grass. Rang always liked to eat well.

"I'll cook a meal while you clean up your pride. You got another shirt?"

"Just mind your own business-and keep your eyes to yourself!"

Outside the weather was growing angry and the horses were growing restless, tied to the rails of the rough yards.

Nell peeled off her checked shirt, aware of Rang's eyes on the other side of the log walls, probably looking between the cracks. She played up to him as she washed herself off, lowering her hair into the tub to rinse it clean, then threw her head back and shook the hair free, flaunting the sight of her breasts at the cracks in the timber walls.

Nell smiled to herself as she washed her shirt clean in the tub aware at how her breasts shook as she leaned forward, wrung the shirt out and fitted it on, still facing the wall. She knotted the wet shirt in front of her, now feeling the cold and turned back towards the door of the hut. Thunder rumbled louder and a few large spots of rain fell as she came through the door.

Rang looked a little awkward. "You got another shirt? You better change that one before you catch your death!"

Nell rummaged through her saddlebag and came up with a worn Tasmania bluey. She turned her back and shrugged it on, then warmed herself in front of the fire, hugging herself with her hands.

"How's that bacon going?"

"The bacon? Oh, I haven't got quite around to that yet!"

"No, you wouldn't."

Outside the lightning cracked, bringing down the limb of a snow gum, the sound like a cannon. Outside Rang's horse broke away and plunged off up the spur.

"God damn, I lost my horse!"

"Then you better go get it, or you'll have a long walk home. Take mine, you might catch him before he gets to Melbourne!"

She laughed as she watched Rang run out into the storm. He tightened the girth and swung into the saddle of the chestnut. Nell closed the door against the rain and bent over the dirty pan to fry the eggs. She liked her food too.

Nell had eaten her meal long before Rang came back. When he pushed at the door it wouldn't open. "Let me in, I'm damned near drowned out here!"

Nell had dropped a length of timber into the brackets that held it shut. The door shook but held fast.

"A little water won't hurt you, Harvey. Might even clean out your dirty eyes!"

"Come on Nell, have a heart!" She ate the rest of the bacon and smiled to herself. Nell was usually more interested in cattle than in men. Usually. But about once a month she had a mood change. And it always surprised her how strong the change was.

So after he was well wet, she felt he had paid his penance for his roving eyes, so she opened the door to let him in.

The mood change was suddenly very strong and it was very cosy in the dark hut.

"Come over here 'till I warm you up, you dirty-eyed young bull…"

Chapter 24

The heifer was in trouble.

Jim found her in a valley above Chalky creek, laying on her side in trampled snow grass beneath a grove of twisted gums, a new-born calf's nose and part of one hoof showing between her legs. The heifer staggered weakly to her feet and turned with all the aggression that she could muster, but Jim quickly had his rope around her and, with little effort, threw the animal. He had her on the ground and was down between the hind legs working on the birth when Emanuel rode up. He swung down from his mount, tied the big roan to the branch of the nearest snow gum and, grasping a front leg, got a boot on her neck to hold the struggling heifer from rising.

The first snow was in the air and fog crept silently along the valley floor as Jim, working in mud and slush, managed to pull first the hoof and then the head free. The head seemed far too big for the mother, a small baldy in poor condition who had put too much growth into her unborn calf and kept little nutrition for herself. The second leg was bent back so Jim thrust his arm inside, right up to the elbow. Finally his groping fingers found the leg, turned it inside her and dragged it free. He had to rest a while on his haunches to regain his breath. He coughed and spat. He had not been feeling well for the past few days.

The heifer had finally lost her fight, so Emanuel took his boot from her neck and grasped a back leg. Using all his strength he rocked the animal from side to side while Jim strained between her legs. Progress was slow. The calf too big for the opening that was supposed to be the passage to life. Jim coughed, spat, then went back to work while Emanuel worked the legs from side to side.

Then the heifer got one leg loose and kicked him in the stomach. Emanuel reeled back on his haunches, the breath driven from him, a great ache below the ribs. The heifer kicked and thrashed with new-found energy. Jim held fast to the calf while Emanuel withered on the grass. Finally, exhausted, Jim roped the heifer's front feet together and tied them to the nearest tree. The animal had by now lost some of its fight. The tongue lolled from the calf's gaping mouth and the eyes were glazed, but a gasp of air proved that life still remained. He rested for a moment then tied a rope around the calf's front legs, hitching it to his saddle.

"Be careful there!" Emanuel, down on the grass, suddenly realised what Jim was about to do. "Be patient or you'll kill the damn calf!" A cough tore at his throat and his ribs hurt. He tried to regain his feet but found the effort beyond him at the moment.

"It's the calf or the damn cow!" Jim eased the horse forward. The calf came by degrees and eventually burst free.

"God damn it you've killed the animal!"

Jim released the rope. "There was nothing else to do, it was either the calf or the cow. We would never have got it with you on the ground!"

"God damn it man show some patience. Give me time, I can get up. I been pulling calves before you were born, you young whelp!"

All his life, Jim had kept the feelings bottled up inside him, but finally everything broke free. He picked up the dead calf, wet and slippery, and flung it at his father, who still squatted in the trampled grass.

"Shove your bloody calf. I quit, you cranky old bugger!"

Jim mounted his horse, turned it into the soft snow and spurred up the hill, the rage still streaming from his mouth.

"You know what you can do with your damn lease and all your damn cattle!"

Emanuel, resting on one arm, watched, stunned, as his son rode away.

It was almost nightfall when he finally arrived back at the homestead. Nell, George and Charley Nash were at the stables unsaddling their horses.

"Seen young Jim?" Emanuel asked, easing himself down from the saddle. His ribs still hurt and he suspected one was cracked.

"Seen him?" Charley replied. "Sure we seen him, up top. Long while ago-long before dinner. Steam coming out his ears, there was. Said he was going to get a job at the mine and said to tell you to go to Hell!"

He threw his saddle on the rail.

"Don't expect to see him around here again for a spell!"

"Bad tempered young bugger!" Emanuel loosened the girth of the big roan. "But he'll be back."

"Well, I wouldn't count on it boss," Charley muttered under his breath. "I just wouldn't count on it."

Chapter 25

Jim had arrived home at the spur two hours before Emanuel. He strode through the house, throwing things about, throwing things together that he intended to take with him, using language that Emily would not usually stand for. But now she just followed him through the house, rubbing her hands on an apron, bewildered at the tone of her eldest son. She had never seen him like this before, and was a little afraid of what she saw.

There was not much that Jim owned. He wrapped it all in an old blanket torn from his bed, took the few pounds and a few coins he had hidden in a biscuit tin in his cupboard, was off on his horse in a matter of minutes, the horse circling and kicking as it felt his rage. Jim had never really drawn wages. Only collected money from his father when he needed to buy something. And that was not very often.

"Tell the old bugger I'll be back for my wages later on!" He bellowed, jamming his heels into the horse and turning his head towards the mine.

The whole thing had changed since Emanuel's day. The stamping mill was mounted on a concrete block, below an embankment built up like a ramp where the drays could unload into the funnel of the mill. The whole thing was driven by a water wheel mounted above a fast flowing channel of water, waste collected from the hose gouging out the hillside. The system had been designed by a man named Eric Mince. A small, quick rat-like man that Major Terry had hired from the mines at Bendigo. Eric, despite his looks was a genius and Terry was well pleased with himself. The only thing was that it had cost the mine a fortune and Terry was not sure how the mine could recoup the expense.

The foreman of the mine was a man named Fleedner. A giant of a man with a brown handlebar moustache, coated with the dark stains from tobacco spit. The top of his head was completely bald with dirty yellow hair down to the collar. He had a fowl temper and was almost as big as Jock Hoolahan. The two men hated one another and Jock longed for the old days when Emanuel was still here.

93

There was a job available on the sluice hose so Fleedner hired Jim on the spot. Not many people, especially those that knew would take such a job.

Jim bought an old tent from one of the miners and pitched it in a vacant spot he found among the trees.

It was miserable work, nozzle man at the mine. They worked in four hour shifts, usually two shifts per day. It took a strong arm to work the timber beam that controlled the nozzle, chewing the earth from the mountain side. He wore canvas clothing, the only luxury provided by the Royal Dargo, but still this did little to keep the water out. The noise was deafening and the cold spray did not let up for an instant.

"If it don't send you deaf, it'll probably drown you!" Jock Hoolahan had told him.

Jim was not in good health when he took the job, and he lasted only a fortnight.

Jock Hoolahan led him home one night in the pouring rain, tied to the saddle of his pony. Jock untied the ropes to help him down but Jim could barely stand. Jock helped him onto the veranda and hammered on the door until Emily answered.

"Good God!" she said. "What have you done to my boy, Jock!"

The family gathered around the small kitchen as rain pounded on the roof.

"Get him into the bed there!" Emanuel shouted, pointing to the open doorway to the next room. "And somebody ride to Dargo and bring back the doctor!"

Nell was the one to go. Dressed In an oilskin coat, she was soaked long before she got there. The track was dark and dangerous, lit up at times by the flash of lightning.

It was near midnight when she hammered at the door of old Dr McGuire. He was slow and unwilling to answer the door, but Nell's hammering was persistent. She helped the old man harness his buggy and load his equipment, wrapped up in one battered old black bag. Then, by the flickering light of a carbide lantern and the scattered lightning, followed Nell back to the log homestead on King's Spur.

Jim lay shaking on a bunk, covered in blankets, white as a ghost. He barely found the strength to cough, and when he did the effort doubled him up beneath the blankets. McGuire lay a hand over the man's forehead and shoved a thermometer deep into his mouth.

"Good Lord," he shook the mercury back down in the instrument. "The man's got a fever fit to blow his damn head off!" He uncovered his chest and tested the heart.

"He's got pneumonia, I expect—and a good taste of it. We've got a sick man here!"

The lantern was low on kerosene, the yellow light darkening the glass as the wick burned low.

"Get another light in here!" McGuire found a package of yellow powder in his black bag.

"I'll ask you for a little clean water, Mrs Trask…"

He drew another bottle from the battered black bag.

"This is as best we have at the moment."

He measured out portions into a small bowl. "A sulphur combination. Give the man a tablespoon every four hours. I'll leave you the drugs and show you how to mix them. It may help bring the fever down. Keep wet towels on his forehead and I'll also give you a liniment to rub on his chest. The next few days will be vital. We must bring that temperature down."

Emanuel sat still beside the bed with his head in his hands. Occasionally his shoulders shook.

Later, in the kitchen warming his hands around a cup of tea, old Dr McGuire spoke softly.

"It's a bad one, Mrs Trask. A bad one. Your husband seems to be taking it hard. I expect we should have got to the man sooner."

They could hear the lungs labouring in the next room. He patted Emily on the shoulder. The sun was just lightening the sky outside.

"Just keep him on that sulphur and maybe pray a bit. Some say that helps."

The fever broke on the third day. Jim had lain in a lather of sweat, shaking violently while he dreamed strange things of racing cattle, of deep cliffs and thundering water. At times, he felt sure he would drown. He called out at times and screamed "Hold the head fast!" His feet thrashed in the wet sheets and his arms flayed the air.

But on the third day the fever passed and Jim lay, white and beaten, the breath still rasping in his lungs.

Emanuel had stayed by his son's bedside the whole time and when he saw the eyes open at last, pale but showing some kind of reason, he almost took his son's hand but found he could not quite do it.

"I expect you think I've been a little harsh on you at times." The apology would not quite come out as it should. "But mostly I don't mean what I say, you know. So we'll put all that behind us. There's work to do and we badly need you back on the run."

Jim was conscious of every breath of air he drew into his lungs. The fact worried him, that he could hear his own breath so loud.

"I dunno Dad." He laboured with every breath. "I feel a man should make his own way." His lungs made a soft whistling sound, "We'll have to see."

"I'll pay you son. I promise I'll pay you a good wage."

"It's not that, dad. We'll have to see…"

The next day, when he was sure the crisis had passed, Emanuel returned to his cattle on the high plains.

Emily and young Frank, were the only ones left at the hut. Jim could hear his mother loading dirty clothes into the copper on the veranda outside his room. Hear the thump of the stick she used to load the clothes into the boiling water, could see in his mind's eye the water bleached stick going in and out, drawing the clothes out into the wicker basket. Jim was feeling a little light-headed. The pain was gone, only the sound of his breathing remained.

So he decided to take a little walk. It was a beautiful day and his legs were weak as he shuffled down along the spur. He rested with a hand to support him at the end of the clearing. From this spot, he could almost see as far as the coast through the haze between the trees.

The thought suddenly struck him that he had never seen the sea. Twenty eight years old and had never even seen an ocean. He had spent most of his life in these mountains and really hadn't seen much of the world at all.

He swung away from the timber and turned back towards the house. Emily was out in front calling for him.

Twenty eight years old and never even seen the sea. He had to take other people's advice that it even existed at all.

There was fog creeping up the valley to the east. The cloud crept like a soft white snake between the timber and rocks. Why was there always fog? Even on a good day.

His mother was standing in front of the sprawling log cabin, calling to him.

Why was she calling to him? Why was fog swirling around her legs? Her voice seemed far away. The sea. He would see the sea. If only the fog would lift. It seemed to be all around him now and he could still hear his mother calling through it, though she seemed a long, long way away. And then the earth and the mud was there.

It was still soft from rain.

Jim died two nights later. They buried him on a small rise between the trees not two hundred yards from the homestead.

There were only a few people at the graveside, for Jim only knew a few people. Emily stood off to one side supported by her two daughters, Nell and Bess. Bess, twelve-years-old, had idolised her brother. Emily kept her head buried in a hanky, shoulders shaking in tiny spasms. Emanuel stood off to one side in a faded, serge suit that hung loose about him. He had once been a big man but seemed to have shrunk over the past few days.

The preacher was from the Methodist church in Omeo and, after performing the ceremony, he turned awkwardly to shake Emanuel's hand.

Emanuel said nothing at all.

Chapter 26

Emanuel was a different man after the funeral. The fight had gone right out of him, and the enthusiasm to go on with his life.

For days, he shuffled around the house and around the yard outside, sometimes wandering as far as the stables, where he went through the motions of repairing harness. But mostly he spent time at the mound of fresh earth where Jim had been buried.

Emily watched her husband silently. She felt the loss of Jim deeply, but could somehow handle it better than her husband, feeling that although the good Lord had taken him away, there must be some good reason to it. All a body could do was carry on. You never really expected to be happy in this world anyway. The next place was the time for that.

She sat Emanuel down one day with a cup of tea and patted the back of his hand. This was an unusual show of affection for Emily.

"It's no good stewing on bad things you know. What is, is."

"It was always my fault, love. I was always too hard on the lad."

"He wasn't a lad. He was twenty seven years old, and you shouldn't think like that. We all did what we had to do. Life's hard, and there's no denying that, and if we made a few mistakes along the way, we've just got to go on with it. We've made our own beds so we have to lay in them."

"And the truth is, Mother, I fear I loved him more than the rest. And I always treated him the worst."

"Rubbish, the man thought the world of you. You only did what you did when you were tired. The world gets to you sometimes."

"Say that as you will, but I'll always feel I was to blame. Nozzle man, no less. Not even a crazy monkey should take a job like that. Why can't they dig their rotten gold out of the hill like the other mines? It's unnatural, blasting the mountainside away. Bloody Terry, Watts and Maloney. Bloody God-damned Royal Dargo mine!"

98

"Twern't them that forced him to take the job." She didn't chastise Emanuel for taking the Lord's name in vain. Instead this time she gently squeezed his hand. "Jim always had a weakness in his lungs. I always secretly feared we'd lose him someday."

He thought he saw her shoulders shake and a little moisture form at the corners of her eyes. Emanuel was amazed to see it.

"I'm going down into Dargo to buy cement. We'll cement the grave and put a fence around it. Yes, that's what we'll do, put a fence around. And I'll get a fine headstone carved!"

He got up from the table and wandered outside to look at the sight and plan the headstone.

Chapter 27

There was a place on the high plains, on the lower southern slopes, where the Trasks moved their cattle at the onset of winter. The valley, known as Clunes run, was just above the four thousand feet mark, and backed up into the mountain, gaining some shelter from the teeth of winter. The valley was covered in short scrub, not like the sweet snow grass of the higher slopes, but at least palatable through the times of heavy snow, when the snow grass was completely covered.

The bite of winter was in the air and soft snow drifted before the wind. Already the higher peaks were blanketed. Emanuel rode his old roan gelding down to the spot to check how work was progressing. Nell and Rang were already there, with a herd of some three hundred cattle. There was a trail of salt laying on a high, barren ridge and the cattle were gathered along it. Some had been coming in by themselves over the past weeks. It always amazed Emanuel how far the animals could smell the salt.

Nell hadn't seen her father on the mountain for quite a while, so she rode out to meet him.

"Glad to see you about, old timer," she said with a warm smile. They rode along in silence, side by side, down towards the cattle. "We miss you telling us what to do you know. Even when we mostly know better ourselves!"

The cattle were in top condition, but would need all the condition they could get over the next three months. The sweet-grass run on the high plains could carry ten thousand head over the warmer months. But the winters were hard when the grass was lost beneath the snow. There was often a heavy loss of calves during a bad year. And not only calves were lost.

"George and Charley are mustering the west side. Should be here in a day or two."

Emanuel shifted uncomfortably in his saddle. Although his backside was sore he felt excited. He didn't know he'd miss the life so much. "I just hope they can beat the weather."

He looked out over the valley, all four hundred acres of it. Not much for cold and hungry cattle when there was only short scrub to graze on. For the first time, he noticed the huge piles of dry timber. They were scattered across the valley a few hundred yards apart. This had been Emanuel's idea, when it first came to him some months ago. He had been planning with some enthusiasm, then. Before Jim died. Evidently the kids had been working on the idea by themselves. They planned to light the fires during the worst cold changes and maybe build up some heat in the sheltered spots. Well, that was the thought anyway. George always said it would be like pissing in the wind and the fires wouldn't do a lick of good.

And maybe they wouldn't. But it was something to try anyway.

William King had already shifted his cattle from the high country to his holdings lower down where the winters were much kinder to man and beast.

That was the way to go. But in the meantime? Emanuel was quietly pleased that his children had at last taken some advice from the old bull. They'd give the fires a go anyway.

Chapter 28

The mine closed in the summer of 1902. It had been winding down for a while, the ledgers in Melbourne spelling the doom of a fading enterprise. Major Terry had sold his part of the company two years before to re-enlist in the armed forces. Considered too old for active service, he served out his time in Africa as an advisor.

Jock Hoolahan stayed on at the mine for a while, to watch the site while the assets were wound up, then moved on to the goldfields of Crooked Creek.

The mountain slowly regained its lost ground. Ferns and bracken grew again, covering the stamp mill that still stood mounted on a concrete block, silent and rusty. Many of the buildings were carried away, or parts that were of some use, like good sheets of iron and the best of the timber. The roof of the administration building fell in and creepers slowly took over.

The Crayes stripped quite a lot of useful timber, then set fire to the main building as Henry considered it an eyesore. Within two years, the mountain had almost totally reclaimed all that it owned. Except for some rusty iron, blackened stumps and a water scoured mountain side, little evidence remained that the Royal Dargo had ever existed.

Emanuel drove his sulky along the dusty track that led from Dargo to Lindenow, the bay mare in the shafts. A foal trotted beside the mare, nuzzling her whenever possible as they travelled along. Nell sat up on the seat beside her father, enjoying the trip into the open country of the lowlands.

The sulky crossed a small rise and rattled down towards a creek that crossed the road then travelled along beside it. A grove of trees grew at the bottom of the rise, hiding the entrance to a farm. An eager young man in a smart new suit, hat, stiff shirt and tie waited for them, holding the gate open. 'Ashburn' was burned into a sign, hanging askew on a slab of red gum over the gate.

Emanuel drew back the reins and turned in through the opened gateway. The young man tipped his hat. "Morning Mr Trask. Morning Nell."

"Good day to you Adam." Emanuel nodded.

"The old man's waiting up at the house, "said the young man, running his eyes hungrily over Nell. "I'll close the gate and follow you up."

They travelled down the corrugated track between a row of pepper trees towards the creek, where a rotten wooden bridge had had once crossed, but had now caved in to the water. The track wound off and crossed below it. There was only a little water and the sulky wheels jumped over the rough, wet stones. They followed the track up to a stand of Elms where an old homestead stood, almost hidden among the trees. A fine place in its day but those days were long gone.

Jack Haynes, the proprietor of 'Haynes and Son', stood at the broken front gate with the widow of Josh Sharrock at his side.

Haynes held a walking stick with a pig's-head handle to support his gammy leg as he shook Emanuel's hand. Used the stick for effect as he tipped his hat to Nell.

"Good to see you Emanuel. And you Nell. Lord, you're looking more lovely every day I swear. Just wish I was a young man again!"

He turned to the old woman by his side. "This is Mrs Sharrock. Mrs Sharrock, Emanuel and Nelly Trask. They are some of the wild cattle people from the hills I've been telling you about!"

The widow acknowledged the two visitors. She was thin old woman with skin the colour of leather, dressed in the clothes of a man. But when she spoke her voice was much younger than her face.

"Welcome, I'm sure."

Jack offered his hand to Nell as she climbed down the sulky steps. Nell, not used to such treatment, thought she was quite capable of getting down by herself.

"Mrs Sharrock will show you around the house Nell, and I'm sure young Adam here will be glad to look after you as well. Meanwhile I'll show Emanuel over the place."

He threw his stick into the sulky and climbed into the seat. He seemed to have no trouble with his legs. He slung one foot over the side of the sulky, threw one arm over the back of the seat and directed Emanuel between the buildings surrounding the homestead.

"A fine property this, make no bones about it." The sulky rattled over the stones. "Bit run down now, but nothing that can't be fixed by you and your boys. She's had a rough time of it as late, Mrs Sharrock."

They passed by broken pig pens, a windmill with a leaking trough beside it, crossed an overgrown lucerne flat, passed through an open gate then up a gentle hill.

"Bit steep this, but good soil. Topsoil goes down three feet in these parts!"

Emanuel was not used to land as flat as this.

"I could probably get it for you at a good price. But mark my words, she's no pushover this woman. Looks a little rough but she knows her way around. Had a hell of a battle when old Josh was dying of cancer. Took two years for him to die. Dreadful thing. She's been trying to run the place on her own since then, and done a fair job of it too, but it finally got too much for her. Got a son too. Useless sod never comes near the place. Often the way, I'm afraid, but she's a fine old lady. You're lucky to have the sons you got. This place would suit you down to the ground."

"But I don't know how it would suit the bank."

"Oh, you'd be alright, you got three sons and a couple of handy daughters, not to mention a fine lease on the high plains. God's country up there! But you need something down here to winter on. It's too damn cold to winter cattle up there!"

"You're damn right about that, Jack. Last year was a bad one. We had heavy losses calving last winter. How many acres are we talking here?"

"About seven hundred. Just suit you fine."

They stopped on top of a rise and looked out across the valley. To the north they could see the rise of the mountain range, covered in mist. And behind the spot where Dargo would be, Emanuel could see the top of Mount Hallibutt. Between the mist to the right, King's Spur and the high plains would be there hidden in the mountains.

As Emanuel climbed down the sulky bent under his weight then sprang upwards as his feet caught the ground. He squatted in the earth and dug at it with a stick. He let the dirt trickle through his fingers as he gazed through the sunlight towards the homestead. Many of the fences were falling down, but they could easily fix that. Old Jock Hoolahan was looking for a job. He was hopeless with cattle, but handy with his hands. Yes, it would be great to be like King and the likes to have somewhere to bring his cattle during the winter snow.

Up on the sulky Jack Haynes sat with one leg flung out over the side, one arm nonchalantly thrown over the back of the seat, his head back with the sun catching his glasses. He had been a fine specimen of a man, Jack Haynes. And knew it well. With chiselled jaw and head thrown back, Jack knew that the hook was well in.

"Horses. You should be breeding horses up on those high plains. The army is always looking for mounts, and those hills of yours are ideal. The war with the Boars may well be over, but there are always more wars. That mate of yours Terry was over there you know. I feel sorry for the bloody Boars."

"Don't think they had much to fear from Terry."

The home, Emanuel thought, old Jock Hoolahan could do wonders there. It was all sawn timber with an iron roof. Emily had never had a real home before. And he could use some free time himself, sitting on the front porch in winter, looking up into the mountains, not having to be up there.

"I know where you could buy forty head of fine breeding animals. Suit you down to the ground."

"Might well suit me, but where would I find the money? Especially if I bought this place."

"We could arrange something, old man. You've always been a good client and I'd be happy to back you. We could arrange something, I'm sure." The sun flashed on the rimless glasses.

"I think that son of mine, young Adam, fancies your daughter, you know. Usually can't get the young bugger out of the office, but today I couldn't get him to stay. Tie and suit you notice!"

Emanuel laughed, letting the soil trickle through his fingers. "Half the boy's luck. But I'm afraid Nell's more interested in cattle than men."

He looked down across the valley. He'd buy a plough to break up that creek flat. Grow lucerne there and maybe a stand of oats up on the higher ground. Emily could have a vegetable garden where the cold wouldn't kill everything in sight. A new pigsty down there, and holding yards to draft the cattle.

Emanuel climbed slowly into the sulky.

Ashburn was sold.

Chapter 29

Emanuel sat at the kitchen table trying to get his records in order, a good fire at his back and paperwork spread out before him. He hated bookwork with a passion and would rather spend a hard day on horseback than try his hand with figures. These things did not come easily to him. A pair of damaged spectacles sat uneasily on the end of his nose, as he worked by the hissing light of the gas lamp.

Across the room, Bess stoked wood into the new stove while her young brother Frank played with a hand-made toy in the corner. Occasionally he made wild noises and kicked the floor which caused Emanuel to lose concentration. He sometimes swore and this caused Emily to call down the wrath of the Lord upon him.

Then in the late afternoon, Adam Haynes rode out of the mist.

He was greeted by a pack of excited dogs as he tied his horse to the top rail of the fence. Stepping onto the veranda he stamped the mud from his boots and shook the moisture from his oilskin coat. Emily met him at the door, wiping her hands on her apron.

"Good afternoon young man. Adam, isn't it. Adam Haynes?"

Adam swept off his hat and almost bent at the knee. "Afternoon, Mrs Trask. I just happened to be in the area and thought I'd drop in."

"You picked a bad day to be out. You better come in and warm yourself up."

Emanuel glanced over his glasses. "What brings you out on a day like this, young Adam?" The young man shucked off his oilskin coat. He was very well dressed in a stiff collared shirt with a string tie.

"The Royal Dargo are having a sale to clean up some of the spare stuff, now that the mine has closed. Thought I'd just take a quick look at what was there in case we got the sale."

Emanuel knew he was lying. "Won't be much left to sell. Most of it has been looted by now anyway. Only thing worthwhile would be the stamping mill, and that's well cemented in. Would take a devil of a lot of moving."

"I daresay you're right Mr Trask. Just thought I'd take a look anyhow." His eyes travelled around the room.

Emanuel spoke around the sly smile on his face. "I expect you'll find young Nell up in the stables, playing with her horse. She's trying to teach the damn thing to do tricks."

Adam's ears turned red as he twisted his hat in his hands.

Emily felt quietly pleased that a well-dressed young man would come courting her daughter. "You had better sit yourself down for a cup of tea, now that you're here. Bess, are any of those scones ready? She's becoming a good cook, young Bess. Like her mother, no doubt!" Emily laughed. A rare thing for her.

Adam sat nervously at the table, playing with his hat brim. "Thank you Mrs Trask. I might take the load off for a while. It's perishing cold out there."

"You don't know the word cold, son!" said Emanuel, loading his pipe. Emily glared at him.

Bess poked more wood into the new stove. It had been shipped up from Omeo just a fortnight ago and she was still getting used to it. A large black fountain sat to the side with a brass tap polished so well you could almost see your face in it. The women were very proud of the new stove.

Bess tested the scones with a delicate thrust of the skewer.

"You can be my guineapig, Mr Haynes," Bess was only thirteen and seldom got a chance to talk to strangers. She had seen Adam in Dargo a couple of times and thought he looked very gallant. Like a lord or Duke in some of the picture books she had. She felt she was making very adult conversation. "I've never poisoned anyone before!" She felt a little flushed under his gaze as she placed the scones on a plate before him. Emily had already supplied the hand-turned butter.

The door swung open with a gust of wind. Nell and Harry were coming in from the cold. "She's got that damn horse kneeling on its front leg!" Harry was brushing the rain off his trousers when he noticed Adam.

"Watch your language young man, we have a visitor." Emily snapped.

Nell wondered idly what Adam Haynes wanted on a day like this. She had a fair idea. Adam knocked over the chair coming to his feet. Bess couldn't help sniggering.

"Inspecting the mine." Emanuel said. "Nothing to see there anyhow, and you'd get your fancy suit dirty." Emily shot him a withering glance, so he went back to his paperwork.

Young Frank, down on his knees on the floor, couldn't take his eyes off the man. Anyone new in the house was an experience. He almost forgot the hand carved horses, whittled for him by Harry on cold and lonely nights. He horses were drawn by lengths of string, wound around a stick made into a crank. You could set the lot up on the floor and by winding the crank, race the horses. He decided to show Adam how the whole thing worked.

"Leave the man alone," Emily said.

Adam played about with a scone and pretended to be interested in the hand-carved horses, but was really only interested in Nell.

The mantle of the light began to blacken so Emily sprinkled a pinch of salt on it to burn it free.

"Lord, I dunno. We'll have to replace that mantle." She said.

It was some hours before Adam at last got Nell alone, away from Bess and her young brother. They sat on the swing seat out on the veranda. He was pretending to get ready to take his leave.

"I just wondered Nell, if I could call on you again sometime?"

"When you're heading to the mine you mean? How often do you intend going to the mine?"

"That was just an excuse. I just hoped to see you."

"I would never have guessed!" Nell laughed. Even when she laughed at him, Adam felt a surge of excitement. He blushed again. It seemed to Nell that he spent half his life blushing.

"You may as well stay the night while you're here. It's much too evil a night to ride home in the dark." She considered the situation for a while. "At least that way you won't be wasting all your time."

"Oh I couldn't do that. Stay the night I mean."

"Rubbish. But frankly I wouldn't waste my time rushing back up here if I were you. I'm afraid I'm just not interested in boys at the moment."

She couldn't admit that she felt like laughing every time he tipped his hat to her in the street. Nell just didn't appreciate what it felt like to be a lady.

The next morning, Rang helped the young man saddle his horse, and when he mounted lay his arm on the pommel of the saddle. "That girl's accounted for you know."

Adam felt a rush of anger. The upstart in the fancy clothes was only a workman. And the clothes were a little worse for wear anyhow.

"I think that's for Nell to decide!"

But as he rode away down the mountain, he knew the girl had already made up her mind.

Chapter 30

The upper reaches of the Little Swiney creek were fed by vast beds of sphagnum moss that spread out across the valley at the foot of the Gavin escarpment. George, Harry, Rang and a brace of dogs circled the beds of moss, driving a small herd of Angus cattle, following the creek down the valley towards the junction of the Big Swiney.

The snow gums slowly cut out as they lost altitude, giving way to Mountain Ash and Woollybutt. It was past midday when they came to a halt at the mountain hut. The hut was a small log building hidden among overgrown vines beneath a stand of timber. This spot was close to the boundary of the Trask run.

The steers belonged to Cecil Jurd, the man who owned the Jindawaddy station, the freehold run on the upper Wonnangatta River.

It was time to square up after the autumn muster, before moving the cattle down to Ashburn to escape the snow. Winter was falling late this year with just small clusters of snow around the rocks at this lower level of four thousand feet. Only the higher peaks held heavy snow.

Cattle often became boxed on the unfenced high plains. At mustering time, the cattlemen checked for clean skins and strays. Restitutions were generally worked out among the neighbouring runs. This practice happened without trouble among the Kings, Pattersons, Boxes and Jurds. Only the Crayes on the Bogong side were difficult to deal with. So generally the Crayes and the Trasks kept one another's cattle with the hope that everything squared up in the long run.

The Trasks had already arranged to meet riders from the Jindawaddy station to exchange cattle at the hut.

They boiled the billy and waited, but it was late afternoon before they saw two riders and a small herd of cattle climbing the track through the wooded valley to the south. From this point, they could see right across the Wonnangatta valley, where mountain rises seemed to flow endlessly into the distance. High peaks and plunging ravines, shrouded in mist and distant haze.

The riders from both groups met where the two mobs were well apart.

"Be careful not to let 'em mix!" One man from Jindawaddy called. "Better hold 'em apart from your cattle too."

He appeared agitated. "Pleuro. I think the boss got Pleuro. Vets out now from Omeo. Better keep your cattle apart. We were told to do the same with these."

"Good God!" said George. "Pleuro!"

"We dunno for sure yet. Got the vet out inspecting the mob—he's down there now!"

George turned to Harry and Rang.

"Drive our cattle up to the holding yards at the head of the valley till we find out what to do. I'm going to ride down to check this thing out!"

Mountains towered to the right as he followed the track down the valley, until it opened out onto a broad plain. He crossed the upper reaches of the Wonnangatta river, where the water flowed only a foot deep, bubbling over polished white stone. He had seen the Wonnangatta much deeper than this, when it flowed half a mile wide, covered in foam and carrying logs and dead cattle with it. He vividly remembered the cattle. He had been just a boy at the time but still the memory remained. A bloated white-faced steer, legs turning stiff, rolling in the foam.

There were Red Gums growing on the river flat, mixed through the Ash and Woollybutt. It was here that he saw the first evidence of Pleuro. A dead steer, bloated and attacked by a dozen crows. They rose in a mass as he passed by. There were two more carcases before he reached the slip-rails.

The homestead stood among heavy timber at the side of a clearing, with outbuildings and sprawling yards further down the hillside. There was a great deal of activity in the yards that were filled with bellowing cattle. Dust was rising like smoke, with men weaving in and out on horseback.

From the homestead off to his left, a young girl with skirt swirling about her legs, burst from the shade of the veranda when she saw George at the slip-rails. It was almost as if she had been waiting for him. The girl ran across the yard and sprang up behind the saddle, as agile as a cat. George and Rachael had been childhood friends, but Rachael was no longer a child, George realised with a start, feeling the press of her young body against his back.

"How you do that?" George called over his shoulder. The way the girl mounted the horse amazed him. He spurred his horse towards the cattle yards.

She bit him behind the ear playfully. "You haven't been around for ages, Georgy boy. We all miss you. Think I'd let you just slip past?"

George and his father had once spent three days at Jindawaddy some years back, cut off by a blizzard when the Wangaratta was in flood. Old Cecil still had a wife then, along with five daughters. Rachael was the eldest.

"Well, for God's sake behave yourself girl, you ain't no kid anymore. What'll your old man think, especially when he's got sick cattle?"

Cecil was on one knee in the dust in front of the yards where a man with the curling stem of a pipe clenched between his teeth, worked his knife in the carcase of a beast lying between them in the dust. He had the carcase opened up, his long knife exploring the lung cavity that oozed yellow liquid. The man straightened up, wiping the knife on the leg of his pants.

"Pleuro. Not much doubt about it, Jurd. You got Pleuro pneumonia."

He acknowledged George and the girl with an indifferent nod. Rachael slid down from the horse and stood beside her father. Cecil, squatting in the dust, threw off his hat and ran his hands through his hair. Snow white, along with his beard. His legs, squatting in the dust were bowed, bent as if to fit around the sides of a horse.

The vet from Omeo tapped the bowl of his pipe on the heel of his boot, then began to reload it with fresh tobacco. His drooping moustache was stained dark brown.

"I'll go through the herd with you, Jurd." The men were already cutting cattle in the sprawling yards. A steer tried to hurl himself over the top rail, stuck half way then dropped back.

"I've already told the men what to look for. Clouded eyes, any beast that looks listless. Difficult breathing. They usually carry the head lowered. Anything with a sign of a cough. You have to isolate 'em early. Get 'em before they show too much signs. Cut 'em out and isolate 'em, not much more a man can do. No real treatment for Pleuro yet. Some will beat it, but most won't. Best thing you could do is to shoot the suspect animals and be done with it, but not many do that. And, who knows, some might beat the damn thing."

He tamped the tobacco into the bowl and held a match to it. When he breathed in, the fire lit up the lower face.

"Gotta keep at it every day. Watch 'em like hawks. First sign, cut the affected animal out and isolate 'em. Only chance you got! Remember man, you can't put any stock through the saleyards till you get the place free. I'll have to inspect your place again to sign the papers!"

Cecil sat in the dust with his head in his hands. "Jesus H Christ!" He said.

He had five daughters, no wife—just a sour housekeeper who he slept with only when he was completely desperate—and now sick cattle. This was a bad day.

George rode back to the sliprails, Rachael trotting at his side. "The old man's upset and I can't say I've ever seen him quite like this before."

"Can't say I blame him. Mind you I don't think my old man will be all that pleased when he gets the news. I'm not looking forward to that at all. His cattle running with a mob full of Pleuro!"

She held onto his leg as he lowered the sliprails. The sun was already behind the peaks of the mountain. Dusk came quickly to the high country.

Clouds were darkening the horizon and a stiff breeze blew down the valley.

"Weather's coming up, so I better get back to the cattle."

There was a little lightning flickering around on the horizon.

"You better stay the night or you'll likely drown out there in the dark."

"'Fraid I can't. Harry and Rang are waiting up on the plains!"

"Well, George Trask, go back to your damn cattle!"

George looked down at Rachael, pouting at his side, and felt a familiar feeling stirring in his loins. He didn't have to get back to the cattle that fast. He'd be travelling in the dark anyway.

Chapter 31

By mid-morning, George and Rang arrived back at the old homestead on the high plains, dreading the meeting with Emanuel, when they would have to break the bad news.

Nell and young Bess were just about to leave the homestead, their saddlebags loaded with food and clothing, blankets wrapped in canvas strapped behind the saddles. Heavy cloud had closed in and the smell of rain was in the air.

"I see you two, but I don't see any cattle—and where's young Harry?" Nell gave the girth of her pony a final hitch.

"It's a long story, Sis. We left Harry to mind the cattle, but we got bad news for the old man. Old Cecil's got Pleuro!"

Nell whistled through her teeth.

"Better you tell him than me, Georgy boy. Meanwhile, we got news ourselves. Henry Craye's wife has done a bunk and the whole mountain's out looking for her. We're about to join 'em. She just took off with the kids, they say. On foot. Old Henry's half off his head by all reports."

Thunder rumbled and a string of lightning trickled across the sky. The horses stamped nervously at the approaching storm. They never seemed to get used to storms. The crack of a whip was one thing, but the clap of thunder was a vastly different matter. Rang spurred up to Nell's side.

"Hold on girl, I'm coming with you," he said. "Could be a hell of a storm coming!"

"We've seen storms before, Rangy old boy. Think of that woman and kids out there. Frankly I couldn't give a damn about old Henry, but the woman and her kids don't deserve this!"

"Well, give me a minute to collect a few things and get another horse. I'm going anyway!"

"As you like. We'll cross the divide at Tabletop. You'll catch up by then. They think she's heading towards Omeo. Probably carrying one of the kids."

By the time they passed by the Craye homestead, the rain was bucketing down with thunder rumbling between the mountain peaks and lightning ripping the sky apart. Rain streamed from their hats and oilskin coats and wet leaves slapped their faces as they forced on through the timber. They were well down the Cobungra River before meeting any other riders.

Nell recognised the pockmarked face of the man who worked for old Ruben Craye. Athol was his name. The water streamed down his face and they could tell he didn't want to be there.

"Tracks look like she's trying to get to Omeo, silly bitch!" he said.

"Shouldn't she be going more to the east?" Rang's words were lost in the thunder.

"Probably got turned around a bit. 'Spect she couldn't cross the river anyhow. We're covering it all this side, got more than a dozen men out here scouring this side of the bloody hills. Don't think the woman's worth it either!"

"The woman's got kids with her!" Nell snapped. "We'll cross down at the junction, 'case she headed off more east."

They found a place about a mile downstream where the woman, carrying her children could have crossed. A huge fallen log almost spanned the stream. And on the muddy bank at the far side, they found a woollen toy half buried in the mud.

"You follow the river downstream," Nell called through the rain. "I'm going off this way." She had a hunch and didn't know exactly why. The tracks were completely lost in the mud. Nell and Bess travelled for another two miles, horses stepping sure-footed through the scrub. Then they came to a place by a gully where a fallen log with a hollow the size of a small wagon wheel lay. Bess saw the movement first, hidden deep inside the log. A muddy white skirt and the frightened face of a child. They were all in there. A wet and bedraggled woman with two terrified children clinging to her.

She looked out with bloodshot, frightened eyes and mud-stained face, unsure if she wanted rescue or not. The rain had steadied and only came in short bursts. Thunder still growled like an angry stomach.

"You, Bess ride off and find Rang. Tell him to let the others know we found them!"

"Don't tell anyone please. I don't want to go back!"

"We'll see about that. Now go on Bess!" Nell reached into the log with her hand. The thin, half drowned woman cringed back, drawing the children as far back as they could go.

"You sure can't stay in there. Here I'll get a fire going, you stay there awhile. Those kids must be near frozen."

Getting the fire burning was difficult. Nell had to forage as high as she could reach in the trees, picking the ones leaning before the wind on the side the rain had not wet as much, peeling away the bark to find the dry strands beneath, shoving each bit, as valuable as gold under the cover of her oilskin coat. Her clothes were mostly wet beneath the oilskin, but there were still dry spots. Finally she had enough fuel to carefully build a small fire behind an outcrop of rock. She broke pieces of dry timber from the lower branches of nearby trees to feed the fire. It was blazing, flame bending before the wind, when the half drowned woman came out from the log. She carried one shivering child while another clung to her wet and torn skirt. The woman's teeth rattled.

"I'll not go back. Nothing will make me go back!"

Nell threw more wood on the fire. "You have to go somewhere."

"I've got somewhere else to go. I'm taking the kids to the Malloy place. I met her once. Mrs Malloy. I'm going there."

"Good Lord, that's ten mile from here, off that way." Nell pointed to the left. "I've never been there, but I think the Malloy's live in the valley below Mt Cope."

"I must have got turned around then. But I met her once. Nice old lady, Mrs Malloy. Old Bevin Malloy seems a decent man, too. Aristocratic old chap, but seems nice enough. They'll look after me and the kids till I work out what to do. But one thing for sure, I won't take the kids back there!"

"Your husband might have a bit to say about that."

"I just don't care anymore. That's where we're going, to the Malloys. Dressed up in my clothes, he did. Caught him dressed up in my clothes. I can take the rest, but I'll not let the kids near that!"

When Rang and Bess arrived, the rain had almost stopped. The fire had burned down but it had done its job. The woman and her two children were dry enough to feel almost human. They loaded the thin woman on the horse behind Rang while Nell carried the two children. Bess, now thoroughly frozen herself, rode along behind.

They had to cross two streams before breasting the rise that looked down into the valley below Mt Cope. A small cluster of buildings were at the bottom of the valley hidden between the trees.

It was then that Henry Craye came through the mist.

Una Craye, turning her head, was the first to see him.

"Don't let that man get me, please! You shouldn't have let him know you found me!"

"Now I'm sure we can work this out."

"You won't work anything out with that man. You, girl, for God's sake get my kids down to that house!"

Nell did not hesitate. She spurred her horse down the hillside. Bess sat sodden and cold on her horse, not knowing what to do.

Henry drew up beside them and clasped Una by the arm, dragging her roughly from the horse.

"Where the hell you taking my wife?" he yelled through the wind. The rain had stopped. "My place is back that way!"

"I ain't going back Henry Craye. I'm never going back!"

"The hell you're not." Henry was handling her roughly on the ground when Rang swung out of the saddle, hitting him hard behind the ear.

Henry Craye came off the ground like a tiger. The two men kicked and rolled, using fists, boots and teeth. Henry had fought and won many fights, but slowly Rang began to get the better of him. They were on the ground, rolling in the mud when finally Rang fastened his hands about the man's throat. Then, with mud-streaked face, twisted in rage he hammered Henry's head back again and again against the earth.

It was then that Una hit him behind the ear with a stick.

Rang slumped face down in the mud, while Henry sat stunned, feeling his throat.

"Well, that settles that. The man's mad."

He twisted his head to see that it still worked. "You better climb up on the horse, girl before that madman comes around!"

He shakily regained his feet, eyes not completely focused.

"I'm still not going back," she screamed and, clutching her torn skirt, ran down the hillside. Terror made her run like the wind. At the bottom of the hill, she could see people gathered. Nell was riding back and the children were not with her.

Henry swore, his boots slipping on the stirrups as he tried to regain his mount. She would reach the bottom of the hill before him.

Bess was cradling the injured man's head in her lap when Nell arrived. She swung out of the saddle and rushed towards them.

"Lord," Rang moaned, nursing an aching head in his hands. "That's the last time I'll ever get involved in a family fight!"

Chapter 32

Old Dr McGuire considered himself a progressive man. Maybe too progressive for Edna, his wife. He had opened the first medical practice in Ballarat as a young man, then married his first and only wife whose parents ran a haberdashery store. Later in life they moved to Dargo where McGuire set up a new practice. They brought three children with them. But his wife soon tired of the place and took two daughters back to Ballarat, where she took over and ran the family store, a feat that was to span the next thirty years. The eldest daughter, Clara, with a temperament much like her father, stayed with him in the small settlement at the foot of the mountains.

McGuire bought the first car in Dargo, an Oldsmobile tourer. He bought the car in Melbourne before driving it back to Dargo, or rather his daughter drove it back to Dargo. The journey taking two full days. He found the car useless in the mountains but Clara, after completing her education in Melbourne, worked with the old man in his practice, driving him about his business in the low country. McGuire was always considered a good doctor and had successfully brought two of the Trask children into the world.

The Trasks were driving a herd of 600 cattle through the streets of Dargo towards their property at Castleburn. Winter was closing in on the high country so the annual move to the warmth of the lowlands was underway.

They planned to draft the saleable beasts at the new property, Ashburn, then drive them to the saleyards at Bairnsdale, a larger centre on the coast later in the year.

There was often trouble moving cattle through the town. People gathered to watch the herd go through with generally enough children in the streets to be a nuisance. Emanuel rode in front with his bag of salt across the pommel of his saddle while Harry and Charley worked the wings. Nell, George, Rang, three pack horses and five dogs bought up the rear.

The cattle milled about the winding streets, mounting the board footpaths in places, rattling the boards and spraying them with dung wherever possible. Billy O'Riley, the butcher stood in front of his establishment, broom in hand trying to protect his property. Billy's face wore the look of a long suffering old dog, a long black moustache hung down each side of his mouth and two dirty strands of hair trailed to his shoulders from beneath a very bald head. The striped, blood-stained apron that seldom saw a wash seemed part of the man. A long horned steer sprayed a line of dung at his feet as he swung at it with his broom, hurling abuse at Rang, the nearest rider he could make out in the dusty street.

They had almost cleared the outskirts of town when the black automobile came up behind the herd, blowing exhaust smoke and quivering with a strange noise. The rubber horn squawked like a wounded calf when the cattle didn't clear fast enough. Two people sat high on the front seat, wrapped in scarves and bound up in dustcoats.

The cattle had never seen or heard anything like this before. Some plunged into the side streets, over a picket fences trampling through several backyards. Over a hundred stampeded into the west fork of the road leading towards Mt Kent, the rest charged towards Bairnsdale.

The automobile had not been moving much faster than walking cattle, but when they ran it was a different matter. Cattle scattered through timber, charged beneath Emanuel's whip, almost unseating him, while George cursed the vehicle with every word he could muster.

Charley, Nell and Rang wheeled about in confusion before charging off towards Mt Kent. Harry jumped what was left of the picket fence, and ploughed through the trampled gardens before the steers smashed through the next fence.

The automobile, lost in the dust while trying to avoid the plunging cattle, wound up in a ditch, the wheels spinning until the motor failed. The driver sat shaken behind the wheel, scarf unravelling about her head. When finally Harry cleared the steers from the broken yards, he rode over to abuse the driver of the vehicle. There was only the sign of dust and running cattle on the horizon.

"What the hell do you think you're doing with that contraption?"

Clara McGuire straightened her scarf and glared at the young upstart on the prancing horse.

"We have every right to be on the road!" she snapped. "My father is a doctor, trying to go about his business. We have more right on the road than you and your rotten cattle!"

Harry was shocked when he saw that the driver was a woman. He recognised old Dr McGuire sitting beside her on the seat. The old man seemed to be in a daze. "My dad has an urgent appointment up the road-so if you'll clear your animals, we'll be on our way!"

"You won't go far stuck in that ditch."

The girl looked closely into his face. "I know you don't I, Harry Trask?"

The girl's face looked familiar. Then he remembered the last two years of his schooling in Dargo. He spent two years there, after Emanuel had got rid of Eric Hare. A new school had opened in the Catholic Church hall and the rebuilt road from the spur made travelling much easier. The girl had been a little older than Harry and had only stayed for a few months before moving to what must have seemed a better school in Melbourne.

"You were an upstart then, Harry Trask, and it seems little has changed since."

When the dust had cleared and the cattle were back from the road to Mt Kent, the drovers gathered to inspect the strange vehicle. Driver and passenger still sitting up on the front seat. Nell held a little way back, hostile in her saddle as the men threw their weight behind the vehicle trying to get it back onto the road. The shaken old doctor still sat in the car but they could see there was no visible damage about him.

"Your old man might need a Doctor!" Rang joked, before he noticed the look on Clara's face.

"I've seen one of them things a few months back in Omeo," George said, walking around the car, kicking the tyres and examining it from every angle. He could see no real damage. He pulled the front mudguard free of the front wheel.

"Shouldn't allow things like that on the roads!" Nell spat, then spurred her horse on after the cattle. The good doctor sat shaken in the seat. He hadn't moved and hadn't spoken since the accident. Harry thought that the old man would be of little use to his patient if he ever got there today. The rest of the men remounted, tipped their hats to Clara and rode up the road after the cattle leaving Harry to help get the vehicle started.

"How do you start this thing?" he asked.

"Oh I'm sure Dad and I can manage, Mr Harry Trask." She looked at him again. "But maybe if you want to be a gentleman, you can grasp that crank-handle at the front and give it a pull while I work the levers."

Harry found what he thought was the handle.

"Now watch yourself," she warned, retarding the spark. "The engine could backfire, so hold the handle carefully. Turn till you feel the compression, then pull up smartly. Don't put your thumb around the handle mind, it may backfire!"

Harry had little time to listen to lectures. He wrapped his fist around the crank and spun as hard as he could. The engine backfired and caught his thumb. He jumped around on the road shaking his hand.

"I'm sorry Sir Galahad, you wouldn't listen." Clara climbed down from the seat to examine the injured hand.

"I think the damn thing's broke!"

"It's only bruised. Here, I'll show you how things should be done." At the front of the vehicle she demonstrated the grip. "Now do it like that and you won't get hurt." She climbed back into the car and readjusted spark and throttle.

"Now go for it!" The car started with the first pull and stood shuddering like a beaten pony in the roadway. The old doctor sat rubbing his forehead and muttering to himself.

Clara adjusted her scarf and smiled at the young cattleman who sat astride his horse, still nursing a bruised thumb.

"Thank you Sir Galahad." She smiled. "If you come back through town in the next few days, drop in to the office and I'll have another look at that hand."

The car lurched away in a plume of smoke.

Harry watched it go, wondering who Sir Galahad was.

Chapter 33

A week later he was back, Charley Nash riding beside him. Charley stopped off at the Dargo hotel while Harry tramped up the boardwalk to the doctor's rooms. Clara, seated behind a desk sifting through paperwork, didn't seem surprised to see the young cattleman from the hills. She tried to hide the smile from her face.

"You said you'd take another look at this hand." Harry stammered, holding it up.

Clara examined the injured thumb among the scattered papers across the desk. She prodded it and moved the other fingers about.

"The doctor's out, but maybe I can bandage it for you."

Harry sat and enjoyed the experience, as she worked the bandages gently with a faint smile playing about her lips.

"I remember you from school," she said. "You know they're trying to build a real school in Dargo?"

"Don't have much time for schools," said Harry "Never had."

"Oh we need schools, don't worry. They're putting on a dance next Saturday to raise money to build a real one. Billy O'Riley, the butcher, is arranging it. They've set up a committee already."

She wrapped more bandages. He wouldn't be able to get his hands around the reins if she didn't stop. She examined the hand gently then let it drop.

"You should come along—they've got this new dance called the fox trot."

"I don't dance."

"Oh I'm sure I can teach you. You can start a car and ride a horse, so I sure I can easily teach you to dance. Pick me up next Saturday night. I'll even let you drive the car."

Harry waved his injured hand. "Dunno how I'd go with this."

"Oh I'm sure you'd manage, Harry Trask. I'm sure you'd manage!"

Chapter 34

It was gently snowing when they arrived back at the homestead. They rode straight past the empty house to the workman's hut further up the spur. Harry had decided to stay at the hut to keep Charley company as there was no one at the main house, everyone was still at Ashburn.

The horses were unsaddled in the stables while the wind rattled the timber doors, a little snow sifting in through the cracks. Charley unbuckled his saddlebag and carried it to the hut, glass clinked when he threw it on the table. Harry gathered an armful of wood that was already stacked beside the front door, and set about trying to get a fire going. Charley lit the lamp and sat it carefully on the table. A rough wooden thing, squared with the deft adze of Jock Hoolahan that rocked on uneven legs. He kicked the door shut then stepped about from foot to foot, trying to keep warm.

"God I feel the cold now. Feel it in me bones!" He unpacked two bottles of blended whisky from the saddlebag, stacking one carefully in the wooden box nailed to the wall, setting the other on the table between two dirty mugs. He handled the whisky more carefully than he handled most things.

"You got enough there to last all winter."

The fire was crackling, but throwing no heat out as yet. The wind rattled the shutters on the window frames.

"Not all winter, but I don't expect to be down there again for a while."

The room was lit up by the yellow glow of the lamp and the crackling fire. Harry threw more logs on. He drew a chair up and threw his legs onto the hob. Already he could feel the heat through his pants.

"I guess we'll have to cook for ourselves without a women to feed us. But I'm gonna God damn warm up first!"

Three bunks lined the wall. Charley peeled off his coat, shirt and woollen singlet. His braces hung around his waist. He drew a tin of liniment from the saddlebag and the bunk sagged as he sank onto one corner, rubbing a yellow paste into his back, as far as he could reach his hands.

"Lord, build up that fire."

Harry watched the man sitting there, fingers working the liniment into the muscles of his back, suddenly realising that Charley was not a young man anymore. He seemed much thinner without his clothes, with bumps sticking out of places where they should not have been. There was three days of whiskers on his face and he winced every time his hands probed a sore spot on his back.

"Don't you know that's horse liniment you're using, you silly old coot?"

"Anything good enough for a horse is good enough for a man. Most horses worth more than a man anyhow."

"Charley, you never married?" Harry stirred the fire with a stick, then threw the stick on too.

"Just never got around to it" The old man's hands stopped as he looked out at nothing at all.

"Just never got around to it. You gotta make things happen yourself, you know. That's just one of the many things I never got around to."

He pulled on the heavy woollen singlet and hitched the braces over his narrow shoulders. "And what brings that up, lad? You thinking of that bit 'a skirt belongs to the old doc?"

"Just wondering Charley. Be handy to have a woman cook for us tonight if we had one." Harry shifted his feet by the fire. "You notice the old man getting old?"

"We're all getting old, son. Thing that happens. 'Cause what happened to young Jim aged the old man a lot. Hard on that boy he was. Dreadful hard!"

He straightened with difficulty and spilled some whisky into the two mugs.

"You're a lot like the old block you know. Same hooked nose, same temper, but you got more brains than him."

"Dunno about the brains, Charley. But there are things I'd like to change around here" He prodded more wood on the fire. They were out of it now, and soon somebody would have to get more.

"We run a lot of cattle up here, but they're a bit the colour of those boiled lollies you buy in the store. All the colours there is. I'd like to breed a good line of white-faced cattle. They do better up here anyway. A good line of white-faced cattle like William King."

"Well, if that's what you believe, then go for it. Your brother George don't give a damn about anything ain't in a skirt. So if you believe in the white-face cattle, go for it. And that bit of skirt you're thinking about, go for that too. Don't be like me and do nothing. If you want something young fella, go get it!"

The next Saturday, Harry arrived at the McGuire house dressed as well as he could manage. He wore a clean pair of moleskins and had shined his boots. A white shirt, buttoned to the neck, and a serge suit top that had once belonged to Jim. George's clothes were much too big. He wore the lot beneath a work hat and oilskin coat to protect him on the ride down the mountain.

Clara met him at the door, wrapped in a heavy coat with a scarf wound tightly about her neck. She had already brought the Oldsmobile around from the shed behind the house and it stood at the kerb with the canvas hood in place. There was only a short distance to the hall and Harry thought they could easily walk the distance, but it was snowing, and Clara was quietly proud of the car.

"Climb in Harry and take the reins, I'll show you how to drive this thing."

"No, you drive if you don't want to walk. I don't know how to work one of these things."

"Rubbish. You're a man aren't you? You should learn to drive a lady!" Harry thought of Charley's words and climbed gingerly into the front seat. Clara closed the door behind him.

"Just turn the wheel where you want to go and use the throttle to go fast. You can also use your feet if you wish, but I think the hand throttle's easier. Now that's the brake beside your foot, turn on the ignition, give it some choke and pull back the spark."

She leaned through the window to show him how things should be done, then went to the front of the vehicle to take the crank. Harry looked at the girl in the swirling snow as she bent and grasped the handle. Her face looked white in the carbide driving lights. The engine started first pull.

Clara climbed in beside him and demonstrated how to set the gears.

"Now keep your foot on the clutch—here, this pedal on the near side, then give a little throttle and let your foot off slow."

They got the vehicle moving in lurches, Harry working the wheel with white knuckles. It didn't seem to go the way he pointed it. Clara leaned over him again and he could smell her perfume. At least, he thought it was perfume. Her fingers worked the small crank handle that drove the windscreen wipers.

The snow fell softly while the carbide lights lit up the road for only a few feet in front. There was a turn at the end of the street and Harry steered for it. He would have been in trouble had he not known where to go. The vehicle made it to the corner and got around alright, then at the end of the street, they could see the lights of the hall. Harry pulled back on the wheel then when that didn't work, stamped on the brake and brought them to a shuddering halt. Despite the snow, he was covered in sweat.

Horses, eyes white with panic, jerked and twisted in their harness at the sight and sound of the car. Harry sat shaken behind the wheel.

He had won. But these things, he thought, would never take off.

Chapter 35

The track was very steep from Matheison's flats to the high plains with about two miles to travel to the old homestead after they reached the snow gum country. The cattle strung out, happy to be back on the sweet grass country of the high plains.

Emanuel rode wearily towards the old homestead, a place in the final stages of disrepair—one of the many jobs in front of them this summer. He tired easily nowadays, the long drive from Ashburn taking a lot out of him. He rode a new horse, a bay mare with an uneasy gait, which didn't help his old bones. The big roan gelding that had served him for many years was turned out to grass at Ashburn. Emanuel felt that perhaps he should have been turned out to grass as well.

As he passed by the stockyards there was a man sitting in the shade of a tree, his horse tied to the fence rails. Emanuel recognised the horse before the man. A sign of his time in the mountains.

The man, with bandy legs and flowing white beard, came off the log on which he sat and offered his hand. Emanuel swung wearily from the saddle.

"How you goin' Cecil." He straightened his legs with difficulty. "I feel I'm getting too old for this life!"

"That's two of us, Trask. I heard you were coming, heard it in Dargo day before yesterday. But it's really young George I come to see."

"George, eh? You'll find him at the homestead on the spur. That's where he was headed yesterday." Emanuel settled on the log vacated by Cecil Jurd. "And how's the pleuro going?"

"We almost got it beat. Lost a lot of cattle mind you, but finally I think we got it beat. That vet bastard from Omeo's coming back to give 'em the last check. Then if they're free, I'm out of trouble."

He found a spot on the log to load his pipe.

"Now young George," He tamped the tobacco and held a match to the bowl. "I really wanted him, the young bastard, but you'll have to do. Him and my oldest girl, Rachael, been playing up. Going to have a baby she is!" The match lit up his lower face.

"The devil she is?" Emanuel was on his feet. "He couldn't have. He's been down in the lowlands all winter!"

"This thing happened before winter. It don't take long, Trask, believe me. Only got it out of her yesterday. Showing up she is. Hard enough it is, raisin' five girls without a mother."

Emanuel sank back on the log and took out his own pipe. He had been trying to give up the pipe lately.

"I'm terribly sorry Cecil, but I'll see the young lout straightens things out. These young bucks—but I expect we were all young once!"

Emanuel's mind began working. This was not all bad. George had been getting restless lately, talking about making his way to Queensland. Maybe this would slow him down.

"I'll send him over soon as I catch up with him. Any son of mine will do the right thing, I'll see to that!"

"It's not that I don't like the young fella, mind. I actually like young George. But five daughters is a handful."

"I expect it is. And you got pleuro and all."

"Another thing on my mind, Trask. I'm like you, not gettin' any younger, and I don't know what to do with them girls up here. I've got my eye on a block near Bairnsdale. Only four hundred acres, mind you, so I'm thinking of putting Jarrawaddy on the market so I can move down to where life's more civilised."

"Probably a good move Cecil."

"You need a freehold block up here on the high plains, Trask, to help keep your lease secure. There's talk of the Government reclaiming a lot of the leases to make more national parks."

"They've been talking that for years."

"Yeah but it could happen. With freehold, you're safe. Make it easier to keep your lease, too. Now I'm not telling you your business, Trask, but my block would suit your boys down to the ground."

Emanuel laughed. "Cecil, I'm in debt up to my ears already." He tapped the stem of the pipe against his teeth. The idea was sound—and it would be another way to tie George down.

"In for a penny, in for a pound as the saying goes. You got a lot of security behind you Trask. And you're lucky enough to have boys. You're a lucky man." He tapped his pipe empty on the heel of his boot. "I'll keep the matter open 'till I hear from you."

Emanuel watched the old man ride away. This was a thing to think about.

Chapter 36

Rachael was well pregnant when George married her. The wedding took place beneath the red gum by the old school hut, where George had often eaten his lunch. Rachael wore her mother's wedding dress. A dress Emily altered to fit, using the sewing machine she had carried from Harrietville all those years ago. The same Methodist minister who had buried Jim, made the whole thing official.

Cecil Jurd stood off to the side with hat in hand. His head was bald without the hat and his white beard shone in the sun. He was dressed in a serge suit that he had found somewhere in the house and his four other daughters stood beside him.

Emanuel felt uncomfortable in stiff collar and tie, thinking that they should finalise things today. He was more interested in Jurd's land than his son's wedding. The plan had already been discussed with Nell and the two boys, and it was decided that they would all have to be involved in buying the Jindawaddy run. Cecil had already agreed to leave a great deal of money in the place at ten percent interest, so the talk with the bank was the next move. By now, Emanuel had become quite proficient at dealing with banks.

It was growing dark when Rang came down from the high country. He could see yellow light through the cracks in the stable walls as he led his mount around to the yard at the back. He removed the saddle and bridle, slapped the horse on the rump and turned him loose. There was an iron roof on the stables now with a skillion to shelter the feed troughs. He could hear the leaves rattling across it in the wind. The horse nudged at his elbow as he threw chaff into the hollow wooden log that served as a trough then, shouldering saddle and bridle, walked through the door into the stable.

Nell was working by lantern light, the light hanging from a peg on the wall, the front leg of her chestnut gelding held between her knees. Her hat was off and red hair hung down as she bent before the task. She held horseshoe nails in her mouth while she pared the hoof with a bone-handled knife.

Rang hung his saddle on a rail and squatted down to watch the girl work. He almost offered to shoe the animal himself, but thought better of it. Nell always liked to shoe her own horse.

"You know," he said, building a smoke, "I been around here a long time now. Only meant to stay for a while, then move on. I always done it that way before, but I been here eight years now. Almost feel part of the family." He licked the cigarette paper and spat into the dust. "Almost."

Nell glanced up briefly, then bent back to her job. She took a horseshoe from where it sat on the anvil behind her and set the shoe in place, drew a nail from between her lips and hammered it through the hard outer hoof. She bent so low that her hair almost brushed the floor. Her breasts strained against the check shirt and Rang could barely take his eyes off her bottom as it strained the cloth of her moleskins.

"Point is, I'm thinking of movin' on. Going to Queensland like George's been talking about."

He peeled a loose strand of tobacco from the cigarette paper, casting his eyes up to judge the effect his words had on the girl. "Thought we might have had a bit of a thing goin' here, but I can see now I couldn't do much good with the boss's daughter. People would just think I was after your money."

Nell raised her head, shook the hair from her eyes and laughed around a mouthful of nails. "Money? All you'd get is debt!"

"No, seriously. I've got to make my own way, and I want you to come with me Nell."

She looked seriously at the young man for the first time, surprised at the shock Rang leaving felt in the pit of her stomach.

"I could never leave the mountains, Rang. You know that. This place is a part of me."

The horse bent his head back to nibble her hair and for a moment she thought that she could see moisture at the corners of Rang's eyes.

"For a while, I thought we had things going." He came slowly to his feet, the cigarette hanging loosely from the side of his mouth, then leaned above her, arms outstretched, hands on the shoulders of the horse.

"Remember that night we were stuck in the storm at O'Riley's hut?" he looked down into her face. "Remember that night?"

"Of course I remember it." Nell reddened behind the ears. She was a confident woman in most ways and felt she could hold her own with any man at work, but with things of a delicate nature, Nell felt quite naive. She had heard the term before. A prude.

"I don't know if I'm looking for in a man yet, Rang." There was definitely moisture in the man's eyes. Maybe a speck of dust got in there. Rang was the smooth and flash one. "We've got a great thing going here, I really like you around. As a friend!"

"Yeah right. As a bloody friend! It don't matter a damn to you what happened in that hut that night. Just a bloody tease!"

"It wasn't just a tease, but it's pretty damn hard living under the eye of the old man, working with you every day!" She could see that Rang, with all of his flash, was really cut up.

"But I can tell you Rang, that you are the closest yet."

Outside, above the wind, they could hear Bess calling, "Nell, are you there Nell?—Rang?—dinner's on the table!"

They closed the door to the stable then walked outside into the dark. "Well, being the closest yet ain't good enough anymore, Nell. I'm going to Queensland!"

Nell threw her head back and strode towards the homestead.

"You're not going!" was all she said.

Rang looked after her. At the haughty back and the swing of her backside. He just shook his head.

Chapter 37

A group of mountain cattlemen, dressed in oilskins, leggings and spurs leaned over the stockyard fence watching the Hereford cattle milling about in the dust. Two horsemen kept the cattle moving, while Jack Haynes leaned heavily on his cane, warily watching the milling stock. He didn't trust his gammy leg to make the fence in time should a beast turn nasty.

Outside the rails Bevin Malloy slumped in his wheelchair, head bowed, a little spittle dribbling from the side of his mouth. The stroke that had confined him to the chair stole the only life he cared for, working his land at the foot of Mt Cope, raising a fine run of Hereford cattle. Now they were all for sale. All his prime steers had gone to the markets in Omeo and now his wife, Betty, stroked his hair and gazed through the fence at the last of the breeding stock.

George, Nell and Harry Trask arrived at the property just before eleven o'clock, the time when the auction was due to start. Jack Haynes, the auctioneer from Dargo, was already well into his spiel.

"Here we have four hundred of the finest bred Hereford cattle in the mountains. They are here for genuine sale and I guarantee you will never get a better chance to improve your herds. But you are all experts here and know your job better than I, so be your own judge as to the quality of the stock. There are twenty two heifers with calves at foot, six well-bred bulls, the rest breeding stock from two to six years of age. All weaned and many already showing in calf. We could sell the mob in sections, or present them as a job lot. It seems a pity to break the mob, so I think this is the way we'll go. You all know their value, so I won't try to teach your grandmother to suck eggs. Now gentlemen, can I have a bid, as per animal. Do I hear ten pounds anywhere?"

George almost fell over as he shouldered his way to the rails. They were interested in the mob, but ten pounds was already higher than he was prepared to bid. Three-year-old steers were bringing little more than seven in the saleyards.

"Four pound ten!" called a bearded, grizzly old man from the rear.

"Well, thank you sir, that is a start anyway. Do I hear five pounds anywhere? Remember you'll not get a better chance in your lifetime—five pound, do I hear five pound? Yes sir, five pound on the left!"

"Jesus, that's Henry Craye!" George noticed their neighbour for the first time, to the left leaning through the rails.

"Five pound ten—I have five pound ten to the rear—any advance on five pound ten, remember you'll never get a better chance, do I hear any advance on five ten?"

"You better put in a bid, George," pleaded Harry, sliding in beside his brother.

"Yes George, give him a run!" Nell said. "You can't let Craye beat you."

"Hell that's ten bob more than we intended to go."

"Yes, but if Henry Craye's got that much money, we have too!"

"Last chance, do I hear any advance on five ten? Yes five fifteen right in front. New blood, five fifteen in front!" George felt a little sick that he had made the bid. Along the rails, Henry Craye threw the Trasks a withering glance.

"Six pounds!"

"Six pound ten!" Nell had jabbed George in the ribs.

"Seven pounds, and that's it!" Henry waved his hand in disgust, then turned as if he had lost interest in the whole business.

"Seven pounds—seven pounds, do I have any advance on seven pounds."

"Seven five," said George.

Henry stopped in his tracks then whirled around. "Seven ten!"

"Seven ten, seven ten, do I hear any advance on seven ten?" Jack Haynes leaned heavily on his stick as his eyes travelled around the yard, sun glinting on his upturned eye-glasses.

"If I have no more bids we'll pass them in at seven ten—going once…"

Mrs Malloy glanced angrily at Henry Craye, then leaned through the fence to catch the auctioneer's eye. He came over and she whispered in his ear.

"Seven ten, going twice…" he glanced over George's head, "Seven fifteen there in front. Do I have any advance on seven fifteen?" There were no more bids forthcoming as he looked around the sea of bearded faces, gazing through the rails.

"Going once, going twice—sold for seven pound fifteen to Mr Trask." He swallowed uncomfortably. "Congratulations Mr Trask, you have bought well today!"

George felt sick.

"That wasn't my bid," he whispered weakly.

When Jack Haynes got them alone a few minutes later, he was sweating behind the collar. "We may have a bit of trouble here boys," he suddenly remembered Nell. "And girls. Seems I got caught with a dummy bid," he whispered, glancing over his shoulder. "Never happened before, but Mrs Malloy got into my ear. Appears she's got it in for the Crayes something fierce. Something about Henry's wife. She don't want any Craye to have her cattle. So I put in a dummy bid and got damn well caught."

Henry Craye was shouldering his way through the crowd. "Somethin' stinks here!"

"Excuse me Mr Craye, I'm talking to these gentlemen if you don't mind." Jack shuffled the Trasks further away. "These cattle would suit you people down to the ground."

"Yeah they'd suit us right enough, but that's more than we're prepared to pay!"

"Look I've been a good friend of your father for many years now. I'm prepared to throw in ten shillings myself. You can have 'em at seven five."

Harry dearly wanted the cattle. "Go on George, take it!"

"Alright, I'll take 'em at seven."

"God, you're just like your old man." Jack said weakly.

"There's something stinking about this!" Henry Craye was bellowing like a wounded bull to anyone who would listen. People began to move away from him. "Somethin' bloody stinks!"

The Trasks were counting the cattle out of the yards when Henry Craye finally got George alone. "Just how do you intend gettin' this lot up to your run?"

"Oh, up past Hotham I expect."

"Not through my run you won't. No Trask cattle will ever set foot on my run."

George looked coldly at the man. "There's not much else we can do!"

"Too bad. Should have thought of that when you cooked up that little deal with that filthy, cheatin' Jack Haynes!"

"Well, you and your Craye run can get stuffed. We'll go another way!"

But when they had the cattle outside the yards, milling around in the dust looking for direction, he thought to himself—*what other way?*

Rain clouds were rolling over the mountain peaks and a there was a murmur of thunder in the east when the Trasks got together to work out a plan of action.

"There's the old Planters track, across the Coburn." Nell suggested. "Go south, cross the divide and down to the Dargo at Matherson's flats."

"That would take a week."

"Well, we got a week." Harry said, well pleased to own the cattle. Getting them home was something that could be solved one way or another.

"I hear they took cattle through that way in the old days," Nell said. "We might lose a few head, but what else can we do?"

"The old man will kill us!"

"He'll most likely kill us anyhow, so what have we got to lose!" Harry said brightly.

So the track was decided. George turned to his younger brother.

"You Harry, ride back to the plains and pick up Rang and old Charley. Bring another pack horse and a few more dogs. And bring a lot more grub. Nell and me will move the mob down to the Cobungra. Should be there tonight, so you should pick up our tracks some time tomorrow."

Chapter 38

The storm was coming closer as George and Nell began to move the herd along. They only had two dogs. Harry slipped into his oilskin coat and turned up into the mountains as rain began to fall softly. It was bucketing down before George and Nell reached the upper fork of the Cobungra river.

The river was very shallow at this point, barely a creek, so George and Nell were able to cross the herd without trouble early the next morning, pushing through the heavy scrub, moving forever south.

Harry and Charley Nash, a loaded packhorse and three more dogs caught up with the mob in the late afternoon. The rain had not let up as thunder rumbled deep in the clouds. Hail spat at them as they came close to the left fork of the river. The water was running deep here, covered with white foam, carrying timber and clumps of weeds. They followed the river downstream, bent before the rain, looking for a place to cross.

"It's rising fast," said Nell. "We better make our minds up soon if we want to cross tonight. If we can't make it, we could be here for a month!"

The hail was pelting down by the time they forced the cattle into the rising water. Cattle that didn't want to go, circling and plunging under the cracking whips, kicking up at the barking dogs. Finally the first animal plunged into the foam. Others followed, while the hail hit the water like buckshot.

"Keep 'em close!" bellowed Nell, her words lost in the sound of hail as she spurred the chestnut gelding into the water, tugging an unwilling pack horse behind her.

The mob were being swept well downstream, calves floundering beside their mothers. There was a bend in the river where they finally reached the far bank, riders plunging about below, trying to keep the mob close. The first wet cattle began climbing the steep bank, churning and slipping in the mud.

The last of the mob were half across when a large clump of timber came around the bend above, like a small mountain, turning and rolling in the water.

Nell, while trying to split the stragglers to let the timber through, lost her footing as the packhorse halter pulled her from the saddle. Rang's voice, full of panic when he saw the accident, plunged his mount towards the struggling girl in the water.

Her lungs were soon full as she grasped the stirrup leather and was dragged towards the bank, never knowing how she ever escaped the timber. She let the horse drag her up the bank like a wet ragdoll.

The packhorse was lost downstream, tangled in twisting timber.

Rang came out of the river, water streaming from him as he bent over the stricken girl. The hail still pelted down as Nell cleared the last water from her lungs. Then George rode up, more relieved at the sight of his sister safe on the bank than he dared to show.

"I always thought that you were the one who could ride, sis!" He chuckled when he saw that she was alright, then turned to Harry. "How many do you think we lost?"

"Two calves and the old packhorse, Barney, you callous bastard!" Harry said, shouldering Rang aside to look at his older sister.

"You don't have to worry about me," Nell spluttered. "Just worry about the cattle and old Barney. Don't nobody worry about Nell!"

The cattle were spreading across the flat, moving towards the heavy timber of the foothills.

"Well, we better get 'em to higher ground before makin' camp for the night, if you lot are finished playing in the water"

George spun his horse around. "We got about five more creeks to cross and a climb over the mountain fit to kill all. But that's another day!"

And that's not the half of it, he thought as he rode away.

Two lost heifers and a packhorse.

And then we have to deal with the old man.

Chapter 39

Harry found the perfect spot to set up his saw-pit, in a narrow gully about two miles from the old homestead, close to a good stand of straight-grained woollybutt.

The rest of the family had shown little interest in restoring the old homestead but Harry, with reasons of his own, became very keen on the project. And when his interests travelled in a certain direction, he followed them blindly to the end.

The only help he could find was Jock Hoolahan, employed full time by his father rebuilding the fences at Ashburn. The old man seemed happy to leave Ashburn to help Harry set up the saw-pit. No longer a young man, Jock Hoolahan was built like an old bullock, capable of working most young men into the ground. His eyes, although a little dimmer than they were in his younger days, were still very accurate with measurements, and he was a deft hand with axe and adze.

They felled a great deal of woollybutt trees over the first month, trimmed the trunks and dragged them up the mountain to the gully, where Jock showed Harry how to lay out the pit. The gully was ten feet wide and about the same in depth. They lay timber across it in the fashion the old man decreed, then built a ramp to roll up the logs, using ropes and a strong horse.

Harry worked in the pit below while the old man guided the saw from the top. Jock drew the line when it came to bottom man on the saw. Although the man below had the advantage of working in the shade, he found himself breathing sawdust all day.

Jock could sharpen the cross-cut saw with an edge like a razor, one of the many talents he had. The saw ran through the timber like butter, guided straight along a string-line, and by mid-summer the two men had cut a thousand feet of timber and lay it in a pile to dry in the sun.

The summer was very dry and the grass and scrub had browned off, almost crackling under the men's boots as they walked. The wind blew almost continuously from the south west. While drinking black tea under a shady tree near the pit, Harry first noticed smoke, a long way off down the mountain.

"Looks about William King's place, down around Drayford," he observed.

"No, that's more to the left," Jock mused. "Dry lightning lit it, I would expect."

Summer in the mountains carried many lightning strikes. Each afternoon the clouds came with the promise of rain but bringing nothing but lightning with them, with occasionally just a light sprinkle. Drought rain, the old hands called it.

"It's a long way off, so I shouldn't think it would get up here."

Harry tossed the tea dregs into the dust, impatient to get back to work.

But by nightfall they could see the glow spread between the valleys and peaks below and by next morning they could smell the smoke. The country to the south was black with it and Harry felt the first signs of alarm.

"We better shift the sawn timber to bare ground near the homestead. Not that I think the fire will come up here."

He tried to reassure himself, but failed miserably. "I think it's more to the west!"

They harnessed a horse to the dray and began loading the timber which overhung the tray-bed by many feet.

"Now's the time we need a wagon!"

But even getting the dray onto the high plains had been difficult, with a track having to be cut through from the Harrietville side. Emanuel had helped with that job the previous year, work that had taken more than a month. At the time, Harry had planned to buy a wagon and bring it in at a later date.

They had shifted half the timber back to the homestead when the others arrived. The smoke was much closer now, carried on a stiff breeze, and the day carried blistering heat.

"If you two are finished playing here," George said, "You can help us shift cattle down to Getty's plain. We'll take 'em down to the river there. Should be safe that far west the way the wind's blowing."

Harry, although much younger than his brother, resented the orders.

"You got enough manpower without us. We've got timber to shift. Seems we're right in the path of the fire here!"

George swore at the young upstart, wheeled his mount and rode off, Nell, Rang and Charley Nash at his side.

The two men drove the dray back to the pit and began clearing as much trash as possible from around it before the fire got there, shovels working like fury clearing the dry grass.

Now they could hear the fire, a low but terrible sound, and could see the flames travelling through the treetops where the timber was much thicker, below on the mountain. They saw the grove where they had felled woollybutt covered in fire.

"I think we better leave the rest and get out of here while we still can!" Jock Hoolahan had witnessed many fires in the mountains. Harry hated to leave the rest of the sawn timber—hated any force of nature that could steal anything that he had worked hard for—but finally he bowed to the old man's advice. The fire travelling close behind as they flogged the horse and dray back to the homestead.

They stood at last on a patch of bare ground to watch the fire burn past, the noise and the heat almost unbearable. The low rumble of the fire brought a fear and a dread of its own but at least there was not enough heavy timber on the high country to carry the fire through the treetops. Instead it travelled in erratic bursts through the dry grass, flaring up with an excited roar, then dying down for a moment but always racing along with a purpose of its own, changing direction at every whim of the wind.

"I think we're safe here, but I wager the sawpit's gone!"

"We can cut more timber, lad. Always cut more timber. But let's hope the others are safe. You better pray if you believe in that sort of stuff!"

The fire had burned through and was up in the foothills below Mt Hotham when Rang rode out of the smoke covering the blackened plain. He had Nell behind him on the saddle, covered in soot, leaning awkwardly to one side. Harry helped her down and she clutched an injured shoulder, seeming deeply shaken.

"Randy trod in a rabbit hole—I think his leg's broken." She clutched her injured shoulder and seemed close to tears. This was a first for Nell.

"Found her on her back." Rang said. "Hurt too, but pig-headed. I had a hell of a job getting her here. Didn't want to leave the damn horse!"

"Harry, lend me your horse and a gun, I can't leave that animal to suffer out there!"

"Like hell, you're not going back into that fire," Rang yelled. "Harry, for Christ's sake, give me your gun, I'll go back in!"

So he went.

They waited through most of the day, then in late afternoon his horse came back alone.

It was almost dark when they at last found a body lying face down in a sphagnum bog, the charred remains of the horse thirty yards away.

Nell screamed and rushed towards the body lying in the mud, the pain of her injured shoulder was gone. She turned the body over and cradled him in her arms, his face down one side, hanging in charred pieces. They could easily see his track through the ashes where he had crawled into the mud. Most of the clothes were burnt from his body, his left arm hung crooked and his hip seemed wrong.

"Rang baby, love, what have I done to you?"

"Give up sis, it's not your fault!" said Harry.

Nell screamed through her tears.

"You don't think he would have gone back for the damn horse if it hadn't been for me?"

"What's done is done! Now hold him while we bandage that face!"

Harry tore his shirt to strips and wrapped the face as best he could. Hard rasping noises came from the injured man's throat. They were not quite human sounds.

Meanwhile Jock Hoolahan cut two long poles of blackened timber and two short ones. They unstrapped the oilskin coats that were forever carried behind the saddles in the high country, threaded two short poles through the armholes and fastened them in place with lengths of rope.

On this crude litter, with rear end dragging through the dirt, they carried the limp and moaning body back across the burned plain. It was quite dark and the glow of the fire could be seen burning across Mt Hotham. The sun was rising, just a red glow through the smoke before they reached the old homestead.

They lay Rang on a bunk and gently removed the filthy bandages. Burned flesh came away from his face and the skin was off most of his left arm. The hip was clearly broken. Nell bathed him and applied all the liniment that she could find, then bandaged him in a torn sheet. Looking like an Egyptian mummy, Rang was unconscious most of the time.

The next morning they brought him down from the high plains. The journey was slow as they had to carry him down Angel's Leap on foot, reaching the lower homestead shortly before lunch.

Bess, alone at the homestead, screamed when she saw the burden they carried in. She had always secretly idolised Rang and, although not as strong as her sister, was a far better nurse. Gentle, with a soft and caring touch, she helped Nell change the bandages and spread more salve.

Jock Hoolahan had lost all hope of saving the man. In a lifetime, he had seen a lot of terrible accidents but had never seen a man live who had been burned like that.

Harry harnessed the sulky and, with the help of the two girls, loaded the injured man onto the seat. Nell sat beside him, holding him all the way to Dargo.

Twenty four hours after the accident, they carried Rang into the doctor's surgery, where Dr McGuire took one look at the man and sadly shook his head.

"Got to get him to hospital in Melbourne. There's nothing I can do for him here!"

He injected a strong dose of morphine. "Here Clara girl, I'll give you the rest of the bottle, you may have to give him a further dose on the way. Only thing we can do is ease the pain. You best take the car."

Old Dr McGuire had seen many burns in his day, but none to match this.

Clara filled the tank of the Oldsmobile with fuel then carried another drum as spare, as there were few places to buy fuel between Dargo and Melbourne. She climbed behind the wheel, adjusted goggles, scarf and dust coat, then with Rang on the back seat, his head cradled in Nell's lap, began the long journey to the city.

Harry sat beside her in the front.

Chapter 40

Six months after the accident, Bess was alone at the house on King's Spur. This was not unusual since Emily had taken to live in the low country and, although no match for her sister at cattle work, Bess kept the house reasonably clean and was a very good cook.

She had more schooling than the rest of her siblings and could read much better than them, devouring books where ever she found them, which wasn't that often. Bess could live between the covers of a book if this were possible and, when she ran out of them, she wrote her own.

Her mother Emily had always called Bess 'my little house girl' as she was growing up, and tried to keep her away from horses, cattle and the high plains as much as possible. But now at sixteen, Bess was feeling a little restless.

She shared many of the features of her sister Nell, but was much softer. As she grew older, she began to notice that when men walked into a room, it was always Nell that they looked at.

Her mind always took her to romantic places. Places where a log cabin in the mountains were not part of the scene. And often Rang was in this other place. She had worshipped him as a little girl, and still worshipped him at sixteen.

There was always something dashing about Rang. Like a pirate. There was no one else like him on the mountain, or anywhere else in the world for that matter.

In the days long ago when he still lived on the mountains.

Bess was at the front door with a broom in her hand, the day he came back.

Bent over in the saddle, the long ride up from Dargo taking a heavy toll. Her hands flew to her mouth when she saw his face and she dropped the broom to help him down, an action that he seemed to resent. But still he let her take his weight while they limped into the house. The horse began moving back towards Dargo so Bess ran after him and led him to the stable.

"Lord," she said, back in the doorway, wiping her hands on her pinny. "You look done in, Rang. You shouldn't have rode up here on your own! Someone would have got you in the sulky. Why didn't you let anyone know you were out of hospital? Here, I'll make you a cup of tea. Put your feet up and take a rest!."

"How would I let anyone know?" Rang said wearily. There was something else in his voice. An edge. Self-pity.

She almost fell over herself filling the kettle and stoking the fire in the stove.

"We weren't expecting you, Rang." She stammered, "Not yet!"

His voice seemed different than it had sounded in the past. There was a flatness there. All the flashiness was gone.

"No, I don't suppose anyone was expecting me." He kept the hat pulled well down over his eyes, even on the chair at the kitchen table.

She was shocked at the sight of the left side of his face. The part of his face that showed under the hat. She wanted to run her fingers over the scars. He seemed lost and vague, fingers tracing little shapes across the tabletop. "Didn't know what to do. Old Doc McGuire loaned me a horse and some clothes, so I came up here."

"Of course you should have come back here. Where else would you expect to go?"

"I ain't one of the family, Bess. Won't be worth a damn now to anyone anymore."

"Don't be so silly!" She slopped the tea while filling his mug. She poured in sugar, remembering he liked a lot.

"Nell came to the hospital a few months back." His hands began shaking and he had trouble holding the mug. "A few months back."

"Pretty hard for her to get down to Melbourne from way up here. I've never been there myself. Always wondered what it would be like." She knew that had it been her she would have stayed by him, no matter how long it took.

She noticed his knees bouncing under the table. He tried to hold them still with his good hand.

"Doc McGuire kept us posted. You should have seen the party we threw when we heard you were going to live!" Perhaps this was not the right thing to say.

"I never knew it was possible to live like that, so long on your back, just lookin' at the walls. Walls, God, I hate walls! And they're all white. White. Why has everything got to be white? A man would be better off dead than to do that again."

Bess sat next to him at the table, turning the hot mug of tea between her hands.

"Nell and the rest are up on the plains. I never see Harry much anymore. He's mad keen rebuilding that old house." She wiped some of the spilled tea from the tabletop, wanting to test the scars about his face with her fingertips.

"He stays up there most of the time with old Jock Hoolahan, then when he does come down he's off to the King farm. That girl of his, Clara, the doctor's daughter, is nursing Mrs King. Harry spends his spare time over there nowadays."

There seemed to be skin missing from the side of his mouth where the teeth showed through. "Nell worries about you all the time. Never talks about much else. *Oh a*nd I don't suppose you know George's got twins!"

Rang laughed, not a very happy laugh.

"So old George's got twins. That'll keep him happy."

"Don't know about happy. They keep him awake most nights. Think it drives him crazy. Both boys too, first boys ever born on Yarrawaddy. He and Katy lives over there now. Practically no one lives over here anymore!"

She caught a look at the other side of his face. Everything looked fine over there.

"It gets awful lonely up here now, with everyone away."

Bess twisted her hands in the folds of her pinny, her throat tightened up until she almost choked. Lord she loved the man. More than before. She could look after a man like that, pamper him something terrible.

Nell and Charley Nash arrived home before dusk. Nell felt a wild thrill when she saw the spare horse in the yard and rushed to the house.

Rang was slowly gaining his feet as she rushed through the door, swung her arms around his neck and her legs around his body. "Baby, honey, you're back!" She knocked his hat off hugging him, tried to kiss him on the lips, but when she saw the mouth she couldn't do it. She hugged him the harder.

"We didn't expect you back for a long time yet. God it's good to see you Rang!"

He tried to regain the hat to cover the head as the hair only grew in patches.

"Can't keep a good man down," he said lamely.

Charley Nash stood awkwardly in the doorway for a moment, feeling like an intruder. He finally went to slap Rang on the back but thought better of it and shook his hand instead. Probably Charley was the only one in the room who sensed how Rang really felt.

"Thought we may have lost you, son, but only the good die young they say. Great to see you back, anyway!"

"Dunno what use I'd be around the place now. Best move on shortly I suppose." He laughed a hollow laugh. "I only planned to stay a few weeks in the first place, now I've been here for ten years if a day!"

"Don't talk rubbish!" Nell snapped. "We'll never let you go, especially now!"

"What good am I? What could I do, make the damn tea?"

"There's lots you can do. Mend harness. You'll be able to ride again shortly. Give yourself time, man. Hell you can even help Harry with his damn house!"

"He's not going up there yet!" Bess snapped. "He's not near ready yet!"

"You keep out of it." Nell, startled at the way her sister reacted, was surprised at her own response. "Nobody said anything about going up there yet."

Charley twisted the hat nervously in his hands, "It's been a long day, so I guess I'll leave you folks too it. Good to see you back son." There were things going on here and Charley didn't want to be around to see it.

After the meal, Nell led her man to the veranda, where the old swing chair was anchored by trace chains from a sturdy rafter. A log fashioned from red gum, shaped by an adze formed the seat. Harry had made it some time back and was very proud of his work. The chains creaked a little as they swung.

"I'm really glad to see you back, baby, I really am." They sat in silence for a while. "I missed you something terrible. For a long while they said you weren't going to make it. I don't know what I would have ever done then!"

He thought he could hear her crying. Nell crying? He squeezed her hand.

"I don't know what I thought in that hospital. Drove me near mad thinking about you Nell. Always looking, but you never came."

"I came once!"

"Yeah, I guess you came once."

"I wrote you nearly every night." Nell couldn't write as well as her sister. Her fingers were much more at home wrapped around a pair of reins than around a pencil. And of course she could only get down to Dargo to post the letters once a week.

"I kept all your letters, Nell. Still got 'em."

The summer air was cool that night on the mountains. The chains moved and the moon threw shadows against the log walls. Emanuel had made many improvements to the old homestead over the years. An iron roof with a water tank beside. Rooms added as they were needed, spread out with little order like a patchwork quilt.

"I just couldn't get to the hospital when I wanted Rang. Honest. But lord I thought about you all the time."

The log creaked on the trace chains.

"It was all my fault that you had that accident. I put you there, in that hospital. That made it all the worse."

"I never blamed you Nell. You know I never blamed you. The damn horse spooked when I let off the gun. Wasn't used to guns, and I guess the fire had him nervous. Threw me right into a burning log." The horror of those moments were still etched into his mind.

Nell's fingers traced the good side of his face. Over the past month Rang had developed a method of facing people so they saw mainly the good side of his face. It had become habit. When she turned to kiss him, Nell saw the teeth and just couldn't do it. She kissed him on the cheek instead.

Rang threw himself out of the seat. His knuckles gripped white to the railing, then he staggered into the yard, almost tripping on the top step, his hip didn't work well anymore.

Nell followed him to the front fence where he stood shaking as he clutched the top rail.

"I'm sorry, Rang, Lord but I'm sorry!"

He pushed her away and limped off towards the stables.

Charley always had a way of seeing things.

Chapter 41

Emily was on her knees working in her garden. She loved her garden at the new property, now that they had water. The previous year Emanuel and Jock Hoolahan had sunk a well close to the house where Jock had divined water. He held a forked stick in his hands as he crossed and recrossed the hillside behind the house and, when the stick bent in his hands, marked the spot with his boot. He swore by the method and, although Emanuel had been sceptical at first, when they struck good water at twenty feet, he thought the old man a 'bloody genius'.

So now a windmill turned steadily in the wind pumping water to troughs around the farm and, more importantly, Emily believed, to her garden.

She rested on her knees, looking contentedly across the valley. Emily had accepted as an act of God everything life had thrown at her. This was what you had to do, but now with the luxuries of a good house, she rarely missed the harsh and cold life on the mountains.

Down on the creek flats, she could see Emanuel stumbling like a drunken man through the clods behind his plough. She buried her fork into the soft earth and for the first time in her life, felt truly happy.

Emanuel rested on the shafts of the plough beneath a shade tree, the half draught gelding resting too, emptying his bladder, urine splashing almost as far as Emanuel's boots. He watched the stream and felt envious of the horse. Emanuel had learned not to drive himself too much lately, since the turn he had taken. It had come on him suddenly with a burst of sweat and a dizzy spell. He found he had to sit down, only to wake up moments later lying in the furrow. The turn passed quickly, so he went back to work, never telling anyone about it. But the turn worried him. He didn't feel immortal anymore.

William King arrived in his buggy one afternoon in late autumn when Emanuel was resting on the front porch with a glass of brandy in his hand. Emily worked in her garden.

"Afternoon Emanuel." King tipped his hat to Emily and rested one foot on the step, "Easy to see who does all the work around here."

"I'll offer you a brandy if you like. Only take it myself for medical reasons, you know."

"Of course!" King laughed. "Don't mind if I do. Got a few medical things myself!"

He took a chair while Emanuel went inside to bring the bottle.

"We see a great deal of that son of yours, Harry, lately. Seems he's sparking that nurse Clare McGuire. Lovely young girl." He watched Emily down among the weeds.

"The wife has been a bit off lately. Young Clara's looking after her. Lovely girl, but your sons are like tom cats. Don't blame 'em mind. I was that way myself, once."

He admired Emily, wishing that he had a low maintenance wife himself.

"You're very lucky to have boys. Never had any myself."

"Got another coming along too," said Emanuel, feeling quite proud of his loins. "Young Frank's fourteen now and goes to the little school up the road. We should be able to get a little tucker out of him in a year or two."

King swilled the brandy around in his glass.

"The reason I'm here, Emanuel, is there's a meeting of the Cattleman's Association in Bairnsdale tomorrow. I stopped by on the way past. We're looking for new blood you know—you should come along and join. Might even be room for you on the board. We need more representation from the high country."

"That's a point." Emanuel mused, looking into his glass. Emily glanced up in surprise. Her husband had never showed any interest in that sort of things before. "They seem to have a bit of clout, from what I hear."

Emanuel thought hard about the challenge, grinning to himself on the inside. It would almost be like going into politics, he thought.

Chapter 42

Harry was striped to the waist in the midsummer heat, balanced on a plank ready to set the roof. The hammer was jammed in his belt, the nails held in his mouth. He held a length of timber above his head while he balanced on the narrow board. Harry was scared of heights, which came as a surprise to him. A mountain man scared to balance on a narrow piece of timber fifteen feet from the ground.

Jock Hoolahan set the first rafter in place and secured it with a four inch nail, then he moved to the opposite side of the building, edging carefully on his own narrow plank.

"Get a move on you old coot, I can't hold this bloody thing all day!" Harry mumbled around the nails.

"Can't move any faster, you young goat. Hold fast there and keep it steady!" Jock fixed the next rafter in place. They had been already cut well to fit from Mountain ash saplings. When four were in place, they climbed down the rough ladder to inspect their work from ground level. It was then that Rang arrived, weary after the ride up Angel's leap. The two men watched him tie his horse to a rail.

"Any chance of a job hereabouts? I thought I'd better check on what you were doing. Thought I might even get a job," he laughed.

"There's always work here Rang. No pay, but bloody good work. I can't seem to get the other lot interested. They don't think cattlemen should be interested in lowly work. Especially when it means getting their backsides out of a saddle."

"I had a hell of a job getting away from your sister," Rang mused. "God she mollycoddles a man—hardly lets me breath!"

"Don't sound like Nell."

Rang paused before replying.

"It's not Nell I was talking about." He wandered around the shell of the building, handling the timber, shaking it. It stood like the bleached skeleton on the open plain. The remains of the old building still lay about. "Nell left early this morning."

Jock Hoolahan loaded his pipe, glad for a chance to stop and yarn. Young Harry was a slave driver.

"Charley and Nell rode through some time back, said they were meeting George down towards Yarrabiddy. Cuttin' some culls or something." Harry could only concentrate on one job at a time. Absorbed in building his house he had almost lost interest in cattle.

He examined their work from a distance. "Should be moved to the left a touch. We ain't got it quite straight. Gotta start off right or we'll run off to buggery."

"Do you have a job for me?" Rang asked hopefully. "I probably won't be much good for anything, but I'll have a go."

"You can put the billy on, for a start." Harry said and, when Rang looked a little downtrodden, Jock Hoolahan noticed at once.

"Lot of noggins to go in yet, son. We're putting 'em two foot apart, you can work on that. Keep 'em flush against the studs so we can fix the wall timber straight."

Old Jock was more sensitive to other people's feelings than was his young boss. They sat in the shade and drank black tea. It was their only lunch. Harry believed in a big breakfast and no lunch, as it only cost time.

"There's a lot more work building a house than I ever thought," he said, looking at the results of a full year's labour. There seemed little to show as yet for their efforts, and there were still a great deal more timber to saw.

"Patience," said old Jock. "You young bucks got no patience! You're just like your old man. When we built the hut down on the spur—and you not a gleam in your mother's eye then—old Emanuel wanted it finished in a week. Woulda' fell down in a week if he had his way. You gotta' have patience to do a job right."

After they had finished the tea, they went back to work on the roof. Rang looked at the object that served as a ladder and was glad not to attempt the climb. Instead he selected a length of timber, measured a space between the studs and tried his hand at a saw.

When the saw didn't seem to go straight, he swore and tore a knuckle. Eventually he had the timber cut, carried it to the spot and tried to fit it straight. The nails kept slipping from his damaged fingers and when he swung the hammer it didn't go straight. He sweated and the hammer landed all over the place. The others watched silently from the roof above. Rang bent the third nail before he threw the hammer away. It landed in bushes fifty yards to the right. He hammered his bloody fist on the noggin, tears of frustration streaming down his face, then he swung away like a drunken man and lurched over towards his horse. The two Men on the roof watched silently, then climbed down without a word to each other. "Lord," Jock Hoolahan said, examining the spot where Rang had tried to fit the noggin. "He even tried to fit it in the space we left for a doorway."

Harry watched the man try to mount his horse. "That's the least of his worries."

Even the horse would not stand for him. But at last he pulled himself into the saddle, then half slumped across it, rode off down the mountain.

Chapter 43

It's hard for a man to outrun his past.

Syrus Craye once owned a hungry block of land in the Cooma area, where he ran a few head of cattle and an assortment of pigs. He had a name for stealing anything that was not nailed down and this included cattle. This ended when he fell beneath a wagon wheel, leaving five sons, a sick wife and a heavy mortgage.

Much later Ruben, the eldest of his sons, gained a lease on the high plains, but the slur on the name followed him there.

Ruben always believed the Craye look had more to do with the distrust than anything else. He was very much like his father—short, heavyset with hooked nose, wild eyes with eyebrows that joined in the middle. Not a face that carried trust. He felt people disliked him on sight, so he always tried to get in first.

In the late summer, Ruben and his two sons stopped on a rise at the north end of their run, when they noticed figures toiling like ants, far down in the valley, trying to free their wagon from a bog. The old spear wound in his hip worried Ruben greatly as he climbed painfully out of the saddle. Of course the weight he carried didn't help much either. Albert tried to help him, but the old man brushed him away. He made his way to a fallen log to watch the happenings below. Henry rolled his leg over the pommel of his saddle to build a cigarette.

"Them's the Trasks down there," he said.

Ruben was still wary of the Trasks. The trouble with Emanuel had happened twenty years before, but he had still managed to avoid the man. "What the hell you think they're up too. Don't they know they're on our land?"

"Been there yesterday too." Said Henry. "Young Harry and that old goat from the mines. Bogged the wagon to the axles trying to cross that gully. Had to leave it there while they went to get more horses and some help."

"Bloody hide."

Albert sat on the log beside his father and tried to cross his legs like Henry.

Ruben wiped the sweat from his face. "Them people think they got the right to come on to a man's land any time they please!"

"They're cutting a road in from Harrietville," said Henry talking around the cigarette. "I seen 'em a couple of days back, way to the west. Got a load of roofing iron aboard."

"Everyone always trying to screw a man!" Ruben rubbed his sore hip and spat into the dust. It had always been the world against Ruben Craye. Honest as the next man, but always mistrusted. The bad name would follow him to the grave. And the way he felt lately, the grave might not be far away.

He found himself thinking back over his life a great deal of late. Drifting back forty years, to the summer when he brought his first wife to the mountains. She was pregnant at the time, carrying a baby almost as big as a young calf in her belly. Ruben sent for the doctor in Dargo, but it was a difficult birth and he always maintained the forceps the man used stretched the baby's head. This was the reason that Albert was always slow. She died a few days later, leaving him with an idiot son and no wife. He always blamed Albert in a way, too.

"Can you see old Emanuel there?"

"Don't see him. There's George, Harry, and that old goat, Hoolahan-and the girl." Henry had eyes like a hawk.

Ruben weighed it all up. He didn't want trouble with the Trasks, but enough was enough. There had been many challenges in his life. Especially in the early years. There was the tribe of aborigines who lived by the upper reaches of the Coburn river near the spot where Ruben chose to build his first cabin. They didn't take his presence lightly, spearing a few of his cattle and eventually putting a spear in Ruben's left hip. He couldn't get much help from the local troopers to move the original owners along. Didn't get far at all until at last young Henry, then in his early twenties, took matters into his own hands. Henry shot two men by Kirkman's billabong and drove the tribe away. But that was never proved, the Crayes always maintaining that the original settlers chose to move on by their own motivation.

The old man was now well rested. "Well, we best go down there and sort this thing out!"

He had difficulty regaining his feet and even more difficulty remounting his horse. He led the animal to the fallen log and tried to remount there. Albert tried to help but was pushed away. Ruben would accept help from no man. Especially a halfwit.

"Let the cantankerous old bugger do it himself!" said Henry, turning his horse down the slope.

The wagon came free just as they reached the gully. It leaned heavily to the side and when the wheels lifted they sucked the mud up and sprayed the men working behind. Four draft horses lurched up the bank dragging the heavy wagon, hooves gouging the gravel, mud spilling from the rims. Harry and George stood covered in mud, clutching the poles they had used behind the rear wheels. Jock with his shoulder to the front wheel, slipped when the wagon burst free. Nell urging the horses up the bank, bringing them to a stop on the clear ground. The wagon had been unloaded the day before, the roofing iron carried by hand up the bank where it lay in untidy heaps. Nell drew the wagon in as close as she could. It was then that she noticed Henry Craye.

"What do you lot think you're up to?" he asked.

Harry Trask was in no mood for stupid questions. "What the hell does it look like? You think we're posting a bloody letter?"

Ruben and Albert arrived at that time, looking at the roofing iron lying on the ground. "Don't you know you're on my land?"

George scraped some of the mud off his pants. "Only passing through a small corner of your block, Mr Craye."

"A small corner? You been on my land for the past five miles!"

"We'll be soon off it, after we cross the next creek," Harry said. "Of course you can use the track. You should be glad to see us coming through here!"

Ruben wouldn't admit it, but the boy had a point.

"Wouldn't hurt to ask permission, young fella. I would think it would be a courtesy to ask before you come onto another man's land!"

George was always the diplomat. "We're sorry, Mr Craye. Just didn't think you'd care."

"Well, I bloody well care when someone takes liberties!"

Nell stood wiping the mud off her shirt. "You didn't seem to worry about liberties when you beat up my Dad—and him in his own home!"

Ruben turned red behind his ears. He wasn't used to backchat from a girl. "That was nigh on twenty years ago. And your old man had no title to the homestead then!"

"We got title to it now," said Harry.

Henry Craye couldn't keep his eyes off Nell. He wished he could help wipe the mud off her shirt.

157

Ruben shifted uneasily in his saddle. "Well, we'll let the matter settle now. You can use your damn road, but pay a man the courtesy to ask next time!"

With that, Ruben wheeled his horse away. Albert followed, but Henry stayed awhile, a strange look on his face.

Then he turned and slowly rode away.

Chapter 44

Charley Nash sat on the edge of his bunk with his shirt pulled up rubbing horse liniment into his back when Rang wandered into the room.

"Hard day Charley?"

"They're all hard days now, son."

Rang wandered aimlessly around the small room. "Charley, you still got that rifle?"

"Sure I got it. Over there against the wall."

"Thought I might borrow it for a while, if you don't mind."

Charley rubbed the liniment in with renewed pressure. "What do you need a rifle for?"

Rang examined the gun as if about to buy it. "I saw a mob of wild pigs yesterday in that swamp below the leap. Thought I might knock over a porker." He tested the breach lock. "Saw a couple of good ones the other day. Long while since we tasted pork."

Charley worked the liniment silently into his back.

"Got any shells?"

"Sure." Charley said uncertainly. "In the top cupboard."

Rang took a few shells and dropped them into his pocket. He shuffled uncomfortably about the room. "Don't tell nobody about this, Charley, I want it to be a surprise when I land home with the porker, I mean."

"Sure," said Charley, closing the lid of the liniment tin, his eyes following Rang's back as he left the room. *Every man had a right to live life as he wished*, he thought, but Rang worried him none the less.

It was lunchtime before Bess realised that she hadn't seen Rang all morning, and when she found his kelpie still chained to the hollow log, she became worried.

Rang never went anywhere without his dog.

She unchained the animal while her eyes travelled around the clearing with its cluster of farm buildings.

"Rusty boy, where's your master!" The dog jumped all over her and panic started to mount as she searched through the stables and the workman's hut.

"Rang! Rang! Where are you Rang? Dinners on the table!" The dog ran in circles before veering off around the red gum then spearing off between a stand of mountain ash. Bess followed, panicking in earnest now. Bracken tore her dress and branches slapped across her face as she plunged through the scrub, following the dog.

"Rang! Rang, answer me Rang!"

She had covered half a mile before she heard the shot, a long way off, echoing between the ridges and valleys. Bess stopped, hands to her mouth.

"Dear God, Don't let it be…"

She plunged blindly through the scrub, the dog now a long way in front.

Dress torn, she came upon Rang at last, sitting on a log, looking out over a marshy piece of land, the rifle resting between his legs. Bess ran to him and threw her arms around his neck. He just sat staring into space, saying nothing, as if sitting on a log with a rifle between his legs was the most logical thing in the world. A dead pig lay in the mud, fifty yards away.

"I couldn't do it," he said at last, vaguely aware that there was someone else in his world, "I just didn't have the guts."

"Rang, Rang, you scared me half to death!" She smothered his neck with kisses. "What on earth do you mean?"

"I just couldn't do it." His words were vague as if he was not fully aware that Bess was even there.

"You know what worried me the most?" It was as if he were talking to himself. "Charley Nash. I thought if I used his gun he'd feel awful bad. I couldn't help thinking of old Charley!"

"Rang you fool, don't you know how much we all care about you?"

He looked at her in wonder. "I just didn't have the guts. I ain't got nothing else and now I ain't even got guts!"

"If you'd done something stupid, I couldn't have gone on living!" Her tears were all over his neck and she shook like a child. Rang got to his feet and stood on shaky legs. The dog licked his hand.

"Rang how could you think to do that to me?"

160

When he shuffled to the other side of the bog and dragged the dead pig out of the reeds, it left a trail through the mud. With the pig in one hand, the rifle slung over his shoulder, Rang wound his other arm around the girl, shuffled through the scrub towards the homestead. Bess was crying softly by his side. He stopped and looked down at her.

"Christ, you're only a child."

"I'm fully growed, you big oaf" She looked up at him through tear-stained eyes. "In case you never noticed." She kicked a toe into a tuft of grass. "I know I got a lot prettier sister, but I always loved you, you big ox!"

"But you're only a child," he said in wonder. He slung the dead pig easily over one shoulder, along with the gun, and they continued slowly on towards the house. They stopped for a while in the clearing by the house.

"Bess, promise me you won't tell anybody about this?"

She snatched the rifle from his back, wrenching his shoulder as she pulled the rifle free.

"Not if you promise not even to think of stupid things like that again!" She hammered her fists into his chest. "Promise you won't ever think of anything like that again!"

Her fists pounded him and her tears splattered across his face. He held her gently at arm's length.

"No, no chance of trying that again. I tried it once and it didn't work!"

He put his arm around her and shuffled towards the house, dragging the pig.

"I never thought of you as more than a little girl. Thought of you more like a kid sister." But feeling her against his side, he realised she was not a little bit like a sister.

Chapter 45

Two men rode out of the scrub at the head of the Cobungra river. One, a small man, dressed in a suit and dust coat, the other much larger, leading a pack horse. There were tripod legs protruding from a saddle pack on the second horse.

They rode across the clearing and tied their horses to the rail in front of the Craye house. The building sprawled in neglect beneath a gnarled old woollybutt. The veranda floor was rotten in places as they picked their way to the front door.

The lumbering mass of Albert Craye met them at the door, while old Ruben sprawled on a chair inside. A chair that barely took his weight.

"Mr Craye I presume?" The thin man asked. "My name's Jones. I'm from the Department of Environmental Affairs, and this is Max Wallace. Surveyor Max Wallace."

He said the name as if this should carry some weight to Ruben Craye.

"And what do we owe this visit too, Mr Jones. We don't have many people come around here dressed in suits."

"I'll come straight to the point, Mr Craye." He completely ignored Albert. People had told him that old Ruben had an idiot son. He spread a large map on the bare wooden table.

"I thought it better to bring the word in person."

The surveyor drew a blackened pipe from the pocket of his seersucker coat.

Outside Henry, down by his hut, watched the visitors arrive as he shaved in a bowl at the back door. He drew water from the water tank to wash the spare lather from his face. The braces hung about his waist and he wore the same woollen singlet he had worn at the beginning of summer.

Henry was not very successful growing a beard, so of late he kept himself clean shaven. A trickle of blood spread down his neck from a nick from the cut-throat razor. He still carried the razor when he entered the room where the men were talking.

"And who are these dandies?"

The small man nodded curtly. He had heard of Henry Craye. "I was just showing Mr Craye on the map the area of land that we are reclaiming for the national park. Of course you are not the only lease-owners affected. The Boxes will lose eight hundred acres of their lease as well!"

"Like hell!" swore Henry. "I don't care what old Julias Box loses, but you're not taking any of our land. You can take your map and shove it up your arse!"

"I'm sorry you take that attitude Mr Craye, but believe me the decision was not mine. This was a council decision. Many different groups were involved, including the high country Cattlemen's Association. I am just the carrier of the bad tidings, I'm afraid. I just felt the word should be delivered personally, rather than by mail."

"Well, I don't care what you think and mail would do you no bloody good up here. We don't have mail. You heard my decision, and I dare say the old man thinks the same!"

"It's not all bad you know," said the surveyor, loading his pipe. "This won't come into effect 'till the leases come up for renewal in the new year. And of course, you won't be entirely banned from the national parks. There are still controlled grazing rights. Limited they might be, but there is a strong push to keep cattle out of the high country. Many people believe cattle damage the natural herbage, and certainly greatly damage the sphagnum beds. These beds are a vital part of the drainage for the river systems, you know."

"Cattle do a damn sight more good than harm, and well you know it. The whole damn place would burn in a few years without cattle!"

"Your opinion, Mr Craye, your opinion," said the surveyor.

"You bureaucrats been stirring this pot for years," grumbled Ruben Craye. "Now you better get out, while you still can!"

"We will go, Mr Craye, but it will make no difference, I'm afraid. The decision still stands!"

They left the map sitting on the table for the Crayes to study later, after they had calmed down.

"We shoulda' shot 'em, Pa," said Albert, watching the two men ride away. "Coulda' dumped 'em in a ditch and nobody'd ever miss 'em I bet!"

"Bloody idiot!" Henry muttered. "Of course they'd miss 'em. Wouldn't make a scrap a difference neither. Be coppers swarming over the place and we'd still lose the lease!" Although secretly he believed there was merit in what his brother said.

He drew a finger on the map.

"Bloody Cattlemen's Association. Notice there's no land resumed from the Trask lease. Old Emanuel, the bastard, he's feathering his own nest!"

"You could be right at that," said Ruben, tapping his teeth with the stem of his pipe. "You could well be right!"

Chapter 46

It was late autumn, just before the winter muster, when Harry appeared at the King homestead. He tied his horse to a rail and William King met him at the front door.

"Taking our nurse away for the day I hear, young Harry Trask."

"Sure, but I'll bring her back in one piece later Mr King!"

"You better lad. You better. That girl's almost a daughter of mine, you know."

Clara stepped around the old cattleman, pinching his arm on the way past.

"So I'm a daughter am I?" she laughed. "I trust you'll remember that in your will."

"It'll be a long while before anyone benefits from my will, young girl. I promise you that!"

Clara was dressed in full riding gear, hat and dust coat. She carried a riding crop and Harry could not help noticing the plaid skirt. He guided her towards the stables, where the pony belonging to Mrs King was already tethered. Mrs King had little need or a horse nowadays and Harry noticed the side-saddle. "You're not going far up the mountain in that gear!" he muttered, helping her to mount.

"Don't you be so sure, Harry Trask!" she laughed, giving the pony a good lick with the crop. Harry could see by the way she sat the horse that she did not ride as well as she drove a car.

Clara had to dismount when they reached Angel's Leap. "Why do you call it that?" She asked, eying the steep ascent with some concern.

"Don't ask me. But I expect if you went over the edge you could ask the angels themselves."

"Well, I don't intend to do that so I think I'll walk!"

Harry dismounted and they led their horses up the narrow path, climbing towards the high plains. "My mother rode this track at night when she was five months pregnant with Bess." He said with a laugh. "Of course she didn't ride side-saddle."

"Well, bully for your mother!" Clara was out of breath, her boots slipping on the loose gravel. It was well past midday when they finally reached the homestead where Harry had been working for the past two summers.

Clara could see that he was well proud of his work as he showed her through the unfinished building, going from room to room, shaking the timber to show how sound it was. The roof was almost in place. "I bought a wagon from Fat Eric, the blacksmith in Harrietville. Old Jock Hoolahan helped me haul the iron. We'll be getting a couple of tanks, so we'll have plenty of water."

Clare noticed the 'we', but said nothing for a while. Finally she could hold herself in no longer. "What's this 'we' Harry?" Harry blushed, a new experience to him.

"Well, you know what I mean," he rubbed his finger gingerly along a piece of exposed timber in the wall. "I thought we might talk about a few things later in the day."

"Yes, I think that would be a very good idea, Harry Trask. I really would appreciate knowing a little bit about what I'm supposed to be doing with my life!" Harry coloured for the second time behind the ears.

"Yeah, well I'll show you a few more things out the back that old Jack and I was planning."

Later they climbed higher into the mountain before turning onto a high plain that they followed until at last reaching a small stream on a plateau, surrounded by snow gums and granite rocks. The stream dropped thirty feet to a rock pool surrounded by large flat boulders, before tumbling down the mountain side.

"I've always liked this spot." Harry said, unloading his saddle bag. "I often stop by here for a bite of lunch." The scenery took her breath away.

"it's a beautiful spot. I've never seen anything like it. So high, it's like the top of the world!"

He found the tablecloth, cutlery and food that Bess had carefully packed for the trip that very morning. He had to promise to buy her some books in Omeo later in the year as a bribe. Bess had excelled herself, but the journey up the mountain had done nothing to improve the food. It had been a very long trip.

"My, you have been a busy little bee, my love" Clara grinned, watching him lay out the tablecloth. He produced knives, forks and tin plates. "And you, a big strong cattleman. Did you do all this yourself?"

"Almost. My kid sister probably helped a bit."

"My Harry, you rough cattlemen never cease to amaze me. Build houses and cook too!"

They had their picnic as the afternoon wound on and by late afternoon Harry found himself resting with his arm about her waist.

"You love it up here on the mountains, don't you?" She said, snuggling in close. He gave her a little squeeze.

"Can't think of any better place to be. Nowhere else comes close to this."

She was silent for a while, trying to think how to get into the subject that was worrying her. "There are plenty of other places, too, you know. Lots of other places. You don't ever want to forget that."

"Nowhere comes up to this."

"But don't you want to travel and see the rest of the world?"

"See no reason for it. What's the rest of the world have that this place hasn't?"

"Quite a lot of things, but you'll never know until you have a look. I've always wanted to travel," she said, a faraway look in her eyes. "Paris, London, all those places." His fingers traced the side of her face, then he bent and gently kissed her. She bent up and saw his face from below. A strong stubborn jaw and the hooked nose of the Trask breed. But friendly eyes. The climate had already left its mark stamped onto his face.

"You know I could well love you, Harry Trask." He kissed her again, more savagely this time.

"That's why I built the house. For us!"

She didn't know how to put the words. "I want you to steady down a bit, Harry love. I said I could well love you, but I'm not quite sure yet. We have our whole lives in front of us to work it out."

"I just don't do things steady," said Harry.

"I said I always wanted to travel," she shifted uneasily in his arms. "Some say there may be a war coming. A world war or some such. I may join up as a nurse or something…"

Harry was shocked to his heels by the very thought. "Rubbish!" he said. "What would a war matter up here in the mountains?"

"That's what you don't realise my love-there's a lot more of the world than the mountains. Lovely as they may be!"

By this time, he was squeezing her waist hard enough to hurt. When he eased the pressure, she settled back comfortably against him. The thought of her leaving for some fool war nobody knew anything about was too stupid for words.

"Just don't get your hopes up too high, Harry. Don't rush into things. I don't ever want you to get hurt."

"What do you mean, get hurt?" He snuggled against her and after a while she snuggled back. Harry was greatly relieved.

"It's just that you take things for granted Harry. I don't think you know what you truly want. You just seem to want things because they're there. Things are not always clear cut the way you want them. Other people have got feelings too. Have dreams of their own."

Harry could not work out the way a women's mind worked. The sun was sinking low. They would have to be leaving soon. It would still be well dark before they even reached the leap.

"You said you loved me. Said it just now. Why waste our lives on things that don't matter!"

"That's the trouble Harry love. You just take things for granted. Why not just slow down a bit while we think things over." She kissed him again, hard on the mouth, feeling the rising in his thighs, "Now I think we best get moving, lest they never find us on this mountain!"

And wouldn't you love it, she thought.

Laying on one elbow, she watched him pack up, loading the gear carefully into his saddlebag. A small smile played around the corners of her lips as the thought ran through her mind—Don't ever take me for granted, Harry Trask...

Chapter 47

Harry lost no time leaving Ashburn. As soon as the last beast was through the front gate he quietly took his leave and rode back down the road towards Omeo. He told nobody that he was going there, merely said he had something to do at home.

He made a quick purchase at the only jewellery shop in town then, only pausing long enough to take a meal at the one cafe that was still open, the Black Dog, he rode back to William King's property in the hills above Dargo.

His eyes were gritty from lack of sleep, something he hadn't tasted in many hours, rain was falling softly with the bite of winter in the air. Heavy snow already covering the high country. Water glistened on his oilskin coat and ran from the brim of his hat as he stood in King's doorway.

"You'll not find your girl here," said King. "The wife's well at last, so we've no more need for a nurse. We let her go about a fortnight ago, so I expect you'll find her back in Dargo!"

So he remounted his horse and rode down into the town after spending sixteen long hours in the saddle.

Dr McGuire met him at the door of his office dressed in a faded dressing gown, looking frail and worn. Harry wondered just how old the man really was.

"If you're looking for my daughter young fella, you won't find her here. She took off to Ballarat about a fortnight ago, had some fool idea to join the armed forces, become a nurse. I just hope her mother can talk some sense into her!"

Harry stood dumbstruck, water running from the brim of his hat.

"When will she be back?"

"Back? Don't know when she'll be back. Or if she'll ever be back. Hard to keep these young ones tied down you know. The army no less. Reckon there's not enough around here to keep her anymore."

The old man tightened his dressing gown against the winter chill and shuffled back to his bed. Harry was wringing wet, but didn't worry much about that. He moved in a daze across the street to the Royal Dargo hotel.

Leaning across the bar with water dripping to his feet, he asked for a beer.

It took him two hours and half a dozen drinks to pick a fight. Harry was not a drinking man nor, up until that moment, a fighting man. In fact, this was his first fight, and had he not been drunk he probably would have won it. But at last he picked himself out of the mud and nursing a swollen jaw, limped back into the bar to try to borrow some money.

"Not on your life young fella. Go home and clean yourself up!" was the only response he got from the barman.

The office of Jack Haynes and Son was closed, but Jack still sat at his desk pouring over his books. He didn't bother to lift his head when the muddy cattleman entered the room.

This was a ploy he often used to keep people uneasy. Give him an edge. Of course he wouldn't use it on anybody he considered important. After a suitable time he shuffled some papers and looked up.

"Young Harry Trask, I see. What can I do for you, young Harry?"

Harry could have killed the man if he hadn't wanted a favour.

"I need to borrow some money, Jack, about ten quid would do. I'm a little short."

Jack shuffled the papers and threw his head back so the light caught his spectacles.

"Ten quid? You are rather short!"

"I'll pay you back in a couple of days. I just need the money urgent!"

Jack found his cane and limped over to the safe in the corner of the room.

He moved slowly, in a bit of a daze, as if some of the life had been taken out of him. His only son, Adam had left the business this morning to join up. Damn fool!

"Ten quid you say. I expect I owe the son of an old customer that much."

He counted the notes carefully. It was almost as hard on him as pulling teeth.

Harry had never taken a train before. Even buying the ticket was a new experience. After riding into Sale, he caught the train and sat nursing a half empty bottle of whisky as the train carriage lurched and swung towards Melbourne. Travelling was a new experience to Harry. At the Melbourne station, he had to change trains to Ballarat, not knowing what to expect there, but imagining it was a large town.

Ballarat was bigger than he thought, with three haberdasheries to pick from. As luck had it the third was the right one. He saw Clara at once behind a rear counter. She recognised him at the same time, rushing towards him, with no surprise, just triumph in her eyes.

Alice McGuire recognised the cattle man at the same instant, although she had never seen the man before. But he was quite obvious, dressed in dirty clothes, unshaven, and he appeared a little drunk. She cut him short before he reached her daughter.

"Clara, don't go near this dirty man!" she said, blocking his path.

Harry pushed her out of the way, surprised at her strength. Alice was much younger than her husband and hadn't aged as much.

"Mind your own damn business, old woman!" Harry was surprised at how his own words came out. He was not used to whisky.

"My business? My business? This is my daughter, so that makes it my business you rude young heathen!"

Clara had him by the arm.

"You shouldn't have come here Harry. Not like this!"

"What do you expect. Don't you know I've worked my guts out on that damn house for two years, just for you?"

"You can do better than this, my girl," the mother said. "That's the very reason I took you away from that place. They're just primitive, those mountain trash!"

Harry shoved her aside again and she stumbled against a bench of clothes. "Here, I bought you this," He had difficulty finding the ring among the trash in his pocket. There was still mud on his face where he had not washed properly. "It cost me a year's wages!"

"Harry, Harry, you never talk to anyone. Just barge forward in your own way. You never even came near me for a month!"

"I was mixed up in the muster—I been flat strap for the last month and couldn't get away. But you knew..." His eyes were desperate. Mrs McGuire stood dusting herself and stood with chest heaving.

"Only you knew Harry. Only you knew. Nobody else comes into it at all!"

Harry looked stunned while the mother looked triumphant.

"Why aren't you in the army anyhow, young man? All the young men I know are joining up. You're just a drunken lout!"

He would have liked to break her face. He swayed on his feet, the top of a half empty whisky bottle showed in his coat pocket.

"I guess I made a fool of myself," he muttered. In the corner of his eye, he saw Clara's two sisters, they had to be sisters, looking agape at the wild mountain man. There were also a group of startled customers looking on.

Clara had lost her look of triumph and was crying.

"You shouldn't have come like this, Harry."

He lurched out of the shop, feeling a fool as he stumbled down the street.

Chapter 48

Harry bought a new ticket and tried to buy another bottle of whisky, but his money was gone. He hated the taste of whisky anyway, but needed something to deaden his mind. So he sat with the empty bottle between his legs in the waiting room. He had no reason to keep it. Perhaps it was just for the comfort. The train didn't leave until ten o'clock that night, so he spent the next hour in the washroom, cleaning himself up as best he could. He hadn't eaten all day and still didn't feel like food. This was not like Harry.

He boarded the train as soon as it was possible and sat in the small compartment, the whisky bottle still between his legs. People took one look at him and moved away to find another compartment while there was still plenty of room on the train. Finally the porter blew his whistle, the train blew steam, shuddered, the carriages clashed as it pulled out of the station. White steam covered the platform and the gas lantern swayed with the lurch of the carriage.

They had travelled some distance down the track when a girl came quietly along the corridor to stand uncertainly in the doorway.

Harry look at her in a dazed sort of way before his mind sorted things out. The girl looked like Clare, but that was not possible. After a while in the half light, his eyes began to focus.

"You crazy big oaf!" she finally said. "You crazy, crazy oaf!"

Harry sat stunned. He tried to hide the whisky bottle beneath a coat on the seat.

"Clara—Clara, I didn't think you wanted to see me again."

"You poor, silly fool," she sat on the bench beside him while her fingers traced the side of his face. "You don't know a thing about women, do you? Why do you think I left Dargo? I had to see if you'd follow!"

His mind could still not grasp the turn of events. "You didn't have to do that!"

"I'm sorry I did it now, love. Honest I am. I just didn't think you'd react like that!"

She sat beside him and smiled into his face, wiping a smudge of mud away with a delicate, white handkerchief. Then she threw her arms around his neck.

"You sure made an impression on my mother!" She found the empty bottle of whisky.

"Aren't you going to offer me a drink?" She wrinkled her nose and choked at the thought of the taste. "I don't know how you drink that stuff!"

"I don't. And it's empty anyway. I don't have anything to offer you. I'm just an idiot!"

"You're not an idiot, Harry, just pig-headed. I don't know if I should hug you or sock you. I just wanted to see if you loved me enough to leave your damn mountain. I didn't know if you really loved me or I was just something in your mind you thought you had to have."

It had been a long day and Harry, confused, didn't know what to think. He threw the coat aside, wrapped his arms about her and wrestled her down across the bench.

The gas lantern swayed above to the movement of the carriage, basking the compartment in uneven yellow light. They were just thirty miles out of Ballarat, passing through the village of Ballan when he managed to undress her, enough for his purposes at least. He was surprised she made it so easy. Her breasts were free and her thighs free of the panties. He tossed them aside as the train rattled and lurched as he slipped inside her.

"My, you are a willing devil, Harry," she moaned into his ear, taking a good lump of it between her teeth, she bit down hard. "You can cook, work cattle, and rape!"

She groaned as he worked inside her, fingernails finding flesh and drawing blood at the back of his neck.

They were finished and exhausted when they first saw the small boy standing gape-mouthed in the doorway. Clara's breasts were damp with sweat as he came off her.

Then a stout woman appeared, gasped, covered her mouth and dragged the boy away into the corridor.

There was barely time to get their clothes in place before she returned with the conductor.

"There—that's the animals there! Disgusting behaviour on a public train if ever I saw it. And my little boy saw it all!"

The boy tried to look around the door frame but his mother pulled him away by the ear.

"I'm sorry sir, madam," spluttered the conductor, "but this will never do!" A thin moustache rode along his top lip like a caterpillar. He had never seen anything like this before.

Clara was still adjusting her clothes and could not bring her eyes to face anyone.

"I'll have to ask you people to stay in your cabin while I telephone the police at the next station!" His hands were everywhere, trying to find something to do to wash the whole thing away. The stout woman stood with legs apart against the sway of the train, holding her son by the ear. "Don't leave the compartment before Melbourne," the conductor spluttered. "I should expect the police will be waiting there!"

"What's the world coming to?" spluttered the woman. "It's the war no less!"

"Dear goodness me," gasped the conductor. "This will never do on his majesty's railways!"

Chapter 49

Two policemen were waiting for them on the platform of the Melbourne railway station.

One was a thin and serious sergeant, spoiling for an arrest. He looked as if he should have been somewhere else, handling something much more important during the war. The other was a heavy set constable carrying a handlebar moustache and the long, mournful look of a Doberman dog. As they led them out onto the street, Clara felt that every person in Melbourne was looking at her. Harry didn't give a damn.

The day was bright and sunny, the street filled with noise. It was totally unlike the silence of the mountains. Harry had not noticed the fact when he came through the day before, but there seemed to be as many automobiles as buggies fighting for space on the streets of Melbourne. He was amazed at the amount of people—and the noise.

They were led two short blocks to the north, then up a side street to the station, an imposing red brick building with wide sweeping steps, covered with litter, leading up from the cobbled street. They were guided up the steps into the front lobby where the thin and serious sergeant told Clara to wait on a wooden bench against the wall.

"No need for you to get mixed up in this, madam." Despite his sour disposition, he liked Clara's looks. "A well-presented woman like you, unless you want to press charges of course. But I daresay we know where the guilt lies on this occasion."

"No." Clara dabbed at her eyes with the hanky, "I don't want to press charges. There's no trouble here. I just want to go home."

For the first time in her life, Clara felt completely lost. She huddled on the bench in shame. "We really meant no trouble, sir. It was just an accident. We've never done anything like that before!"

"Be that as it may, Madam. You just wait there while we sort this thing out." He ushered Harry into a rear office where he slumped into a chair behind a desk. The heavyset sergeant looked as if he wanted to laugh, a strange look on the long mournful face. It didn't seem like a face built for a laugh.

"You cattlemen can't behave yourselves can you?" The detective bounced a pencil against his teeth. "You are a cattleman aren't you?" He liked to think of himself as a perceptive man. He certainly deserved better than this when there was a war on. "Couldn't control yourself, eh? Too long in the hills? Of course you'll have to be charged. Have to be charged!."

The fat constable felt his stomach shake as he tried to control a laugh. "Full of sass, ain't we son. Young whelp like you should'a been in the army anyhow. That would knock the sass out of you!"

Behind the desk the thin detective rattled the pencil against his teeth. "This sort of thing will never do you know—on a public train no less!"

He fixed Harry with a wicked look. "Charge them Fred. Charge them both. Indecent conduct!"

Fred shook with silent laughter. "How could you do it on a train? The friggin seats is only a few inches wide!"

It took Harry and Clara a full day to find a justice of the peace who could marry them. They found two passers-by in the street to stand witness. One an elderly lady with a poodle and the other a drunken soldier in uniform. That night they used the last of the little money Clara carried with her in her purse to book a hotel room for their honeymoon. It wasn't much of a room, as she had little money. The window, when they could at last open it, looked out onto an alley filled with garbage cans.

But it became a standard joke between them over the years, although they could share it with no one else, and it wasn't quite true anyway, that they had spent the first night of their honeymoon in jail.

Chapter 50

Emanuel died in his sleep.

Emily had noticed him acting strangely of late, perhaps he had a premonition that something was wrong. Although he had not ridden into the high country for months and would have found the going difficult anyway, all of a sudden he could speak of nothing else. He craved for the feel of his horse in the high country, grass as high as the horse's stomach in spring after the winter snow. He wanted to stand on the outcrop of rock that seemed like the end of the world and look out to the south where you could see through the mist the curvature of the earth. Sometimes he mentioned a horse named Atlas and a stamping mill. Spoke of a Major Terry, and wondered where he was now. Was he still alive or in Hell where he belonged. He sometimes fingered the place on his jaw where the hair would no longer grow and cursed old Ruben Craye. He should have killed him at the time along with his rotten son. Unfinished business that had not worried him much over the years but did now. Often he thought of Jim, and found himself talking earnestly to him, asking if he wanted a beer in the pub at Wangaratta. Jim seemed more real to him now than the sons and daughters who were still alive. But always it was the high country, the snow and the cattle following the trail of salt.

He tired easily of late and it was not unusual for him to go to bed at sundown. Emily sometimes heard strange sounds during the night. They slept in different rooms because Emanuel's snoring would rattle the rafters and he often jerked and stopped breathing for a short period of time, then draw a sharp breath then back into the snoring again. Emily couldn't stand the strain of waiting for the next breath so moved into another room.

The night he died, a strange sound woke her from a sound sleep. There was a crash of broken glass and the sound of the bedroom light thrown to the floor by a thrashing outspread arm. Emily tangled in her bedclothes as she stumbled out of bed, only to find her husband, arms spread, eyes wide open, mouth hanging ajar, skin as pale as pipe clay, lips already turning blue.

Emanuel was sixty nine years old.

They buried him in the small cemetery on the side of the hill near Dargo.

A great many cattlemen gathering to show their respect. Quite a few people Emanuel would hardly ever known. No man in the world would have been more surprised at the turn out. William King was there, Levi Paterson, members from the Cattlemen's association. Even Ruben Craye, sitting quietly in his sulky some distance away. A man forgave everything at a time of death. Probably he knew his time was not far away himself. He didn't climb down from the seat, just sat there quietly.

George choked out a few words over the grave and William King, hat in hand, gave a long talk of the loss of one of the pioneers of the high country.

The family stood huddled close by as Nell and Bess cried softly. George's shoulders shook as the first shovelfuls of earth hit the coffin.

On the tombstone was carved:

Emanuel James Trask

Born 17th July 1845, Died 27th November 1914.

R I P

Cattleman

Survived by wife Emily and sons George, Harry, Frank (Jim deceased) daughters Ellen, Bess.

When the funeral was over, the family gathered in the homestead at Ashburn—George, Nell, Harry, Bess, Frank and Rang, Rang now considered part of the family. Clara was also there but George's wife, Rachael, was too heavily pregnant to make the trip. Jock Hoolahan and Charley Nash sat on the front veranda, smoking cigarettes.

Emily had taken the loss of her husband very well, as would be expected of the woman. Life was always a challenge to her, a whole heap of challengers, one after another. She felt you just had to deal with them then get on with it. You weren't supposed to really enjoy life, just get on with it as the good Lord meant you too, expecting a better life in the hereafter. The only time in her life she had been a little happy was the last few years in her garden. And she felt a little guilty about it.

The death was God's will and so be it. Just another stumble in the journey of life. But she missed the man she had lived with for the past forty years more than

179

she expected and certainly more than she could show, and would miss him more as the days dragged by.

The family gathered around the dining room table, A heavy wooden table that Emily was immensely proud of, and kept polished until you could see your face in it. Emanuel had bought the table and six chairs for five pounds at a clearing sale. No one was ever allowed put their boots on it.

Emily sat at the head, folding her small hard hands on the polished timber.

"I suppose now is as good a time as any to settle things. Tidy our lives up, as the saying goes."

"Now's not the time, ma." Nell said. She had taken the loss far harder than anyone else. She had always been Emanuel's favourite. "Dad's not even cold in his grave."

Emily twisted her knuckles. "There's no good times for these things, so we best get it over with."

"Nell's right, ma. This ain't the time." George said, moving uncomfortably in his chair.

There was a moment's silence, then Harry asked: "What have you got in mind, Ma?"

Emily lay a sheet of yellow paper on the table.

"This is your father's will. He left everything to me." This seemed fine after forty years. There was a slight tremor in her voice as she said, "Now this is how we should cut things up." She tapped her fingers on the yellow paper as if to make a point. "There's still a heavy debt to clear on this place, and Jindawaddy is still not paid off. We have to clear that up. I will still have complete control." Emily was a hard woman, even at a time like this. "You lot can work the place as one, share the spoils and pay me a retainer each year. I suggest we have a bangtail muster on the high country in the Autumn. I've got a figure set down here that I think is fair to all parties. You boys, and girls, should form a partnership to take over the lease on the high country then pay me off over five years for the stock. That should handle the debt on Ashburn. You can agist your cattle here during the cold months. I'm sure we can set a fair figure on that."

George whistled between his teeth. So much for motherly love. "Jeez, you got it all figured out Ma!"

"No need to use that language son. No need to take the Lord's name in vain!"

Nell shifted on her chair. She didn't think the Lord had anything to do with this. "That all seems a little stiff, Ma. We are your kids and we've spent our whole lives working for damn poor wages on the place!"

"And I spent a whole lot more life than that young lady, working my but off, raising a bunch of kids running the household and still working on the place!" Emily choked something back into her throat.

"Course there will be no need for lawyers. We need nothing in writing. Just a family agreement."

Clara spoke for the first time, to the surprise of everyone present. "That won't do at all Mrs Trask. This has to be set out on paper. Nobody knows what will happen down the track!"

Emily was truly shocked that anyone could stand up to her. Especially one so new to the family. Clara's metal had never even been tested.

"I don't see the reason for lawyers. This family always trusts one another. Why give lawyers our good money?"

Harry thought the time right to back his new wife.

"Clara's right you know. We should have this set down on paper."

Emily twisted the yellow paper in her hand.

"Well, don't forget young Frank. He's just out of school and hasn't had time to do much as yet, but he's still part of the family and should get his share. Oh, and I'll keep old Jock Hoolahan to work the place down here."

"Jock might have something to say about that, Mother," said Nell. "Jock may well have something to say about that!"

Outside on the veranda, Charley and Jock heard it all. Jock screwed up his face and spat into the dust.

They worked at the muster for almost a week, gathering the cattle from every part of the run. This wasn't a complete waste of time, in a few weeks they would have to take the cattle down to lower country.

They sat on the ground and drew figures in the dust. Six hundred breeding cattle with four hundred calves at foot, twenty bulls, three hundred steers. They drew the figures in the dust with sticks. Short butts of cattle tails lay everywhere.

"Well, that's it then," said Nell, making adjustments to the figures. "We'll all be old and grey by the time we pay that lot off."

Harry was more positive.

"Grey or not, we're still be in better shape than the old man ever was!"

He looked around the high plains. "And we still got all this!"

"We got it for a while, anyway. Unless the government decides to take it all over and turn the lot into a national park!"

Harry spat in the dust. "You always were a cheerful bugger weren't you George. If anybody ever decides to take this over it will be over my dead body!"

Chapter 51

Harry and Nell pored over a parish map spread across a table in the registry office in Omeo. The map completely covered the table and hung over the sides. Nell traced her fingers over the part where the Trask run joined the Craye's.

"I could never understand how the Craye's lease cut in there," She stabbed the place on the ridge line with her finger. "I always thought we should run down to the river."

"Well, there you have it in black and white. The way I read it, that land is ours, and it takes in that place called the Gap, where they pen their cattle. Also forty acres of good country that runs down to the river."

"Then why didn't Gordon Jones claim it?"

"I suppose he was like us, just accepted the boundary as it always was. The old man never questioned the boundary either, after he bought the lease from Jones."

"Well, all that changes now. We're taking back what's ours." Nell chewed her lip. "Although old Ruben Craye won't like it!"

"Too bad. What's ours is ours. We're going to take the land back."

"I suppose we best talk it over with George. I don't think he'd be happy to tread on the Craye's toes, especially after they've run cattle there for the past forty years."

"I don't care about George, and I'll handle Ruben Craye. Or Henry—whoever we have to deal with!"

It was late in the afternoon and they were weary when they rode up the mountain to the old homestead on the spur. Rang's horse was standing in the yard, unsaddled but still carrying some sweat, after coming down from the high country. They found Rang inside, a towel wrapped about his shoulders, fast asleep in a chair by the table, Bess trimming his moustache with a pair of scissors. She was so engrossed in her task that she didn't notice her two siblings enter the room.

"There," she said, talking to herself. "Trim it that way so it hangs down thus and you never even notice the lip." The moustache had grown to a fine length and the way she had trimmed it certainly hid the offending gap in the lip, caused by the fire.

"There sweet, you look quite dashing. Like a pirate no less!" She spoke to herself, still unaware of the company.

Harry and Nell stood in the doorway, one amused while the other was not amused at all. Rang lay fast asleep in the chair, head thrown back, snoring softly. He had quietly enjoyed the pampering.

"So this is what you get up to when we're not around?" Harry laughed. Bess dropped her scissors and Rang woke with a start. Bess had shaved his head too, which was an improvement on the patchwork way his hair had grown after the fire.

"Creep up on people, won't you. But don't you honestly think this is an improvement?" She stepped back to admire her handy work.

"You seem to spend a lot of time making improvements, while I'm away that is!" Nell snapped. Bess noticed the edge in her sister's voice.

"What do you mean by that?"

"You know what I mean. Keep your hands off my man. I seen you dove-eyed lately, fawning all over him!"

"What do you mean, 'your' man? You haven't paid him any mind for months!"

Rang shifted uncomfortably in his chair.

"I haven't had time, if you'd ever noticed—not that it's any of your business!"

Rang threw the towel off his shoulders, knocking over the chair as he came to his feet.

"Now see here, Nell, there's something you should know."

Bess was crying now, so he put his arm around her. "Bess and I plan to get married!"

Nell's mouth dropped open.

"Married? Married? To that young bitch? She's young enough to be your daughter!"

"She's older than you think, Nell." Nell's throat worked, but it took time for the words to come out.

"But what about us?"

"There's been no us. There's been no us for the past year. You can barely stand to look at me. I'm damaged goods, Nell, and you just can't stand nothing damaged."

The door almost fell from its hinges as she slammed it. Nell mounted her horse and it reared from the sense of her fury. She spurred it savagely up into the mountains. "The bitch!" she screamed. "The bloody backstabbing bitch!"

The next day, riding with Harry on the high plains, her mood had cooled considerably. They rode quietly side by side across the high plains, the grass knee-high, the white-faced cattle spread over the plains between the snow gums and the outcrop of rocks. Ridges and valleys stretched off through the mist as far as the eye could see. Although Harry was much younger than his sister, she felt that he was the only one she could really talk too.

"She's right you know. Although I don't mean to, I just can't stand to touch his face. I thought the feeling would pass in time, but it hasn't."

They rode along quietly, Harry feeling useless in these matters.

"You know I really care for the man, but I just don't know. I just feel ashamed of myself sometimes. I'll be an old spinster you know. One of those old maids people talk about."

Harry glanced across at his sister. She was still a fine stamp of a woman, as Emanuel would have said, but there were hard little lines growing around her eyes. Her features had grown a little harder as the skin weathering in the elements. Age was creeping up silently while nobody noticed.

"I guess you're looking for the perfect man, Sis, and there probably ain't any of them left. Probably wasn't any in the first place."

Harry was proud of the philosophy he had just sprouted. "You're better than any man, Sis, at anything you do, and I guess you just can't stand weakness in anyone else. You ain't ever going to find a man to come up to your standards."

They rode quietly along. "An old spinster," she mused.

"You're still in your prime, girl," Harry laughed. "What are you, a bit past thirty?"

Nell dug in her spurs savagely and her mount plunged off scattering the white-faced cattle, red hair spilling from beneath the brim of her hat.

"Let's see what an old maid can still do!"

Chapter 52

Fertility is an amazing thing in the high country. Perhaps it has something to do with the clear mountain air. Or perhaps nothing at all. Bess had only slept with Rang twice. The first time was the night after he had tried to take his own life.

The next morning after the act, she felt shocked and ashamed of herself. She had betrayed her sister and herself, her own morels, everything about herself she had believed in. Good Lord, what would her mother think? She had never thought much about sex. Had always lived in the world of books. She read old romances cover to cover maybe thirty times. Books George picked up for her from time to time in the little store in Dargo. But there was no mention of sex in the books. Only love, romance, sorrow and great gallantry. No mention of sex. She felt so ashamed of her weakness that she went out of her way to avoid the man for months. Rang could not work out what was wrong.

Bess had no great seat on a horse and little interest in outside work, especially cattle. But she could cook, keep house and sew with stitches that were almost invisible to the eye. 'My little helper' Emily called her. My little home girl. She spoiled her brothers rotten, mended their clothes and cooked for them. There was not an ounce of malice in Bess. She could see fault in no one. She just lived a life of make believe in some outside world she knew nothing about, filled with romance and chivalry. So the second surge of hormones came as a shock, one cold wet day when she found herself alone with Rang in the barn, among the straw, shortly after she had words with Nell. When Rang said he wanted to marry her, the words came as a total shock. Perhaps he didn't even mean them. But it was the first time in her life that she felt angry with anyone, especially her sister. Perhaps that brought it on, but the rush of emotions came in the straw on that cold afternoon.

When she missed her first period, she was not greatly concerned. The thought never entered her head that she could be pregnant. Never even considered it. Periods had only troubled her for the past year or so and were pretty irregular anyhow. But when they failed to arrive a month later, she noticed she felt a little different in the way she carried herself. A strange feeling in her stomach that she had never felt before. Her mother would have noticed the sickness in the mornings, but such a thing would never even enter her head about her own daughter.

It was another month before she got Rang on his own, in the barn about dusk, while he was rubbing down his horse after riding rode down from the mountain. They were not quite alone at the time, Frank was there too, unsaddling the sway back bay mare that he rode. Frank was inches taller than the rest of his brothers. Thin with the pronounced hooked nose of the Trasks. Too young for a beard. He was not a natural cattleman, but he applied himself and learned things the hard way. Working cattle did not come easily to him. He was more interested in things of a mechanical nature. His mind was not tied up in the hills, but in the country below. There was not much call for a mechanic on the mountain, except fixing sheds and fences so he drove Harry to distraction from time to time. The rest of the family didn't seem to worry about it. Frank was what he was.

Bess wished the boy would go so she could talk to Rang. Her eyes followed him impatiently around the barn as he unsaddled his horse. There was not much time left as she would have to prepare the evening meal.

The boy shoved the mare into a stall and slapped her on the rump with the bridle. Rang, tired from his day in the saddle, was not patient with the boy.

"Rub that horse down well before you turn her loose. You've ridden her hard all day. A man looks after his horse up here!" Frank was the only one of the Trasks that Rang was game to talk to like that.

"Why don't you mind your damn business," Frank said tossing his bridle against the wall.

"I make it my business when a man don't look after his horse!"

"What's it to you. And what's goin' on here anyway. Am I interrupting you two sparkin' or something?"

Rang's horse had dropped a large pile of manure between its hind legs. It was still steaming when he reached down, gathered a handful and hurled it at the retreating boy. Frank ducked out through the door. Some of the shit got him, the rest splattered against the wall.

"Cheeky young bugger!" The sound of the door shook the wall. Rang wiped his hands clean on the straw, then finished the job on his pants.

Bess moved closer and lay her hand on his arm. "The boy was interrupting something." The wind was picking up strength outside and rattled a loose sheet of iron on the roof. "I got news, Rang. I think I'm pregnant!" The tears came and she threw herself into in his arms. Rang didn't know what to do with his dirty hands, so he just used them anyway.

"But how?" He didn't know what to say, "We barely did it!"

"It seems we did it enough." She shook against his chest "Did you mean what you said that day? About marring me?"

Rang was still lost for words. He hadn't really considered marriage. It was not one of those things a man thought about. And there were so many problems in this. "Of course I'll marry you!" He had no money and he felt only half a man nowadays. What would the old mother think? She'd probable kill him. If Nell didn't do it first. Or Harry. Maybe George would understand…"What else could we do?"

Outside there was the sound of horses. Charley and Jock were coming down from the mountain. There never seemed to be much time alone to settle these things. That was the trouble with the world. Never enough time for anything.

It surprised Bess how well Nell took the news. Perhaps Nell had been giving a lot of thought to the matter. She'd said some rough things to her sister. A lot of rough things. They had never been close as far as sisters go, and they were in no ways alike. Nell loved the outside life of a man. She loved competing with men. She loved competing with anybody, including herself.

She had only slept with Rang once. That night in McGovern's hut. Rang thought they were an item after that, but Nell held him at bay, more of a game than anything else. The strange thing about Nell was that she was really a prude. Despite her wild personality and her love of the outdoors, and the fact that she really enjoyed to taunt men, she was really a prude at heart.

Her sister was always a gentle soul. She loved everybody and she loved her books. Nell resented that. But she knew this was wrong and someway deep inside her, she felt a little sorry for the little things she had missed out on herself. She had been hard with Bess, but found it difficult to admit this. Saying she was sorry was very hard to do.

She hugged her sister, probably for the first time in her life. "I'm so glad for you sis. Honest I am." She felt a lot of other strange thoughts too, run through her mind. "I guess I said a lot of rough things to you the other day. And I was wrong. Jealous I guess. You and Rang were always right for one another."

Bess was crying softly in her arms.

She went on, "I certainly didn't treat him right!" There were a few strange tears in her eyes, "I wish you all the luck in the world honey. I really do." She patted her sisters stomach, "We Trasks certainly breed well. Dad would be proud of you!"

They were married at the old homestead a month later, or rather outside the old homestead under a stand of mountain ash overlooking the valley.

The only blemish on the whole thing was Emily. Nobody had told her Bess was pregnant. She only found out when Harry brought her up from Ashburn a few days before the wedding.

Bess's condition was quite obvious by then. Emily was stunned and disgusted at the sight of the girl. She moved around the kitchen with her mouth a little open, in a daze, shifting pots and pans aimlessly into the sink. Then she sank quietly into a chair holding her head in her hands.

Not her own daughter? Her little helper! Nell perhaps-Anything was possible with Nell. And George was bad enough, but he was at least a man. But Bess? Anyone but Bess!

Later when she finally got Bess alone in the bedroom she let all her feelings spill out, "Your father and I never considered such a thing before we were well married!" She choked out the words "He never even saw me with my clothes off in our whole married life!" She tried to hold back her rage. "It's a sin you know." She wanted to hold her daughter in her arms but could not bring herself to do it. "What will the minister think? What will all the neighbours think?"

Bess had been expecting much more, "We don' have any neighbours, Ma." She said dryly.

So that was it.

Bess had sewn her own wedding dress, one to fit the baby bump, but the workmanship was still something to behold.

Harry had never seen his sister so radiant.

Rang stood awkwardly beside his bride, uncomfortable, scrubbed clean wearing a new suit, high collared shirt and tie he had found somewhere. George had brought the Methodist minister by sulky up from Omeo. A tall stiff man called Brady, who was quick to notice the growing bump in Bess's stomach. He gave it a quick, disapproving look but went about his business just the same.

The food that Bess had slaved with for the past month was laid out on tables, and handmade trestles beneath the trees. The food was magnificent, she'd practically done the whole wedding on her own. But Bess was like that. No seat on a horse. No good with cattle. But capable at all other things.

She stood beside her man, heavily pregnant but proud, radiant in a way nobody had seen her before, outside the old homestead on King's spur.

Chapter 53

It would be the most expensive bull to ever pass through the Bairnsdale saleyards. Harry was leaning through the rails as the last bid hung in the air. "What do you think?"

Rang stood beside him, chewing on a piece of matchstick. "I think it's way too dear."

But Harry badly wanted the magnificent Hereford bull displayed in the yard before him, so he threw in the final bid, and with forty miles to travel back to Ashford, too far to drive the bull alone, he bought a dozen aged but well-bred cows to walk with him.

"George's going to kill us," Rang mused as they trailed the cattle through the dust.

"Don't I know it. Nell won't be happy either. We're already up to our ears in debt, but this bull will do wonders for our breeding stock. Price is off because of the war, but things will come back when it's over, you'll see. The whole thing will take time though, so we'll have to be patient."

They rode along in silence for a while, Harry watching the rise and fall of the bull's magnificent rump, almost having a fit when the animal stumbled on loose gravel. A buggy pulled to the side of the road to watch them pass as the news had already spread far and wide about the price 'young Trask' had paid for the prize bull. There were three other incidents like that before they reached Ashburn.

Harry's mind had plenty of time to wander aimlessly as they rode along.

"Rang," he mused. "That's an unusual name. Where did you come by that?"

Rang screwed up his face. "I was christened Harvey. But nobody called me that. The last name is Bell, so I've been Rang for as long as I can remember."

Harry laughed. "You don't look like a Harvey." He studied the rump of the bull. "Lord Harvey—that's what he'll be called. Lord Harvey!"

The drive to Ashburn took two days, camping at night in a stock reserve beside the road. When they finally reached the property, Frank was enlisted to help cut out the thirty best breeding cattle, all white-faced, to run with the new bull. "We might as well keep him busy for the winter—maybe he'll even pay for his keep."

"That bull will have to work many winters to pay for that much keep," Rang muttered dryly.

So they left Frank in charge for the winter, threatening to kill him if anything happened that might harm the bull.

As they rode back into the mountains, Harry found time to plan his defence against George and Nell. He thought it needed to be a good defence.

Chapter 54

Back at the homestead on the high plains, Harry sat beside Clara in front of the fire, his boots in the hearth, almost singeing the leather from the soles. Although he had always lived in the mountains, he never handled the cold easily. He held a mug of black tea in his hands, speaking idly into the fire.

"You know we used the same door from the old house to build this place. That's it there in the front." He nodded to the doorway.

"That's the one Ruben Craye kicked in the night they beat up the old man. Jock Hoolahan wanted to chuck the door away, but I fixed it up again. My mother sat in this very spot when she held the Craye's off during that first winter."

Clara sat sleepily beside him in front of the fire.

"So you've kept the history intact. I suppose the old place had many stories to tell."

"Yeah, I guess it had. This is still the old fireplace, you know. We built the new house around it."

The tea cooled in their hands as the snow built up outside, covering the huge woodpile beside the front door, beating softly against the windows.

When the weather permitted that winter, Harry spent a great deal of time breaking a new horse, a powerful gelding, sired by the same wild stallion that Emanuel had bought from Rang all those years before. He knew the stallion sired the horse by the thumb-sized indentation in the base of the neck.

The horse was hard in the mouth and difficult to break, but sure-footed with a fine bone structure. Harry grew very fond of the animal during the cold months of winter and enjoyed the challenge of quietening and bonding with it. He felt the gelding would develop into the best horse he had ever owned and, because he was hard in the mouth, called the horse Emanuel.

Clara spent her part of that first winter under Harry's watchful gaze, learning to ride well, with her legs astride the saddle, like a true mountain woman, Harry said. He watched her so closely in fact, that he reminded her of an old mother hen.

Spring, when the cattle were driven up from the low country. Ashburn, overstocked for a few months, had been eaten bare. Harry had been away from his new wife for almost a fortnight and had missed her terribly. They had lived in one another's pockets for the entire Winter.

Clara stood at the front door watching the herd coming out of the timber after the long climb up from the river, passing close by the homestead before spreading out to taste the soft new grass of the high plains. She watched the riders coming out of the mist and at last saw her husband, trailing the obstinate, slow-moving, Hereford bull.

"Keep him close and cut out forty of the best white-faced cattle to keep him amused." Harry called to Frank.

George and Nell didn't take their young brother's orders kindly, still finding it hard to forgive him for paying so much for the bull.

"We'll move him and his harem up towards Hotham tomorrow. Try to keep 'em apart so the other bulls don't raid his lot!"

Clara watched all this with a satisfied smile, before throwing herself into his arms. One week apart was a long time. She patted her stomach wearing the same satisfied smile.

"I've got a surprise for you, Harry my love. Old Lord Harvey might have some competition before this summer is through!"

Chapter 55

The men from the Craye run paused at midday at the old hut, high up on the Bogong high plains. The hut had been abandoned for a few years, and now a large limb lay across the roof. After looking inside, they decided to boil the billy in a sheltered spot by an outcrop of rock outside.

Henry was now fully convinced that they were losing cattle. The suspicion had been in his mind for quite a while but when he noticed the white faced heifer with a curiously twisted right horn was missing, the suspicion turned to fact. He sat on his heels drawing a map in the dust with a stick, planning the next move with his men while the billy boiled.

Albert took himself off into the trees while the others sat around talking.

Athol Creed, the man with the pockmarked face, had been with the Craye outfit for many years. He got up to stretch his legs, then wandered inside the tumbledown building, turning things over with his boot. He stepped back suddenly when he turned over a piece of corrugated iron and found a red-bellied black snake lying beneath it. The snake was slow moving and, although it was only mid-April, was about to go into the winter hibernation. Athol ran outside then pulled his stirrup leather free from his saddle, then swung it at the slow moving reptile. He had to make a few attempts to succeed as the stirrup swung unevenly. He wished that he had found a stick. Carrying the smashed and still squirming reptile outside, he threw it among the feet of the cattlemen. He was surprised at the reaction he got.

One said, "Jeez, don't let that thing near Albert. He'll freak. Can't stand the things!"

That sowed the seeds in Athol's mind. It was sometimes hard to amuse yourself on the mountains, so he picked up the snake and curled it around in Albert's saddlebag.

Albert came out of the timber, still hitching his trousers, the braces still around his waist. He was slow moving like the snake and looked as if he needed

195

more sleep. Albert always looked that way. When he wandered over to his horse, his hand groped around in the saddlebag for quite a while before the reaction came. He flung the dead reptile thirty yards into the bushes and let out a scream that echoed around the mountain peaks.

Athol and his mate almost split their sides, but Henry was not amused. Although he often despised his slow-witted brother, he didn't like others taking liberties with him. Of course Albert was big enough to ring Athol's neck with one hand had he wished. But the thought would never enter his simple mind.

Henry tossed the dregs of his tea in the dry grass and began to mount up.

"Alright, that's enough!" He roared. "Try anything else smart on my brother and you can draw your time!" With that he spurred his mount up the incline.

They crossed the divide and rode down onto the Dargo side, still finding no sign of missing cattle. It was then that they saw Nell and Harry working a small mob out on the plain. Henry drew up by a stand of snow gum, looking down at the scene.

"Now that's some bit of ass," he said, eyes all over Nell. "Too bad she's a Trask."

Usually Henry would have stayed well clear of the Trasks, but he wanted to check their cattle, so they rode down towards them.

"A good day to you gentlemen and lady," Henry greeted them jovially, tipping his hat to Nell.

"A good day to you too," said Harry uneasily. He was deeply suspicious when Henry Craye was in a jovial mood.

Henry ran his eye over the cattle from a distance.

"I'm worried because we're losing cattle," he said. "We been looking for any sign."

"Well, you won't find any here. You're welcome to look through this mob if you please."

"No, no nothing like that. We just thought you may have been losing some too. There's been a lot of funny business up here in the past. Been very quiet lately, but maybe that was too good to last!"

"Well, we haven't noticed any missing yet, but we'll know for sure after the muster next month. If we find any of your cattle then we'll let you know."

"That's all I ask." Henry was unusually cooperative and this made Harry very uneasy. Perhaps, he thought, this would be a good time to mention the lease.

"Look Henry, I hate to bring it up, but there seems to be a misunderstanding about the way the leases have been worked in the past. Nell and I been going over the Parish maps, and it seems that parcel of land over by McGregor's is really ours. We should run right down to the river."

Henry's face darkened. The parcel of land he was talking about took in the Gap and the fine sloping hillside that ran down to the river. "We been working that land for nigh on forty years. Nobody queried it before!"

"Maybe," Nell thought her brother might need help. "But nobody bothered to check the map before."

"Don't take our word for it. Check it yourself," said Harry.

They could see Henry chewing his lip, turning his horse in a circle as he regained control. He knew it had been a mistake to come near these shits of people.

"I'll certainly do that!" But they could see by the way he took the news, Henry Craye had already known about the land. Most likely old Ruben had discussed it with his sons many times before.

So he nodded curtly, turned his mount and rode away with his men.

Chapter 56

They rode down from the high plains just before dark.

Darkness fell early in the late autumn, so they worked by the light of a lantern unsaddling their horses in the stables. The lantern hung from a peg on the wall. Nell was rubbing down the foreleg of her pony with a cloth as Rang turned his horse loose in the yard with a slap on the rump. He came over and stood behind Nell.

"Thought I'd better tell you that me and Bess are moving on. Going to Queensland."

Nell froze, bending down, the cloth around the horse's fetlock.

"Why, you can't do that. You're part of the family now!"

"I'm not you know. The rest of you got a share of the land up here. I'm just a blow-in. Bess and I gotta make our own way."

"Bess has got a share. And why Queensland? That's a hell of a long way to go-and hot!"

"Year, hot. And won't I love it. They say there's plenty of opportunities up there too. Places where you can get a grant if you just clear the land, they say. It's one way for a man to get a start."

Nell went back to her job with little enthusiasm. She was used to having Rang around. It suddenly struck her that she would miss the man more than she would have expected.

"How about Bess? Wouldn't it be a little rough on her. Especially in the condition she's in."

Rang bucketed chaff into the hollowed out log that served as a trough. The horse nuzzled the chaff and blew into it.

"We won't go till after the baby comes. I thought we'd take off early next year."

There was silence for a while.

"What do the others think of that?"

"We haven't told anyone else yet. Thought I'd let you know first."

He moved over and stood behind her, resting both hands gently on her shoulders. He still felt strange feelings for Nell.

"There's another reason we should go. Bess is a wonderful girl and the last thing I want to do is hurt her."

Nell froze, twisting strands of the pony's mane between her fingers.

"I still think about you, Nell. I know I shouldn't, but I damn well do!"

Nell's fingers worked through the mane of the pony. It worried her that sometimes at night she still thought of Rang. Sometimes even at work, seeing him in the saddle. She always imagined that Rang would just be there.

"I guess it would be the right thing to move on. But I'll miss you. God I think I'll miss you!"

She pushed the pony away, slapped him on the rump and began bucketing chaff into the trough.

"Yes, it would be best if you went. Sooner rather than later, I'd say."

As they walked through the darkness back to the homestead, there was a tear in the corner of her eye.

Nell hoped he didn't see it.

Chapter 57

Charley Nash was always a great authority on the weather. He had the knack, or always thought he had. The ache in his bones told him things, so did the behaviour of the birds and the ants and the fact that he had lived through all the seasons so many times before. He crouched on his haunches, back against the railing fence of the stockyard as he built a smoke. "We're in for a bad winter lads, mark my words. A bad change is coming!" He ran a rough tongue along the cigarette paper. "We should start the muster soon to bring the cattle down to the low country."

"Bullshit!" George leaned against the pommel of his saddle. "It's way too early yet."

"I remember the year of 'eighty seven. Snow on the ground two foot deep and only the end of April. Blizzards, Lord there were blizzards. People lost a heap of calves that winter!"

"There's still good feed up here. You know how we get eaten out down below before the end of winter."

"It was just like this in '87!" The air was crisp, the sky clear.

"Frankly, I don't see it, Charley." Harry was busy building his own smoke. He glanced at the sky and could see no sign of the change. Still, the springs had opened up strongly on the mountain. "But I have to admit you've seen more summers than I have. Perhaps it would be a good idea to start the muster. Get the cattle close then see how things turn out."

George was a little tired of the way his young brother was trying to take control latterly. Still, there was no doubting the old man's instinct. He was usually right. "I still think you lot are panicking. But I expect we could get 'em close, just in case."

George liked to hedge his bets…

They rode along, trailing a herd of about two hundred cattle. Harry, his blue cattle dog and Charley at the rear, Rang at one wing, Nell at the other. Whenever they came close, Charley's voice ran on, "Snow three feet deep everywhere. Lost hundreds of cattle—" He was getting worse. But Harry did notice the sky was darkening. A wind had sprung and there was a bight in the air.

Angus, the blue-healer swept backwards and forward, his nose just a few inches behind the cattle's hooves. Harry never went anywhere without his dog.

When they moved the herd over a rise the wind hit them full in the face. It carried a little sleet and it was difficult to see through. Well, in the distance they could see the old cabin known as Grant's hut. It was very small with a rough lean-to at the back, almost hidden behind a strong stand of timber. This was to be the meeting point with George and his crew, who were mustering the run to the north.

The sleet stung Harry's eyes and he could see a large mob of cattle milling about in the clearing to the left of the hut. Charley stood in his stirrups for a better view. "That's not George. I think we have the Craye outfit sharing our cabin. That's old Henry on that hammer headed gelding he rides. I can tell how he sits a horse, all slumped over!" Harry was always envious of the old man's eyes.

"I don't mind sharing a hut with another crew. Especially if they keep their peace. We must be close to their run anyhow. I think I'll ride down and have a chat to friend Henry. I want to keep in good with that lot anyway!"

He turned his horse down the hill, then stopped and came back. "Look, George should be along soon. If you see him, ask if he picked up that bull I bought. I thought we would have found him on our side!"

He turned and spurred into the wind, for his meeting with Henry Craye.

"Afternoon, Henry!" He bellowed into the wind.

"Afternoon," Henry didn't know which way this conversation was going.

"I don't mind sharing our cabin on a night like this. Providing we can keep the cattle apart!"

"It's a matter of opinion who's cabin this is, young feller."

"Well, that's as it might be. But I thought you might have picked up a few of our cattle in your muster. I know we got a few of yours." Henry was about to bristle, when he noticed Nell riding towards them.

"Maybe we have a few. Your men are welcome to ride through 'em and take a look. Meanwhile we'll have a pick through yours." He nodded politely to Nell. "Do it in the morning if you like. Weather's closin' in a bit now!"

"I'd rather do it right now Henry, if you don't mind. Clear the whole thing up."

"Suit yourself!"

It was skilled work. In the driving wind, they forced each mob to circle. Some riders forcing the mob to the left while others rode against the flow, edging the foreign cattle to the outside perimeters before cutting them out. They worked the two mobs like this until both groups were satisfied with their work. Nell was greatly surprised just how cooperative Henry Craye could be. The man always kept people off-guard.

There was almost a blizzard blowing by the time the work had finished. The Trasks moved their cattle across the plains to a sheltered grove of snow gums, where they planned to hold them for the night. George and Frank arrived with a further three hundred just before dark. They boxed the two mobs by the snow gums then set out pickets for the night. The Crayes moved their cattle further to the east. With two riders holding the mob fast, the remainder gathered under an uneasy truce in the small log cabin to shelter for the night. The men left outside to brave the elements would be relieved every two hours.

A fire was soon built in the corrugated iron fireplace, throwing the only light in the small log cabin, while an old black pot was set among the flames to boil. The rough timber door, buffered by the wind, continually blew open, until someone jammed a heavy log against it.

Harry and Nell carried saddlebags and blankets to the end of the small room where they settled down to eat cold meat and damper, covered in the treacle that they always carried in their saddlebags. The Crayes were first to the log hut and had lit the fire, so Harry thought they'd better let them have access to the fire. The two groups sat on their blankets, eyeing one another from different ends of the small room. A sheet of loose iron rattled on the roof.

Harry knew Henry, his brother Albert and Athol Creed, the man with a pock-marked face who had worked at the Craye holding for as long as he could remember. The space was so limited that they were almost on top of one another, so Harry thought that this was not the time to mention the disputed land he and Nell had found on the Parish map.

Laying back on his blanket, he spoke quietly to Nell. Somehow, despite the age difference, Harry seemed to have taken charge.

"We still haven't found Lord Harvey, though he was sighted up this way a week ago. Tomorrow at first light, providing there is a first light, I'll take Charley and head up towards the headwaters of the Dargo. The bull has to be up there somewhere. You and the rest of the crew start back with the mob towards the homestead."

The wind blew in between the cracks of the log walls and the sheet of loose iron rattled on the roof.

After he was well rested and warm again, Harry thought it time to relieve Frank. When he lifted the log from the door, wind and snow buffeted in. Albert Craye and the man with the pock-marked face decided to go as well while the door was open. When Henry threw the log back in place after they had gone, he had to use all his weight to force the door shut.

His eyes wandered over Nell in the flickering light, and she realised for the first time that she was alone with the man. She hoped Frank would come back real soon.

"Now ain't this cosy" Henry offered a tin mug and held a half empty bottle of rum. "You like a little something to keep out the cold?"

Nell was surprised at the gentleness of his tone.

"No thank you Mr Craye."

"Drop the 'Mr' business. My name's Henry. No need not to be friends. We live on the same mountain, have done for years."

"Things have never been that friendly between the two families in the past. I seem to remember you and your clan beat my father to a pulp in the beginning of it all. That's not exactly what you'd call friendly."

Henry decided to take more of the rum himself. "All in the past, that was. Wasn't my idea anyway. Frankly, I tried to stop it. The old man just settled us on to your dad that night. But that's all in the past!"

"Maybe," said Nell.

Henry sidled over to squat on Harry's blanket. "That's too long ago to hold a grudge, anyway. No need at all, not to be friendly now." He had yellow teeth and a crooked smile. "You know, I've always fancied you a bit, Nell."

The skin crawled on the back of her neck.

"Ever since I saw you working your cattle out on the plain. I even write a poem about you," He fished around in all the pockets of his oilskin coat, and the coat beneath.

"Should have it here somewhere. Writin' helps me pass the time on cold nights."

It was amazing what he found in the pockets of his coats. An old pocket knife, pencil stubs, even a broken comb. "Probably didn't think I wrote poetry, did you?"

"No, you never cease to amaze me, Henry Craye. Most people up here on the mountain can't even read, let alone write poetry."

"Don't like to mention it myself, neither, lest people don't think you're a real man."

He proffered a crumpled piece of yellow paper. "Don't ever underestimate a man, lest you get to know him."

Nell lay propped on one elbow, wishing Frank would come. It was hard to move further away from the man without being obvious.

"Go on, read it," he urged, thrusting the crumpled piece of paper into her face.

Nell smoothed the paper so that she could make out the words. Henry wrote with a surprisingly good hand, but she read the words with difficulty in the dancing light, the pencil smudged in places.

"Is this supposed to be me?" She was a little startled and very embarrassed. "I'm nothing at all like that!"

"That's the way I see you, Nell." He looked down at his hands, turning them over in the light. "I think if we got together, you and me, we'd really be something. My old man won't last much longer and you're the brains of your outfit. Why someday we could own half the country up here!"

Nell came quickly to her feet, the blanket tangling about her legs. "Just what are you suggesting, Henry Craye? Good God, don't you remember I was there when you caught up with your wife?"

"That was nothin'... That was another thing and you don't know nothin' about it!" He had been so enraged at the time that he had completely forgotten Nell was there. "I ain't suggesting nothing. Just we should be friends for now. No harm in that. No harm in being friends!"

"You're old enough to be my father, heavens forbid... and I loathe the sight of you!"

"You ain't no spring chicken yourself, Nell." This touched a raw spot. She twisted the paper into a ball and flung it into his face.

"That's what I think of your stinking poetry, if that's what it's supposed to be!" She stumbled around him to the door, straining to remove the log.

"Here girl, no need to carry on like that!" Nell was having trouble with the log.

"Henry Craye, if there was no one else in the world, no other toad or snake, I wouldn't have you!"

The log finally came free and the door flew open.

"Who the hell do you think you are, you snotty bitch?"

"Go dress up in girl's clothes!" Nell screamed as she stumbled into the storm.

Henry's face twisted, black with rage, as he tore the paper into little strips.

Chapter 58

Henry Craye was still in a dark mood when he stepped out of the hut at first light the next morning. Three of his men were still inside finishing their breakfast. "Get saddled up and move those cattle!" he bellowed into the wind. "The faster we get away from these Trask shits the better!"

The wind howled through the trees carrying sleet and a little snow with it. The sheet of loose iron still rattled on the roof.

At about mid-morning, they drove the herd over a crest and down into a long valley, following a granite ridge to the left that ran right down to the river. Half way down the valley a gorge cut through the ridge, leading to an old, rough trail that followed a crocked spur down some two thousand feet into a valley below. The place was known as the Gap. It was said that miners often used the pass in the old days to gain the next valley. The gorge was a hundred yards wide with sheer walls thirty feet high, a natural shelter where the Crayes often worked their cattle. They had thrown a rail fence across the north end of the gorge making a perfect corral. Henry called a halt so that they could boil the billy under the shelter of the cliff face. Then he noticed something wrong with the rail fence at the far end of the gorge. One of the rails was not set in straight He spurred his horse up to the fence and saw the earth churned up by the hooves of many cattle. He threw down the rails then rode carefully to the edge of the cliff face where he pulled the hammer headed gelding to a halt. In front of him, the track followed a crocked spur down the mountain side into the valley some two thousand feet below. The way was heavily timbered and the track swallowed up by fog, laying like a swirling white cloud. Henry felt the full force of the wind and driving snow on his face as he circled his horse, chewing his bottom lip. He rode back to the camp.

"I think we may have found where the damned cattle have gone. You, Athol and Frank and Jacko, come with me!" He wheeled his horse around, feeling better than he had all day, "Albert, you stay with the cattle. Look alive men, you can drink your bloody tea later!" There was fire in his belly as he spurred his horse down the track.

The track was dangerously steep as it wound down between the timber. Athol was the first to catch up, his horse sliding on the loose shale, sometimes almost sliding to his haunches. The snow was falling heavily now and was already coating the earth. "Gees' boss, you really think anyone drove cattle down here?"

"Well, them tracks weren't done by mice!"

They skidded and slid down into the fog. They could barely see but in the protection of the timber the wind had dropped. At last, they broke through the blanket of fog onto the valley floor. The wind was just a low moan above them.

They made their way up the valley, weaving between the timber. The fog closed in at times making it almost impossible to see, then lifted again to make everything clear. The snow settled softly now and there was no wind. The silence was eerie. This was a wild and unsettled area, the habitat of wild horses and stray cattle. A man named Willis once owned a track of this land. But that was well before Henry's time. He had only ridden down into the valley twice in his lifetime.

Now well into the Willis run, picking their way carefully between the timber, the fog cleared for a moment and they caught sight of three men and as many dogs, driving a small herd of cattle up the valley. The Trask bull was with them, lagging and stubborn. Henry recognised the animal at once.

Silently Henry drew his rifle out of the scabbard.

The attack caught the thieves by complete surprise. Four men, charging with rifles drawn. They scattered in panic, two spurring their horses into the scrub as if shot from a gun, while the last man circled his horse, bewildered, unsure whether to fight or run. The dogs circled too. Henry covered the man with his rifle.

"Get down off your horse you thieving bastard!"

The man dismounted, angry and unsure. He wore a wild beard and heavy eyebrows that met in the middle. His eyes flashed like an insane man. He wore no coat, but a blanket wrapped about his shoulders to hold out the cold.

"I know you, don't I? Bloody German or something, as I recall?"

"I ain't German, I was born here," the man said in a heavy accent. "Born in Hawker, South Australia. Folks had a farm there. We weren't doing nothing wrong mister. We found the cattle." As he uttered the words, he realised how ridiculous they sounded.

Craye's men returned from the scrub empty handed. There was little hope of catching the other two in this terrain when they knew where they were going.

"You still sound like a German, but you just weren't fast enough either." Henry waved his rifle. "Bad luck."

He ran his eye over the chestnut mare Haselburger was riding, throwing itself about as if it were not broken in properly as yet. A sturdy looking beast. Henry liked the set of the legs under it.

"That's not a bad looking horse you're riding. Where did you steal that?"

The man cursed Henry and stared down at his boots.

"I'll take that off your hands. You can travel on foot." He turned to Athol.

"Round up that mob if you can find 'em in the scrub. Take Jacko and work 'em back up the track. We'll follow this piece of shit back to where they were heading. They're probably got a lot more penned up back there."

He ordered the man to dismount, then trading horses, leading the hammer headed mare, prodded the bearded man along.

"Lead the way, cattle thief!"

"There ain't no more cattle, honest this was all we got!"

"Like hell it is. Move along and, for your own sake, don't give me a chance to blow your bloody head off!"

They travelled some miles up the valley, picking their way between the timber, Henry setting a fast pace, prodding the man along with the rifle barrel. Haselburger stumbled from time to time, and Henry prodded him with the gun and nudged him with the shoulder of his horse. At last, they came to a clearing in the trees where a tumble-down log cabin stood with a wisp of smoke rising from the chimney. Behind the cabin were rough and broken yards, propped up with sticks, barely good enough to hold the cattle that were penned inside.

"Check out the house, there's probably more of the scum in there!"

He had barely uttered the words when a man with braces down about his waist, wearing no boots, broke from the door and sprinted wildly, into the scrub.

On horseback, Craye's man could not match his speed through the timber and between the rocks. Up a cliff face he went, scrabbling in the shale, his feet leaving a trail of blood, still he didn't slow. After a while, the Craye man came back empty handed.

"He's like a bloody jackrabbit, boss!"

"Well, looks like you're it," Henry spoke grimly to his unfortunate captive. He unwound his whip carefully and slid the gun back into its scabbard.

"What do you think your gonna do?" Haselburger pleaded. "We'll give back the bloody cattle. A lot of 'em ain't yours anyway, so you'll do alright on the deal. No need for the police!"

"No we won't worry about the police." Henry unfurled the whip. His first strike spun the man around and brought him to his knees. The blanket fell free.

"Christ, let up!" Haselburger screamed.

Henry was merciless. The whip rose and fell. The crack of it reverberated around the valley. The shirt was torn away from the man as he wheeled and stumbled, and when he ran the whip followed and brought him back to ground. He tried to cover his face, but this was useless. The whip rose and fell, drawing blood and tearing the shirt to ribbons.

Haselburger lay whimpering on the ground as Henry's horse circled him. The whip tore at him.

"That's enough boss, you're killing him!"

"So what!"

But by now Henry was exhausted. He folded the bloodied whip and wound it around his saddle horn. The man lay twitching in the snow caked mud.

"Turn those cattle loose and take the spare horses. We'll take the lot. I don't expect this scum will go to the police!"

Henry rode over to search the cabin. He kicked the abandoned boots into the fireplace, emptied the contents of a kerosene lamp on the floor and dropped a burning log into the liquid. Haselburger was painfully regaining his feet, hugging his torn shoulders, slobbering in pain as Henry rode past, the cabin roaring in flames behind him.

It was well into the afternoon when they caught the other cattle. The Trask bull was surly and giving trouble. He resented the whip and charged at Athol, almost dismounting the man. "Leave the bastard!" bellowed Henry. "And cut out the rest of the Trask cattle, we ain't down here to wipe their bloody noses. Let 'em find their own bloody cattle." They began the hazardous climb up to the high plains. The snow was falling heavily before they were halfway to the top.

The cattle stumbled and slipped on the loose stones, bellowing, protesting between the rocks. Henry was riding the new horse, a powerful beast, only half broken. It shied once and drove his foot against a rocky outcrop. The pain was so intense that Henry was sure that he had broken something. Working through the pain, the afternoon was fading before they reached the summit.

"We'll hold 'em here until morning, men."

He sat on a rock to removed his boot. His toes were crushed and his boot full of blood. He rocked on his rump and nursed the foot. Henry had not had a good day.

Chapter 59

Although he hated to admit such a thing, Harry was beaten. They had searched the marshland that was the headwaters of the Dargo river, then backtracked much of the area George had already mustered with still no sign of the missing cattle. Harry did not quite trust his older brothers mustering. He felt he didn't quite have his mind on things sometimes.

"It's got me beat, Charley. Cattle can't just disappear!" He slumped dejectedly in the saddle while he built a cigarette, Angus the blue cattle dog settled between the horse's feet. He was almost out of tobacco. The wind tore the flame from the matches. Nothing seemed to go right. "Only seen the bull some two weeks ago." But somehow it was impossible to give up. "Look, it's no good both of us wasting our time out here. You best head back to the others, they're probably almost to the homestead by now. I'll swing up to the left fork for another look. Probably be too late to catch up then, so I'll spend the night in the hut and catch up tomorrow."

"Just you be careful boss. Nasty weather to be out here on your own."

"I'm a big boy now Charley. I paid a fuckin' lot of money for that damn bull!"

Charley had just cut the tracks where the Craye's had shifted their cattle that morning. The snow had almost obliterated the tracks but the old man's eyes could still pick them up. He paused for a while in deep thought. What if the cattle were down in that area, towards the gap. They Crayes would be well gone by now, but what if they had picked up Lord Harvey on the way through?

So he followed the tracks down towards the Gap.

But to his surprise, the Crayes were not gone. Charley could see their camp fire through the driving snow.

Henry Craye sat hunched on a rock examining his foot when Charley rode into the camp. Henry glanced up with a puzzled look on his face. The foot was a mess.

"What the Hell are you doing out here old man?"

Charley could see the cattle penned up towards the back of the gorge. The rest of the men milled around; They were curious to know what Charley was doing here as well.

"We're still missing that Hereford bull. Thought you maybe picked him up on the way through."

Henry's face darkened as he held his injured foot and glared up at the old man.

"I've about had a gut full of you lot saying I've stolen your cattle." His voice was low. "But I do know where your bloody bull is and a heap of your cattle!" He tossed his head towards the North. "They're down there in that valley where Willis had his run. That German scum had 'em—along with a hundred head of mine." Henry went back to his foot. "But we dealt with him. You're welcome to go down there and get yours. We didn't feel like wet nursin' you lot. Time you did your own damn work!" The foot hurt like Hell. "Course you're probably too damned old to ride down there. Should be home riding a rocking chair I expect!"

"You lousy bugger. You mean you brought your own cattle up and left ours down there?"

Henry was on his feet in an instant, clutching at the horses bit. "I'm sick and tired of being insulted. Piss off out of my camp!" Henry was surprised at how fast the old man sprang out of the saddle. Charley was old, but he moved like a fighting cock. However Henry was a much bigger man. He had the height. And despite the fact there was no science in the punch, the fist travelled down taking a large part of Charley's face with it. His jaw seemed to just slide down. When he came too, Charley found himself with his backside against the cliff face, a dazed look on his face as he examined the broken tooth he held between his thumb and forefinger.

"Now get the Hell out of my camp. And next time don't start something you can't finish old man!"

Charley's horse was backing away, reins trailing in snow. When he groped towards it, the horse turned away then broke into a trot. Charley stumbled after it like a drunken man. He could hear laughter behind his back.

It was night now. The snow hit him in the face as the horse put more distance between them. Charley's legs didn't seem to work right while the blood froze on his chin. It was only then, as he staggered through the snow, the horse lost from sight, that Charley knew he was in trouble.

Angus, the blue cattle dog was the first to find him. Bounding like an Angel out of the night. The old man knew that Harry wouldn't be far away. Then sure enough, there he was, leaning forwards in the wind, leading Charley's horse.

"What are you doing on foot, old timer?" Harry was so relieved to find the old man safe that he tried some kind of humour. "It's too bad a night for a walk! Did you get thrown?"

Charley was about beaten as he clutched feebly at the horses reins, then hung against the saddle. "No I've never been thrown. It was that bastard Henry Craye. Ten years ago I would have had him!"

Harry could not see the face, but he could hear by the voice that something was wrong.

"I found your horse back aways and followed the tracks. Thought you'd have been back at the homestead by now. What did Henry Craye have to do with it?"

In halting breath, Charley told his story.

"Don't worry about Henry, we'll deal with him later. But you found the bull. Good man!" Harry found himself more elated by the news of the bull than saddened by what had befallen his old mate. Harry felt a little ashamed of himself. He climbed down to help the old man back into his saddle. He was surprised at how little Charley weighed, "You did good, old timer. You did real good!"

They turned back into the wind. "We'll head back to the hut and I'll make you a cup of tea. Haven't got much tucker left, but I've got tea!"

Chapter 60

Henry was in a foul mood when he returned to his homestead block. He could not fit his damaged foot back into the boot, and instead had bandaged it as best he could. The bandage was now unravelling and trailed in a bloody line from the stirrup. Albert and the others were trailing behind with the cattle.

From the chair on his back veranda Ruben watched his son ride by. He didn't move far from the chair nowadays. "Where's my cattle?"

"They're coming." Henry didn't stop.

"What happened to your foot?"

"Mind your own damned business!"

He stumbled into his cabin and lit a fire to heat water, then bathed the foot, grimacing in pain, as he poured iodine on to the wound. He wrapped the foot again and settled it into an old and well-worn slipper. He didn't know where the slipper came from. When he remounted his new horse he rode back passed his father's house. Ruben met him out in front, resting on a stick.

"Where did you get that horse?" Ruben noticed the foot but didn't comment on it.

"From the thieving bastard who stole our cattle. But he won't try that again, mark my words. I fixed the Trasks too. The thieves had that bloody bull they paid a fortune for. Won't be worth a plugged nickel when they get him back!"

"I don't want more trouble with the Trasks!"

Henry had taken enough for one day. Nothing he did could please the old man. The pain in his foot was intense. "Look old man, I've had enough of this shit. I work my guts out on this place all my life and for what? All I ever get is wages!"

"And that's all you're worth!" A blind rage was rising in Henry's throat.

"Your cattle. Your cattle. Never 'our' cattle. I got to wait till you die to get my share!"

"Well, you can always move on if you don't like it!"

Henry spurred his horse on and the shoulder sent the old man flying. "Then go to buggery!" Ruben raised his fist from the ground. "And don't come back!"

But as soon as he said the words he regretted them. But still, he was sure, the boy would be back.

When the cattle finally arrived, Ruben watched them go passed from his chair on the veranda. Albert saw at once that there was something wrong with his father. The old man gained his feet, his mouth moving silently, chewing his teeth.

"You alright, Pa?"

"Do I look alright, you bloody fool? Your brother near killed me—ten years ago I'd have broken his back!" The old man watched his cattle go by. "I've a mind to throw the young cur off the place when he comes back!" It was an idle threat. Albert was as strong as two men and could follow orders, but left to his own devices could barely feed himself. Without Henry, Ruben knew, the place would grind to a halt.

The weather was closing again as Henry spurred the mare through the new snow. His mouth muttering jumbled words into the wind.

God-damned old fool. 'My' cattle—have I got 'My' cattle back!

He spurred the horse's flanks.

All my life I've busted my back for the old fool. Not ever a damn thank you! Not the Trask's cattle's fault? Damn the Trasks! Look like a bloody snake or a toad, do I? Damn that snooty Trask bitch!

A limb snapped under the weight of snow, half a mile away, but the sound carried like a bullet. The mare stepped sideways, fully a yard in a single bound and Henry lost his seat. Had he been concentrating the accident would not have happened, but his thoughts were scrambled. He landed awkwardly, stunned, on his back, his left leg caught in the stirrup.

His knee seemed bent the wrong way.

The mare shied away from the shifted weight, pulling Henry along with her. The foot had slipped right through the stirrup. A boot would not have gone through, but the slipper was lost and the foot held fast. The pain of his twisted knee tore at his throat and when he cried out this caused the horse to jerk back.

"Hold-hold…whoa girl-whoa there…" The horse reeled back for a moment, then plunged down the hillside, Henry bouncing through the snow covered rocks, screaming like a child.

Then the screaming stopped. The horse reeled and turned, the twisted weight pulling the saddle off centre, dragging a useless dead weight along with it.

Through the long afternoon, through heavy snow, the horse dragged its load down the ravine, through the snow gums and snow-covered rocks. The load dragged along like a heap of rubbish, silent now, twisting and turning, trailing a track through the soft snow. The horse climbed onto the next spur, followed it down into the valley beyond. Through the long afternoon it dragged the burden along, the saddle now under the belly. It stopped for a while, turning and circling in a gully, kicking at the dead weight, then passed through a throng of bracken and thorn bushes. The body tangled, then at last pulled free.

The horse, relieved at last of its burden, floundered through the snow up the next slope, saddle still beneath the belly.

Chapter 61

The sheet of iron had blown from the roof while a dusting of snow-covered part of the floor. Harry threw the two saddles, packs and camping blankets, onto the only dry spot he could find. Charley was so spent he could hardly walk. The only light in the hut came from the open doorway and the hole in the roof, with snow drifting through it.

But there was dry wood lying by the fireplace so Harry soon had a fire burning, which lit up the place in a flickering yellow light. Then he saw the old man's face.

"Good god, man. Craye sure gave you a working over!"

Charley ran his fingers over the jaw that seemed to hang lower at one side. He found it difficult to speak. "I'll fix him next time, you bet-with a bloody pick handle!"

"You won't have to worry about next time, old timer. I'll settle that score for you, myself!"

Harry went outside for water, then slammed the door shut and jammed it with a log. He put the billy on to boil but by this time Charley had found the half empty bottle of rum in his saddle bag. "Don't worry about the tea. This 'll do just fine."

So Harry sat beside him on the blankets while they shared the rum.

"Do you think you could make your own way back to the homestead tomorrow?" Harry felt a pang of conscience, sending the old man back on his own. The cattle it seemed, meant more to him than his old friend's safety. Harry knew himself well enough to know that this was a very bad trait. But it was the way he was. He was born that way.

"Sure boss, you don't have to worry about me. I seen enough summers not to let a busted jaw stop me!"

"Well, when you get there, send Nell and Frank back to the Gap. I should have the cattle up by then. Oh, and send back a heap of tucker. I'll be starving by then!"

He prodded the fire with a stick, still feeling the prick of conscience.

"I'm going to leave at first light, but you have a good sleep in. No need at all to hurry."

The wind had died down, while snow fell softly through the hole in the roof.

He found no sign of Haselburger and his men in the valley the next morning.

Only the remains of the burned-out shack, now just a pile of rubble, still smoking.

Harry rode deeper into the valley before he found the cattle, grazing quietly, nuzzling the snow aside to find the fresh grass.

Lord Harvey, stubborn as usual had to be moved with the whip. Harry hated to use the whip on the animal, but he was fast losing patience. With the help of the blue cattle dog, he moved the small herd back down the valley. There were only thirty of them. But still he had Lord Harvey.

Cracking the whip, the dog at their heels, he forced the cattle up the perilous slope. They tried to break back at every chance, slipping and sliding on the loose shale. The whip tangled in the dense timber while the cattle bellowing, tested man and dog at every turn. The task would have been hopeless, working alone without the dog.

They had moved the mob barely halfway up the track when Angus caught a good kick in the head. He was tired and not quick enough to avoid the slashing hoof. It was quite a sickening sound, but still the dog worked on.

Late in the afternoon the end was in sight. Harry could just see where the trail broke away from the cliff face. Then the cattle turned with one last effort to break free. Harry turned the horse sharply and felt its feet give way on the loose gravel. The gelding went down, carrying Harry with it. He scrambled clear and with the help of the dog still held the cattle. The gelding regained his feet with difficulty, lame in the front leg. Harry cursed as he stumbled along, dragging the limping horse.

But Charley always said that bad things come in threes.

Angus, his loyal dog and friend, dropped dead.

Harry was stunned. The dog just lay on his side and died. A little blood ran from his ear. As close to weeping as he ever was, the man just stood there.

The cattle probably knew that he'd had enough, they scrambled up the slope and finally made the high ground. Lord Harvey leading the charge.

Harry expected.to find the rest of the crew waiting at the gap. But there was no sign of them. The cattle were already at the end of the gorge as he examined the gelding's leg. He ran his fingers over the fetlock then slowly straightened his back. "I'm sorry old friend," he spoke to the horse's face. "I guess this is the end of the line."

He looked around at the place. He could not shoot the horse here. So he lifted the reins and led the animal out of the gorge.

The cattle were almost out of sight, heading up the slope, spreading in the wrong direction. Still there was nothing he could do to head them without a horse. So Harry turned towards the homestead, for the first time in his life, beaten.

Night was closing in and it was snowing heavily. There was no sign of the cattle now as he led the limping horse along.

In the failing light, he could just make out a small gully and a stand of timber. He settled on this point and stumbled towards it. His hands were too frozen to loosen the cinch of the girth, so he removed a glove and held it in his mouth as he pulled the saddle free. He dropped the glove and didn't bother to find it. He pulled the gun from the scabbard.

"I'm sorry old friend," he spoke into the horses face, then shot it between the eyes before he had a chance to think. He turned his back as the animal fell and just stood there, tears running down his face.

This was the first time Harry had ever cried.

He tossed the gun aside, shouldered the saddle and the sleeping pack, then climbed out of the gulley without looking back. He had no reason to bring the saddle, but that was the way he was. Exhausted, hungry and freezing he stumbled towards the homestead. It was still snowing heavily.

When he could go no further, Harry found a stand of twisted snow gums. He threw the blankets down, spread them as best he could, then pulled the saddle over his head and shoulders. Cold, hungry and exhausted. Wet from the legs up, under the oilskin. It was only then, before he drifted into sleep, that the thought struck him: *I wonder if Charley made it home?*

Chapter 62

The fire was out, the door wide open when Charley awoke that morning. It was almost as cold inside the hut as it was outside. He had slept in until very late. Harry had long since gone.

Charley staggered the doorway to empty his bladder, watching the steady, warm stream cut holes in the snow. His jaw was a dull ache and he didn't feel right in the legs. He staggered back to the blankets and found the bottle with a full finger of rum in it. He finished the rum, rolled up in the blankets deciding to rest a little longer. Charley didn't awake till mid-afternoon.

In panic, he rolled his blankets and searched for his saddle. But the saddle was gone. He found it on the horse outside, tied in the rough shelter at the rear of the hut. Harry had saddled the horse for the old man so that he could get an easy start first thing in the morning. The horse had waited patiently all day.

Charley had difficulty regaining the saddle, and with one blanket wrapped around his shoulders, rode slumped forward towards the homestead.

The day was crystal clear and a heavy covering of snow covered the ground.

George had brought Rachael and the twin boys with him to the homestead on the high plains. He didn't care to leave a heavily pregnant wife alone on the mountain while they drove the herd down to the lower country.

He had lost most of his hair during the early years of his marriage and his stomach had swelled. His features that of Emanuel without the beard.

The men were gathered in the stables, preparing for the drive when the weather closed in again. Sleet spattered on the iron roof as they lay the equipment on the dirt floor. The two new hands braved the weather, holding the herd together out on the plains as the yards were not large enough to hold them.

There was a great deal of equipment to gather. Enough to load two pack animals. Chaff for the horses, food for the men. Salted meat, flour, sugar, treacle and tea, cooking utensils, tarpaulins, blankets, axes and shovels. The piles rose ever higher on the dirt floor.

George threw a bag of salt onto the pile and wondered where his damn fool brother was now.

Satisfied with their work, the men were on their way back to the homestead, hurrying against the sleet, when Charley rode out of the darkness.

While at the open fireplace of the homestead, Nell stoked the fire until the sparks flew. She was not particularly interested in the conversation at the kitchen table. The talk was all about babies. It seemed like some kind of competition among the women, comparing their bumps.

The lamp glass blackened at the centre of the table; the wick turned too high. Something smashed in the next room, probably a bedside lamp as the twins ran wildly through the house. There was a strong smell of kerosene and Nell wondered why Rachael didn't control her kids.

Why was it so hard to control kids? Nell hammered at the fire.

Rachael just drifted along while things unravelled around her, and Clara still had stars in her eyes—didn't know she was alive as yet!

Nell jammed the fire until the sparks flew. She kept her horse under control, her dogs and her cattle. Why was it so hard to control kids? Bess was still at her home on King's spur, just a little bit pregnant. All the Trask women seemed that way. They should bring Bess up here too, to make the whole thing complete.

In this weather, driving the cattle down the mountain without losing any was a thing to worry about. Not babies.

Good men had lost their lives out there in conditions like this.

The door flew open with George and Rang, trying to fit through, holding Charley up between them.

The old man slumped at the kitchen table as they all gathered around him.

"Jesus," said George, "Charley you smell like shit!"

"I don't care how the man smells," snapped Nell. "Let's get the wet clothes off him. He must be near frozen! Look at the man's face?"

"Don't you worry about my face, love. Go back out and give your fool brother a hand." He almost fell off the chair. "I should have been here hours ago. Should have been hours ago!" He was almost asleep. But in halting voice, through broken jaw, he told the story.

Chapter 63

Out on the high plains the next morning they found a horse standing still in the soft snow, with saddle hanging beneath the belly.

Nell was the first to see it. "You know the horse?" asked George.

"No, never seen him before. How about you, Rang?"

"Nope!" This hurt Rang. He thought he knew every horse on the mountain. He unhitched the saddle and let it fall to the ground. What was left of it was useless anyhow. He examined the shoulder and flank but could find no brand, so he removed the bridle and turned the animal loose. But the gelding had lost all interest in going anywhere.

"At least, it's not Harry's horse, but the rider, poor bugger, must be somewhere."

"We don't have a clue where. That animal's come miles. I expect nobody will find him before spring, when the snow melts. Maybe they won't find him then."

"Well, I guess we better leave her here and go on. Not much more we can do at this time, except tell someone about the horse soon as we can!"

The change had finally blown through and the air was clear, the sun glaring white on the plains. Finally, back towards the gap, they found Harry, a black speck in the distance staggering through the snow. He didn't seem to be walking straight, prodding himself along with the help of a stick. He had an old scarf wrapped around his lower face, unravelled and almost touching the ground. His eyebrows and eyelashes coated in snow.

He clutched at the pommel of Nell's saddle. His eyes didn't seem to function in the glare of the sun. "What took you lot so long?"

"You crazy, crazy young bugger!" was all Nell could say. She hugged her young brother. "What happened to your horse?"

Harry was completely spent, hanging on to the saddle. "I don't want to talk about it." He turned weakly towards the two men. "I found the cattle. About thirty head…and the bull. You'll find 'em back that way somewhere. Probably headed before the wind. Maybe you can still find some tracks."

"George, help your silly young brother up behind me and I'll try to get him back to the homestead before he dies on us! Then you can go look for his bloody cattle!"

"Don't worry," Rang said to Harry, circling his horse. "We'll find your cattle!"

Chapter 64

Albert found the horse struggling through belly deep snow in the late afternoon, He could see it was almost done. No saddle or bridle, but Albert knew the horse. There were many things he didn't know in life, but he knew horses.

And he knew his brother.

Everyone else said that Henry had just taken off. But Albert knew he hadn't. So he rode aimlessly through the snow, calling his brother's name.

"Henry?" The words carried away in the wind. "Henry, where the hell are you Henry?"

His voice was strangely weak for a big man. He rode on, floundering through knee-deep snow, up out of one valley onto the next plain, weaving beneath the snow gum, where sometimes a limb cracked under the gathering weight.

"Henry, where are you, Henry?" But Albert would not find his brother that day. Or the next.

In fact, his body wasn't found when the snow melted the following spring. Only two years later a group of bushwalkers found the remains in a remote, overgrown gully.

"Henry?" Albert called into the snow. "Henry?"

Chapter 65

They heated a drum of water over the open fire, filled a tub and somehow manage to get Harry's half-frozen body into it. He was much heavier than they had imagined, still shivering violently and muttering incoherently. He had passed out, on the way back to the homestead, his arms still wrapped around his big sister. But she managed to keep him there. They kept the water topped up to his chin and soaked him in it for the best part of an hour.

Moving the dead weight from the tub was the hard part. It took the three of them with the twins hindering as much as possible, to do this. Finally in bed, they dressed and wrapped his hands. When he finally regained consciousness, Harry looked about the room with wild, bloodshot eyes, muttering words no one could understand. The sheets were soon wet, almost as if he were still in the bath. At times, he sat bolt upright with bloodshot, unseeing eyes, muttering to himself. Something about Emanuel. But they were at a loss to know if it were his father or his horse that he was talking about.

"Hold on love, we're all here now," Clara said softly, cradling him in her arms.

His eyes were a little crazy as he gripped her arms. "I had to shoot my horse!" Then he finally sank into a troubled sleep again. The three girls sat exhausted at the kitchen table, while the twins, silent now, peered around the doorframe at the strange, wild man lying in the bed, tossing and screaming out from time to time.

Nell tried her first attempt at levity. "I guess he'd kill us when he realises I helped undress him. He's a terrible prude you know, that man. Thinks I've never seen anything he has, though I almost reared him as a baby!"

Clara began to sob softly. "I think that would be the least of his worries"

"Frankly," said Nell, "I don't think the crazy fool would give a damn what he looked like as long as his bull was safe!"

Nell placed her hand gently on Clara's arm. "Love, why don't you get some rest? You've got a bub to look after you know."

Gentleness came hard to Nell. The tears leaked from Clara's eyes. "I should have gone out to look for him myself!"

"You wouldn't have been much help in the condition you're in."

"I could have lost him, Nell. Only had the man for less than a year, and I could have lost him!"

Nell patted the back of her hand. "We Trasks take a lot of killing, especially that one. Got a hide like a bull. Now all we have to do is worry about you. How does everything feel now, down below?" Nell found the sensation strange, worrying about babies. She usually found calves more interesting. Perhaps she was developing maternal instincts. The thought shocked her a little.

In the next room, she heard the weird noises Charley made through a broken Jaw.

And here she was in a house full of broken down crocks and pregnant women.

Chapter 66

Two days later, the cattle drive started down the mountain.

Nell watched the men go, wanting to be with them, but thought she had better stay a little longer with the women.

Frank had gone ahead, taking the shorter path down the leap taking Charley with him. The sooner they could get the old man to the doctor the better, though Charley preformed at having to miss the drive.

Clara was like a mother hen around her patient. The sheets had to be changed a dozen times before the fever broke. By this time, he had stopped screaming and was even a little coherent and they could make some sense of his wild ranting about Emanuel and the horse. He could see a little. Dimly at first, but at least some kind of sight. At times, he was even quite rational.

By the third day, they thought he was well enough to mount on horseback, to try to get him further down the mountain, closer to medical help. With Nell supporting him, the three Trask women carried their burden down the mountain to the cabin on King's Spur. Clara rode down Angel's leap, heavily pregnant, as Emily had done years before, but going a different way this time. Nell led the horse on foot with Harry clinging to the pommel of the saddle. She felt she would have to have some crack at him, later about being led down the mountain by a woman.

The next day, Harry was not as well as he thought he was, but there was still some improvement. His sight was coming back and when he held his hand in front of his face he could see it. Two fingers on his left hand were turning black, which was a worry, but he convinced himself he had more fingers than he needed. He climbed out of bed to roam through the house driving the women mad, saying he should be back with the drive, but every so often he felt weak and was forced to lie down until the feeling passed.

Clara didn't know what to do with the man. Nell told him bluntly he was a fool. Bess was much more sympathetic, telling him to settle down and have a hot cup of tea.

"I should be on that drive you know." He stumbled as he got out of bed. The wild shaking took him again for a moment. "I'm alright now. I can ride."

"You're a fool," snapped Nell. "You couldn't ride a rocking horse. You think more of your damn cattle than you think of your wife. Don't you realise you nearly died? It not only affects you. It's your wife and baby. You could easily have lost that baby you selfish idiot!"

Harry dropped into a kitchen chair, stunned by the outburst.

"Thanks for the sympathy, sis. I did what I had to do," he said lamely.

"Rubbish. You did what you pig-headed wanted to do. Why didn't you just come back for the rest of us?"

"Because I thought you'd be half way down the mountain by then. Besides, I couldn't leave 'em when I found 'em in that weather!"

"No, it would be better to lose the baby than the bull!"

Nell tossed her head while Clara cried softly. The full force of the thing was hitting her now, days after the event.

Bess slammed a batch of hot scones on the table. "I don't know why you don't let up on the man. He's been through a lot you know!"

"We all have," said Nell.

Clara stroked the back of his hand as the tears still ran down her face. "You just didn't have to do that, Harry. You just didn't have to do that."

Later, Nell found her sister alone in the kitchen. She had been waiting for the chance to get a few things off her chest for some days.

"Rang tells me you're going to Queensland."

"Yes, in the new year. It'll be hard to leave, though." She gazed out through the kitchen window at the rocks covered in snow. "I hate to leave, but Rang wants to go, and he is my husband."

Nell moved up close up behind her and threw her arms around her sister's waist. "I guess we haven't always been much of sisters."

Bess was surprised by this sudden affection. She continued to gaze out at the snow. "I guess we haven't. But I don't quite know what sisters are supposed to be."

"Not like we've been. Maybe it's time to sort of mend our fences. Before you go. We might never see one another again."

"Never is a long time. We're only going to Queensland."

"Only to Queensland! It would take a month to ride there!"

To Bess, with her books, distance was not the daunting thing it was to her sister even though she had never left the mountain in her life.

"I've said a lot of things to you I shouldn't have. I don't want you to go away for ever with that hanging between us."

It was easier for Nell. Her feelings could change with the wind. But for Bess, things went much deeper. Or so she thought.

"I've been a bitch to you a lot of times. You do the housework while I work the cattle. But I suppose you really had the toughest job in the end. I only ever did what I liked. I suppose in a way it was a way of avoiding things. I can't cook a lick to save my life you know. Anyway, I wish you all the luck, sis. And look after that man, you were always better for him than me."

"Oh I'll look after him." But looking out the window, Bess let her mind run back over her life. She was not quite as forgiving as her sister.

The next day, Nell rode off to catch up with the drive.

They had to take the cattle the long way down from the high plains to avoid Angels leap, circling way to the east, down to Macpherson's flat on the Dargo river. Nell caught up with them well before they reached the low country. Riding wild and free, she galloped down the steep incline, swinging her hat in her outstretched hand. Nell was home again among her cattle.

Chapter 67

At Ashburn, Emily carried a plate of scones and a mug of tea to the old man resting in a cane bottomed chair under the shade of an elm tree in the garden.

"They'll be coming down with the cattle any day now I expect."

Jock Hoolahan took the mug from Emily's hand, no longer afraid of the woman.

The summer, and perhaps age had cured him of that. In fact, a strange affection had grown up between the two.

She still kept Jock soundly in place, but Emily had grown fond of her husband's old friend.

"I miss it all you know, Jock. Didn't think I would, but I still miss it. Yes, I expect they'll be coming down soon."

Chapter 68

The road down into Dargo was only a track, heavily eroded with ditches knee-deep in many places, running with water. Clara guided the sulky between the ruts, the track so steep that the mare slid on its heels at times.

Harry sat hunched beside her, wrapped in blankets, as she tried to keep the ride as smooth as possible on the trip down to the doctor where McGuire still operated his ancient practice.

Harry's hands were still heavily bandaged and he was afraid that he was going to lose at least two of his fingers.

Still they were only on his left hand, and surely, working cattle, a man didn't need all his fingers.

Finally, Clara drew back on the reins, bringing the sulky to a stop on a rise overlooking the small town.

They had almost caught up to the drive and could see the last of the Trask cattle moving into the town, while the front of the mob had already passed well through. A crowd had gathered in the streets to watch the cattle pass, almost a thousand head of them. Some were in the side streets, worrying the gardens, some mounted the boardwalks under the shop verandas, dropping their dung at intervals as if to mark their passage, hooves slipping on the wet floorboards.

Harry could just make out the short figure of Billy O'Riley, local butcher and long standing self-appointed mayor of the town, standing in front of his shop, waving the cattle away, dressed in his trademark blood stained apron as they clamoured across the boards, spraying his feet with shit. Despite his eyes, Harry could tell the man at the distance by his striped apron. A few boys and dogs were running around creating havoc. Whips were cracking and dogs barking.

Lord Harvey took up the rear, obstinate as usual, like an aristocrat, resenting any part of the drive, preferring only to travel at his own speed in the general direction he choose himself.

Harry's eyes were improving by the day. He could make out the form of Nell on a prancing pony, putting up a fine show for the crowd, red hair spilling out from under her hat.

As Emanuel would have once said, "A fine stamp of a woman!"

Lightning Source UK Ltd.
Milton Keynes UK
UKHW022216270223
417768UK00006B/38